THE SOUL KEEPERS

THE SOUL KEEPERS

DEVON TAYLOR

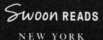

Swoon READS

NEW YORK

A SWOON READS BOOK

An imprint of Feiwel and Friends and Macmillan Publishing Group, LLC
175 Fifth Avenue, New York, NY 10010

Our books may be purchased in bulk for promotional, educational, or
business use. Please contact your local bookseller or the Macmillan Corporate
and Premium Sales Department at (800) 221-7945 ext. 5442 or by e-mail at
MacmillanSpecialMarkets@macmillan.com.

Library of Congress Cataloging-in-Publication Data is available.
ISBN 978-1-250-16830-6 (trade hardcover) / ISBN 978-1-250-16829-0 (ebook)

Book design by Carol Ly

First edition, 2018

1   3   5   7   9   10   8   6   4   2

swoonreads.com

For Kelsey,
who says she's designed for evil, but has only ever
shown me patience, inspiration, and support.
I love you, gorgeous.

"I AM THE AFTERMATH."

—CROWN THE EMPIRE

ONE

ONE

The fall was slow.

Through one mangled opening of the car, where a window had once been, he could see the earth and the sky tilting into one another, falling over each other with a weird sort of grace. Pine trees bristled against the cloudless sky, bruised and leaking color as the sun sank below the hills.

In another one of those slightly crooked, slightly grinning holes—a mouth with teeth of shattered glass—there was the gray asphalt of the road, rising to meet him, open and flat like the cracked palm of a steady hand. It was there to crush the car, with him still inside it. It was there to end him.

And it did.

When time unstuck itself from whatever ringing echo it had been momentarily captured in, he felt the raw pull of gravity, the unfiltered attraction of the earth. He felt it pull the car down, with him still inside it and the steering wheel tight in his hands.

There was time for one last glance in the rearview mirror, where his father's cornflower-blue tie had been snapping back and forth in rhythm with the tumbling of the car. But the tie was gone. In the mirror he saw only the blackening sky and the first makings of constellations brave enough to show themselves on this horrendous night.

Then the car smashed against the road, his soul was torn from his body, and his life was suddenly, unceremoniously, over.

The edges of his vision rattled with an oncoming darkness.

He held it back, concentrating on the pain, on the sight of his own body wrapped up in the tangle of metal and plastic that had once been a newish Volkswagen Jetta—his mom's car. The forest-green paint was scraped and stripped and wrinkled like a dirty shirt. All the windows were blown out, the glass strewn along the road behind the vehicle.

There was also the semitruck another few feet up the road, its trailer crumpled like the mangled spine of some long-hunted animal. It burned there, charring the road beneath it and sending an unhealthy-looking cloud of dark smoke into the air. He could see the FedEx logo peeling away from the metal of the trailer, flaking off and fluttering away on the rising heat of the flames.

He sat there with his legs under him, the uneven surface of the road digging into his knees and palms, registering all this with only a slight pinging against his senses. What he was really focused on was the *other* him, still hanging upside down inside the wreckage of his parents' car, his face and hands white, his eyes vacant. A little trickle of blood escaped out of the corner of his mouth and ran up his cheek, across his forehead, and into the thicket of his brown hair. The body was a warped reflection of the seventeen-year-old boy he'd previously been. And *previously* had been only moments ago, when his world was normal and right, empty of ruined cars and burning trucks.

And yet . . . he was still here. His lungs burned with the air he was breathing in. His body cried out from a million white-hot pinpricks of agony. His head thudded and throbbed like the backbeat to some terrible house music. But he was also . . . *there*.

He could feel the accident, could feel the impact. His limbs and muscles ached with the force of it. But the body dangling inside that tomb of crushed metal was no longer his. It looked like him—it had his smallish nose and his wide, sometimes haunted-looking eyes. But it definitely didn't belong to him. How could it when he was sitting right here, breathing, aching?

Even as he thought it, though, the ache was fading, replaced by a bizarre numbness, a *nothingness*, as if the inside of his body had suddenly gone hollow.

On both sides of the concrete barrier that ran down the center of the highway, cars were pulling over, people leaping out, staring at the carnage with shocked eyes and open mouths. Some people were weeping, some were coughing from the smoke and the heat . . . heat that he suddenly could not feel.

A couple of men ran over to the car, to his body, and were reaching in. One of them looked like he was trying to find a pulse. Within the crowd, he could see other people holding their phones in the air, trying to get a decent shot. He was a spectacle now. Soon he'd be all over the internet, a viral tragedy.

"Hey!" he yelled at them. "Hey! Don't do that! Can't you see that I'm dead? I'm fucking *dead*!"

He didn't need anybody to tell him that they couldn't hear or see him. There was a part of him that already knew. It was the same part that knew he had "crossed over." Or whatever the correct phrase was. Maybe someone caught the moment that the spiritual was peeled away from the physical. Maybe there was a picture on one of those phones that showed a ghostly fog in the shape of a human, hovering just above his body as it hung there behind the steering wheel in a horrid imitation of life as it was, as it would never be again.

He felt his arms and legs begin to shake. He fought to still them, afraid now. Afraid that he might shake himself into a billion little particles of mist and get carried away by the cool evening breeze.

Was he a ghost? A spirit? Was he just a memory, firing off in one of the last living neurons of his brain?

Something was going to happen soon. Either he was going to poof out of existence, or he was going to fade into a shadow, or he was going to follow a brilliant white light down a tunnel into oblivion. But *something* was going to happen. It had to. Otherwise he might go insane waiting. He shut his eyes. He waited for infinity to swallow him.

Meanwhile the *whump-whump-whump* of blood in his ears was beginning to fade—not necessarily slowing, just getting quieter—as if someone was turning the volume down on his heart. He was able to hear the world again: the animal trumpet of horns blaring and brakes screeching as traffic came to a halt along the road, the whispery murmur of panicked conversations among the crowd, the haunted cries of distant sirens.

Someone—a woman from somewhere in the back of the crowd—had called 911. She was still on the line with the operator, describing the scene: ". . . a big FedEx truck and a . . . a sedan . . . I can't make out what kind of car it is. It's too . . . it's too messed up . . . I almost got caught in it, too. It just happened out of nowhere."

Nowhere.

Was that how they were going to remember this? Had he been flung out of "nowhere," right into the middle of these peoples' lives, maybe to linger there forever? Him and his parents?

His parents.

He opened his eyes and the destruction slammed into his senses all over again. The burning truck, the tinfoil ball that had been the car he'd learned to drive in . . . had *still* been learning to drive in. The sky was even darker now, bordering on black, and the fire lit the scene with its unsteady orange glow.

Peering in through the empty windows of the car, he braced himself for the sight of one of his parents' bodies, trapped in the car the way his was, looking cold and empty. But he couldn't see either one of them. In the backseat, where his father had been sitting, there was only a gnarled hole through which he could see the crowd gathering along the shoulder of the road, still trying their best to look more scared than interested, trying not to look like the rubberneckers that they were.

His father should have been there, in that space where there was now only empty air ringed with the ragged bite that had been taken out of the car.

He flicked his eyes to the front again and tried to look past his own body (someone had shut his eyes, at least) and into the passenger seat, where his mother had been sitting . . .

Nothing. The seat was empty, and the dashboard was covered in bits of broken windshield and streaks of something red that he wouldn't allow himself to believe was blood.

Panicking, he tore his eyes away, let them sweep over the spot in the backseat again, over the sight of the enraptured crowd on the far side of the road, and . . .

On the shoulder, in the front row of the gathered onlookers, there was a guy in a black blazer and dark jeans. He was around the same age, maybe even a bit younger, but with immaculate hair and one eyebrow cocked up in a slightly curious, slightly irritated expression. The guy was looking right at him.

He looked around at the other people, who were all fixated on the tangled metal and billowing smoke. He looked back at the guy in the blazer. Still staring.

He didn't know what else to do—he raised his hand and waved.

"Oy!" the guy yelled over the din. "C'mon, mate! I'm not gonna wait all day!"

"I . . . uh . . ." He pointed at himself in a silent question. Blazer Guy groaned and twirled his finger impatiently.

"Yeah, mate, I'm talking to you. Who the hell else would I be talking to?" The guy turned and sidestepped into the crowd, disappearing behind a wall of bodies.

"Wait!" he called. "Hold on a second!"

He struggled to his feet. His legs felt rubbery and not quite his own. It took a moment for everything to balance out, but as soon as it did, he darted around the car, leaving his body there on its own, to the shoulder of the highway. The crowd stared past him, *through* him. He paused before going after Blazer Guy, looked back at the only part of his body he could see from here: a pale hand, open and dangling, frozen in a silent good-bye.

He turned and shuffled into the crowd.

Nobody noticed him.

He slipped between a few people, bumping into some, but none of them seemed to realize they were being touched. It creeped him out. He hurried through the crowd and left it behind.

On the other side there was the rocky shoulder of the highway and a shadow-littered tangle of trees. The highway itself was a mess of cars and people, with traffic completely halted and angry honks rising into a chorus.

He turned, staring up the highway, back in the direction of the city, peering past the glare of headlights. He was still looking for the guy that had called to him—Blazer Guy. In the dimness of the night it was hard to tell what anyone looked like. He scanned the collection of bystanders that he'd just come through, but there were no blazers.

He considered waiting there for Blazer Guy to come back. Maybe if he stayed put, the guy—or someone else like the guy, someone who could see and talk to him—would show themselves. But going back to his body, looking at that mess again . . . the idea gave him the shivers.

And there was still the problem of his parents. Where were they? Were they like him?

The trees stood by, as if waiting for him to decide—look for his parents, or keep looking for Blazer Guy. The shadows among the branches and around the tree trunks had turned to full-on patches of black now, hiding the fallen leaves and pine needles and bits of debris from the wreck that were scattered here and there. He wondered if somewhere within that curtain of darkness he would stumble upon his parents. He wondered if he really wanted to find out . . .

Ready to give up, he was prepared to just start wandering around, when he heard "Oy, mate!" from right behind him. He started, whipped around.

Blazer Guy stood in front of him, grinning, hands in his pockets, looking back at the wreckage, focusing, it seemed, on the burning hunk of metal that was the FedEx truck. He whistled.

"That's quite a mess you made there, mate," the guy said. "Not sure if you know this or not, but fire is usually not great for a vehicle's overall state of being. Personally, I try to avoid fires when I can. I grew up in London, so I'm partial to the rain. You know what I mean? Well, I suppose not, given . . . well, this." Blazer Guy gestured with a wide sweep of his arm at the entirety of the wreck, at the car and the truck and the onlookers.

"You're . . . British?" he said. They were the first words that popped into his head, and they found their way to his mouth before he had a chance to stop them.

Blazer Guy looked offended.

"First of all," he said, "I'm technically Welsh. And what, you've got something against British people?"

"What? No! I mean . . . I just . . . We're in New York. I didn't expect . . . I mean, I didn't think . . ."

"Less than twenty miles from the international hub of the world, and you didn't expect to see a British person?" Blazer Guy folded his arms and began tapping his foot. "You know, mate, it could be that I'm here to decide your fate. As in whether or not you end up . . . there." He pointed up, at the black canvas of sky. "Or . . . there." He pointed down, cringing. Blazer Guy leaned in and whispered, as if sharing a secret. "And you're not off to an exceptionally good start."

"Oh my God . . ." he started.

Blazer Guy hissed in a breath, cringing even more.

"Shit . . ."

Blazer Guy did it again.

He felt his legs give out, and he squatted down, covering his face with his hands, panic crashing around inside him.

But the guy was laughing.

"Don't worry, mate," he said, squatting down with him, leaning back on the balls of his feet. "I'm not here for anything like that. That was a pretty good laugh, though, right?"

He dropped his hands and glared.

"Maybe not," Blazer Guy said. "How about we start over? I'm

Basil. Basil Winthrop. Pronounced with a long *A*, mind you. And you are?"

"I'm . . ."

For a second he couldn't remember. He grasped for it, but it wasn't there. He stood, and Basil—formerly Blazer Guy—stood with him.

"It's all right, mate. Some of it gets lost in the transition. The name especially."

He turned around, back to where the crowd stood and where there was now an ambulance and a number of police cars parked along the concrete barrier, their warbling lights making the whole scene look shimmery and unreal. Cops were pushing members of the crowd back. He looked past them, at the car, at the spot where he'd been sitting, staring at his own body as the last of his life slipped out of it. He thought about the tie—his father's tie, cornflower blue, jerking around in the rearview mirror like the head of an electrified snake.

"My name is Rhett," he said. "Rhett Snyder." He turned to Basil. "My name is Rhett Snyder," he said again, this time hearing the relief in his own voice.

"Rhett," Basil said, almost questioningly. "Rhett. Sounds like something you'd name a pet. Like a dog, or possibly a small, help-less rodent."

"My parents' favorite movie is . . . was *Gone with the Wind*," Rhett said, for some reason feeling the need to explain. "They named me after Clark Gable's character."

Basil pondered this, then said, "Ah. Yes, well, there's no account-ing for taste, is there?"

"Listen, I don't know who you are or why you're here or what's happening. I—" Rhett stopped short. He felt dangerously close to cracking. Confused, alone, afraid, invisible. This guy—Basil fucking Winthrop—was about as compassionate toward the recently deceased as a vulture is to a zebra carcass. "Shouldn't I just be . . . dead?" he went on. "I don't know what's going on, but this . . . this isn't anything they ever went over in Sunday school."

Basil chuckled and leaned in, grinning. He said, "Oh trust me, mate. I know. When I took the old dirt nap myself, I hadn't expected any appendices to my time line. But here we are."

"I . . . sorry. You . . . ?"

"Yeah. I can regale you with all the perfectly unfortunate details later. But right now we have a boat to catch. Shall we?"

"Wait," Rhett said. "What about my parents?"

"Your . . . ?" Basil looked confused and then worried. "Oh. Then we really have to get moving," he said. "The others will be along soon. Your parents are . . ." He gave Rhett a serious look. "They're in good hands, mate. I promise."

Rhett glanced over his shoulder and considered the scene one last time. The crowd had been all but dismantled, pushed back behind a yellow perimeter of police tape. There was now a white sheet draped over the crumpled mess of the car, hiding the carnage and the sight of Rhett's body. The sheet fluttered in the breeze for a moment, catching the light of the fire-ravaged semitruck, now surrounded by firefighters dousing the flames with a hose.

Somewhere nearby, Rhett was now sure, his parents' bodies would be found and covered with sheets of their own, turned into vaguely human-shaped spaces of emptiness, erased from the universe.

But if that was the case, why weren't they with him now?

Rhett turned back to Basil, the only person who seemed to have any of the answers. He was a pain in the ass, but he was going to take Rhett where he needed to go. He could only hope that his parents were there, too.

"Let's go," Rhett said.

TWO

Basil navigated the highway and Rhett followed. They kept to the shoulder, following the road back toward the city. For a while they were entangled with the people who had abandoned their cars to check out the scene of the wreck, and Basil had an irritatingly graceful way of maneuvering around them. Nobody spoke to either of them, nobody *saw* them. Rhett knew that if he were to bump into someone, *he* might feel it—but would they? Basil swept through the clutter of bodies and cars like an ice-skater, hands behind his back, leaning forward with a determined hunch. Meanwhile, Rhett was having a hard enough time just keeping his feet under him.

"It takes a while to get used to, mate!" Basil called over his shoulder.

"What does?"

"Walking. Running. Eating. Anything, really. You're essentially an apparition now. It's all sensation and no feeling. Anything you think you feel is just made up in your head." Basil said all this over his shoulder while dodging the confusion that had overtaken the highway.

Behind him, Rhett was still trying to match Basil's pace. They were moving up a short hill now, with the halted traffic beside them and the clear, glimmering night sky above them. Rhett felt like he should be out of breath—and was almost acting the part—but he didn't feel anything. Basil was right. He expected to *feel* the walk, the aching muscles, the burning lungs. Even though he was a mostly healthy teenager—or had been—Rhett was sure that by now he'd be running out of juice. And yet . . . nothing. Not even his bad ankle, which he'd broken in the sixth grade and had always bothered him after long walks through the city, was giving him any trouble. It was a weird sort of miracle.

Or maybe it was a curse.

After a while they came to the top of the hill and, finally, to the place where the traffic was thinning out. The honking horns and humming engines faded, replaced by the sound of rustling leaves and chatting night-birds. The highway stretched away from them, slipping into shadows, pointing the way toward the city skyline, which hung like an electric splash on the horizon.

"Nearly there," Basil muttered, and continued down the hill.

They went on for so long that Rhett began to believe they would make it all the way back to New York City before getting to wherever Basil was taking them. But finally, at some seemingly random spot on the side of the highway, Basil turned off and trudged into the smothering darkness of the woods. Rhett stopped and stared after him, listening to the crunch of his feet.

Basil must have realized that his new travel companion was no longer behind him, because he stopped and turned back.

"Coming?" he said. His face was only a flicker in all the black.

Rhett hesitated, but only for a second, before wading down through the detritus of the forest to where Basil stood waiting. He thought to ask questions. He thought to throw Basil into a tree and pummel him with his fists until Basil simply told him what he wanted to know. He thought to run.

But he didn't do any of those things.

The highway quickly vanished behind them, lost for good behind thick trunks and waving branches. Ahead of them there was only more woods . . . and what else, Rhett had no idea.

Until he watched Basil step through a curtain of branches into an open area, thick with tall brown grass and dominated by what at first looked like an ancient ruin. In a way, that's exactly what it was, but Rhett soon realized that it wasn't as ancient as he'd first thought.

It was the collapsed shell of an old brick house, thick wooden beams creating an empty box in the middle of the clearing, with puzzle-works of moss-smothered bricks filling in the squares. The only mostly intact part of the house was the northern wall, the one facing Rhett and Basil, and the chimney, sad and crooked and pocked with holes. There was a wooden door in the one good wall, hanging on by only one rusted hinge.

Rhett was suddenly afraid that he'd made the wrong choice to follow Basil.

"Ready, mate?" Basil said, dusting off the arms of his blazer as if they were about to make a grand entrance at some party.

"If I knew what I was supposed to be ready for, I'd tell you," Rhett responded.

Basil only grinned, then kicked the old door in.

It swung away with a brittle *crack* into strange, murky light. Rhett saw bits of the door fly off and go spinning away. He expected a dusty, must-scented puff of warm air. What he got was a stormy breeze and a spray of brackish water. Behind the door, where more weeds and dirt and fallen bricks should have been, there was instead a craggy stretch of rock ending in a jagged cluster of stones. Beyond that: ocean and sky, gray and churning both, for as far as he could see.

Rhett opened his mouth, closed it, opened it again. Whatever words he might have had to describe what he was seeing, they were lost on him now. His head swam. He looked around at the woods, the trees only standing there, bathing in the moonlight, uninterrupted by the bizarre wonder taking place right in their midst. If there had been any other person here—any other *living* person— he wondered if they might see the open door, hear the waves smashing hard in a burst of white foam against the rocks, feel the cold mist that came floating through.

"You're not crazy, mate," Basil said. It sounded like he was trying to be comforting, and it was surprisingly effective. "You might feel like you are right now. You just have to give it some time. Are you ready? We have a very small window of opportunity here, and if we don't make it through in time, we'll get left behind. I assure you."

Back in the direction they had come from, Rhett could hear the far-off wail of sirens again. They were for him, for the body he'd shed and left in a broken heap inside his parents' mangled car. He stared through the door, at the endless ocean and endless sky that met in a dark line at the horizon. It wasn't what he'd expected—it was no light at the end of a tunnel—but this was what he'd been waiting for. This was infinity, ready to swallow him.

"Let's do it," he said to Basil.

"Good deal." Basil looked pleased. "Now, the first step can be a little disorienting. If you just close your eyes . . ."

But Rhett ignored him. He stepped past Basil, through the whispering grass, and then ducked into the doorway.

The ocean would have taken his breath away, if he'd had any breath to take.

It stretched out in every direction from the lone patch of rock he was standing on. It roiled and chopped and spat, like an angry animal. The sky was layered with dark, sagging clouds, bubbling and shifting as constantly as the ocean. In the great distance, Rhett saw jagged flickers of lightning.

He turned around, and there was the rectangular patch of woods, just hanging there, like a badly Photoshopped picture. Basil came through it, stepping onto the rock like a passenger boarding a train. As soon as he was through, the doorway faded, dissolving into specks of dust that crumbled and were carried away by the bitter wind. Now it was just the two of them, alone on a narrow shard of rock in the middle of this vast, unsettled ocean. Even though, according to Basil, he was probably just imagining it, Rhett felt his stomach churn.

"Did you forget who your tour guide is?" Basil asked, looking a little offended. "What if I was just putting you on about all that boat stuff? Maybe this is actually purgatory and you just willingly leapt into it with utter glee."

Rhett had to yell over the crashing waves. "That would have been an awfully elaborate joke."

"You severely underestimate my comedic ambitions."

"You're right about one thing, though."

"What's that?" Basil looked almost taken aback.

"Being stuck on this rock with *you* forever? That would absolutely be purgatory."

For the first time since Rhett had met him, Basil cracked a genuine smile, and Rhett had to smile in response, in spite of the morbid surroundings.

"Well, lucky for you, the only thing I don't joke about—much— is my job," Basil said.

"Which is . . . ?"

"In due time, mate. In due time."

"So what do we do now?" Rhett felt his impatience biting at him. None of this was what he'd had in mind back there, when he'd opted to leave his parents behind.

"Now," Basil said, "we catch our ride." He nodded over Rhett's shoulder. Rhett turned, and his heart lurched. It might have been an imagined sensation, but to him it was really his heart. He felt the awe and the panic and the uncertainty and the fascination in that lurch. He wanted to say something, but, again, there was nothing to say.

It was more than a boat; it was a ship. A massive one. The biggest Rhett had ever seen. Bigger than anything that could have actually been built by human hands. It was all black iron and rivets, with two monstrous smokestacks on top that sent columns of coal-black smoke punching into the sky. It cut through the water, moving with slow, sure progress. It was taller than most of the skyscrapers Rhett had grown up looking at, and it had portholes dotting the sides with sparks of light like stars in the night sky. Metal groaned, engines hummed. It was more like a giant aquatic mammal than a sailing vessel. Rhett could think of only one decent word to describe the ship: *otherworldly*.

"Get ready to board," Basil said.

"Board?" Rhett tore his eyes away from the ship. "As in get on that thing?"

"Well I'm not telling you to go beat at it with a two-by-four, am I?"

Rhett struggled for words. "Where . . . where is it taking us?"

"Patience, mate. There are colleagues of mine on board that are probably better equipped to explain all this to you than I am. I'm just here to collect you."

The ship was closer, taking up most of the view on that side of the rock. The nearer it got, the more it started to blot out the sky. Rhett was in awe of it, but he was also frightened by it. It was all black, surrounded by a constant dark fog, and, despite the lights on in some of the portholes, there was no sign of any actual life on board.

There wouldn't be any of that, anyway. *Not here*, Rhett thought, once again picturing the death that he'd only just experienced.

They waited.

The ship grew, a colossal shard of metal slicing through the water until it was nearly on top of them. Rhett could *feel* it—a low, steady thrum. The iron moaned as it bent and stretched, sounding more haunted than anything else Rhett had encountered so far.

The hull was only a few feet away now. Rhett and Basil were deep in its shadow. Above them, the hard black exterior and warbling columns of smoke were like a second sky. Within those columns, Rhett was sure he could see bolts of blue lightning.

A horn blew then, deep, deafening, so loud that it was almost like being submerged in water, a constant roar that blotted out every other sound. Rhett fought to not cover his ears. Basil already thought he was an idiot. He didn't need him to think he was pathetic, too.

The horn cut off, leaving only the comparably quiet sound of the ocean, and the ship stopped moving. It floated there, looming over them, a monument to darkness.

"What now?" Rhett asked, unable to stop himself.

But before Basil could respond, a door on the side of the ship opened with an iron screech. It swung outward. Behind it, there was a square of light that was nearly blinding against the obscurity of the ship. But Rhett could make out a metal ramp extending out of the doorway like a rusty tongue.

The ramp crunched into the rock at Rhett's feet, an invitation—or maybe a lure. He looked to Basil for guidance, raising his eyebrows. Basil just stepped onto the ramp, hands clutched behind his back, and began closing the gap between himself and the ship.

"Coming, mate?" he called over his shoulder, just as he had back in the woods.

Rhett glanced around. If he didn't get on board, the only other option would be to hang around on this damned rock for the rest of eternity. Or go for a swim . . .

He stepped onto the ramp. It only took fifteen steps to get to the ship.

And to his new life after death.

THREE

The light swallowed him up, and so did the ship.

Rhett waited for his eyes to adjust, but they didn't need to. They didn't burn or water from the brightness. He could see just fine. Nevertheless, the light was so intense that it hammered into his retinas, shining off the white metal of the walls. If he had been alive, he might have been blinded.

He stepped farther in, following the foggy shape of Basil's shoulders into the brilliance. Their feet clanged on the floor. Rhett felt himself reaching out in front of him, prepared to slam into some oncoming mass.

Then he did run into something: Basil.

"Oy! Watch where you're going," Basil hissed. Rhett took a step back. He heard an iron screech and Basil's voice again. "Through here."

And all at once the light was gone, replaced by an unsettled orange glow that was constantly wrestling with the shadows. Firelight.

Rhett shifted on his feet and heard the creak of wood beneath him. Whatever metal hallway they'd gone through to get inside the ship was gone. They were now standing in a large, open cavity.

There were splintered wood floors and wooden railings that went all the way around the periphery. The most curious thing was in the middle, jutting up out of the floor and connecting with the ceiling, almost like a support. It was a ship's mast, complete with the worn-out, weather-beaten sail. Up at the top, where the mast met the ceiling, Rhett could see the crow's nest, a rickety basket that leaned precariously to one side.

Rhett didn't quite know what to make of it. And in the gloom of the torches that were leaning away from the outer walls, it was hard to say that he was still on the same boat. Had Basil performed another one of his party tricks and sent them somewhere else? To another point in time altogether? Was that even possible?

He didn't know. He didn't know anything about how any of this worked. Was this hell? Was this some kind of punishment?

All at once, Rhett wanted to weep. But when he imagined the pressure behind his eyes, imagined the tears falling down his face, it was only an image that floated up in his mind. His body stayed calm and still and . . . lifeless. There was no sweat on his hands, no tremble in his fingers. His body betrayed nothing of the chaos that was erupting in his head.

Desperately, he looked to Basil, who had given him that tiny bit of comfort back in the woods. But Basil was smiling, watching Rhett and allowing that internal panic to play out.

Basil said one thing, leaning in with his arms folded: "Welcome aboard the *Harbinger*."

For a while they passed through halls made of gray, rotted wood, freckled with barnacles, and swollen with moisture. As the ship leaned and swayed with the waves, the wood groaned and cackled in response.

Then they stepped out of the smoke and mildew into a long passage of metal bulkheads that were lit by sickly yellow bulbs. The passage was narrow, suffocating. Rhett had always had a touch of claustrophobia and could feel it raging around inside his mind now. But, again, his body was quiet—no hyperventilating, no damp forehead. Somewhere within him, a connection had been broken.

At the end of the passage, Basil spun the handle on a door and pushed it open. Beyond it, there was a massive ballroom with thick, polished wood columns and a wide staircase leading up to some other part of the ship. The floor was some elegant, decorative carpet, covered in flowers and swirls of gold fabric. Above it all was an enormous, twinkling crystal chandelier, wide at the top and tapering to a point. *Here. You are supposed to be here*, the chandelier seemed to say. *This is the dazzling landscape of your dreams.*

Yeah, right, Rhett thought, and for one horrible second, he believed that he wasn't dead after all. Maybe he was just unconscious, lying on some gurney back in New York, wandering around the bizarre confines of his psyche—not the landscape of his dreams, but of his nightmares.

Basil caught him gaping at the chandelier.

"Magnificent, isn't it?" he said.

Rhett looked back through the bulkhead door, at that long

yellow tunnel. "I just . . . I just don't understand. What is this? What's happening?"

"Nothing's *happening*, mate. It's just the ship. The *Harbinger*, at some point well before either of us was even a speck on the genetic radar, was just a lowly rowboat. Now it's . . . all this."

Rhett blinked at him, and Basil laughed.

"It's true! The rowboat is still here. Somewhere. I'm sure the captain will show it to you sometime. He showed me, but hell if I can remember how to get to it. Anyway . . . over the centuries—the *eons*, I should say—the *Harbinger* has . . . well, grown." He sighed, admiring the chandelier. "I suppose I've said too much, though. On our way."

And with that, Basil took to the stairs, ascending them with his strange grace to the point that he appeared to be floating rather than walking.

Rhett shook his head, squeezed his eyes shut, trying to elicit some kind of response in his body to the fretful storm going on in his mind.

But he got nothing.

Basil disappeared up the staircase, beyond the glimmer of the chandelier. With no other options, Rhett followed him.

The stairs wound their way up through the ship, changing their appearance seemingly at random as they went. One moment they were the same polished wood and carpet as the room with the chandelier.

At another, they were solid steel with diamond grooves and flaking paint. Then they were made of gray and decaying wood, like the room with the mast in it. Finally, they were made of metal-lined glass, beneath which was the wavering, ethereal glow of water—some kind of tank or aquarium, although Rhett couldn't see any fish.

He expected to be tired after all those stairs. But of course, when he finally caught up with Basil at the top, his lungs continued to take in air normally, the thing that might have been his heart pumped obliviously along, and his legs—his bad ankle—never made a peep. In a weird way, Rhett wondered if this was how it felt to be Superman— ignorant of pain and yet somehow longing for it.

Basil was waiting for him, hands in his pants pockets, leaning back on his heels. He was whistling some old-timey bandstand song.

"Take you long enough?" he asked, eyebrows raised.

"Sorry . . . I . . ." Rhett hardened his gaze and swallowed whatever the rest of that statement was going to be. He was done apologizing. Why should he have to be sorry for being freaked out?

"Ah . . ." Basil said, sounding amused. "He's got a bit of tough skin on him after all. Good for you, mate." He smacked Rhett on the shoulder. "You ready to meet the rest of the gang?"

"The . . . rest . . . ?"

The stairs had led them up what must have been a few dozen or so different decks of the ship. Now they were standing outside a set of polished steel doors, a look that was a little more modern and familiar. They reminded Rhett of so many doors in New York, battered and commonplace. Here, the sight just freaked him out. He willed his skin to break out in goose bumps and, miraculously, it

did. They crawled across his arms in a delightful chill. He could see them breaking out and then fading away. It seemed that the mind still held an insurmountable amount of control over the body. If Rhett *wanted* a physical reaction, he could force himself to have one—feeling with the senses was no longer involuntary. Deep down, below all the layers of confusion and anxiety that had been settling in on him like strips of tight, smothering gauze, he was fascinated.

Basil pressed a button near the doors and they split apart, disappearing into cavities in the walls. Rhett stared.

Beyond the doors was an entirely different part of the ship, an up-to-date, twenty-first-century paradise. It was a large atrium, wide open, with winding stairs to different levels that went back down into the ship for as far as Rhett could see. Here there was no rapid change in decorum. Everything was polished steel and glass, lit by a soft, bluish glow. Rhett felt like he was standing in the belly of a starship rather than some rusty old sea vessel. And besides that, there were *other people.* Throngs of them, milling about, working behind the glass walls of some of the rooms, talking together with folded arms and invested stares. They were all in darkish clothing, and they all appeared to be human. At least, on the outside they did. There were races and ethnicities from all over the world. But no space aliens or monsters that Rhett could see. For now.

Here was a group of middle-aged men, hunched together around a wide sheet of paper, pointing at it, commenting, nodding in agreement.

Here was an elderly woman, trotting up a set of steps to another deck with the same stamina as a twenty-something jogger in Central Park.

Here was a little kid, tinkering under the light of a workbench in another room, her hands busy with some kind of contraption, putting it together or taking it apart.

Rhett stood at the railing, peering down at the hivelike commotion, feeling the ship list and pull. He wanted to be nauseous, and for a moment, because his brain made it happen, he was. But he was also excited. More and more, the notion that he might be dreaming, that this was all just some sort of mental interpretation of the damage he'd suffered, was fading. His imagination did not have the capacity to think any of this up. He hadn't been a jock, but he hadn't been too deep into creative arts, either. He had no talent for artistry or writing or music. He couldn't catch a football to save his life. Rhett Snyder had been a pebble wedged into the tiny divide in the concrete pillars of high school, dropping between the cracks and vanishing there.

But this. This was no product of Rhett's—or anybody else's—subconscious. And the fact that there were other people, people who were like him and would understand him and might even be able to explain what was happening to him, was more exciting than anything he'd seen so far. It gave him hope. Hope that his parents were here somewhere, waiting for him.

"We call this the Column," Basil said. "Pretty much the only part of the ship that we stick to unless our . . . uh . . . duties take us elsewhere."

Rhett glanced sidelong at Basil and caught that irritating, know-it-all grin.

"And these fine folks," he continued, gesturing around at the busy clusters of bodies, "are the crew of the *Harbinger*. Myself included. And now you."

He was so matter-of-fact about it that Rhett almost missed the last part. But he did catch it, and his resolve hardened again.

"I'm not going to be part of any crew," he said. "I don't know why you brought me here or even who the hell you really are. But I told you, I'm just interested in finding my parents. I . . . I don't think I'm supposed to be here, and I don't plan on staying."

Basil's cheery demeanor was unfazed. "We'll see, mate. How about you come have a chat with my team and you can see how you feel after?" He was gesturing across the open part of the atrium, to the other side of the deck, where there was a tiny collection of people who looked close to the same age as Rhett and Basil—two girls and one massive guy. Basil was already moving in their direction.

When Basil approached, one of the girls rolled her eyes at him. She had dark hair, brown eyes, and long legs in a pair of dark pants. She was also muscular, toned through her arms and shoulders—obviously not a physique that was gained after her death but something she must have had prior to it. In other words, not someone that Rhett would have had the courage to ask out on a date.

The other girl was scrawny, probably the youngest of them all, and up close Rhett could see that she was probably closer to middle school age. There was a smattering of dark freckles across her cheeks, some of them the same color as her red hair, half-hidden by the too-big pair of glasses she had on. She was hunched over some sort of tablet—an actual electronic device, from the look of it—poking at it, biting her lower lip, not really acknowledging anybody but still appearing to be tuned in to the conversation.

The guy, who was standing beside the girls with his arms crossed like a dam about to break, was an easy six foot seven, six foot eight, maybe. His arms were roiling pockets of sinew and wiry veins. His neck was a bunch of dense cables, popping and flexing. His skin was thick, and his skull was probably thicker. You could have sharpened a knife on the guy's bicep and he wouldn't have noticed.

"So you've returned from your supersecret mission," the first girl said to Basil, the malice on her tongue almost visible. "And it appears to have gone well. Not sure why it needed to be such a big secret, though." She turned the malice in Rhett's direction. He didn't waver. He might not have been brave enough to ask her out, but he knew how to stand up to people like her. "We just got back from there," the girl continued, eyeing Rhett with a mixture of fascination and repulsion. "We got his—"

"Mak, Rhett. Rhett, Mak," Basil said, cutting her off without any deficit in cheer. He patted the scrawny girl on the shoulder. "This is Treeny, our resident technological empress. And that enormous chap, whom you might have mistaken for a large tree, is Theodore Sampson Tinderbuff the Third. We just call him Theo."

Rhett looked up at Theo, who was holding his hand out. They shook, and Rhett swore he heard something in his hand crack under the force of the grip. But he didn't feel any pain, barely felt the handshake itself.

"Pleasure," Theo said in a dense, almost comic New York accent.

"You lookin' for a spot on our crew?" He spoke like a 1940s gangster. Rhett was mystified.

"I . . . uh . . . I don't . . ."

"What? Words ain't ya strong suit?" He said *words* like *woyds*.

The first girl—Mak—interjected. "He absolutely does not have a spot on our crew, Theo. What he needs is a spot with someone else. Or maybe out in the water." She smiled in a way that looked more like a grimace.

"Whoa, whoa, whoa there, ninja princess," Basil said, stepping between Mak and Rhett. "I told you I had a feeling, didn't I? I gave you as much information as I had. I didn't know where I was going until I got there . . . and found *him*." He jerked a thumb over his shoulder at Rhett.

"You didn't know where you were going, but you had to get *off* the ship to get there?" Mak asked. She squinted her eyes at him and licked her lips—a predator waiting out her prey.

But Basil just laughed. "And how exactly did *you* get aboard this luxury vessel?" he asked her. "Hmm? Did you ride in here with a cloud stuck between your legs?"

Mak's mouth twitched, just slightly, and Rhett imagined that now would have been the time that, in the living world, her face would have flushed with color. She said nothing.

"That's right, love," Basil jabbed. "I came and rescued you, too, didn't I?"

Mak dropped her arms and stuck a finger in Basil's face. "You did *not* rescue me."

Meanwhile, Theo stared on from his separate altitude, and

Treeny prodded her screen. Rhett stood just outside the confrontation, not sure what to do. He looked around at some of the other crew members lumbering around. A few of them glanced in the direction of the argument, but nobody spoke up or seemed bothered by it. *What the hell did I get myself into?* Rhett thought.

The exchange between Mak and Basil continued, with each of them poking the other with their verbal swords, most of the content going right over Rhett's head. Mak asked Basil why he couldn't have just used one of the *regular* doors on the ship to go run his "little errand." Basil asked Mak why she was so "nosy and disrespectful." Mak told Basil that they were supposed to be on the same team, that "gathering" was a "group effort." To that Basil said only one thing: "Not this kind of gathering, sweetheart." This seemed to set ablaze a whole new kind of fire in Mak.

Theo and Treeny stood by like a couple of witnesses to a fistfight, not really wanting to get involved but thinking that they might eventually have to.

Rhett decided he had two options: turn around and try to find his own way off this damned boat, or . . .

"Hey!" he yelled at the squabbling pair, feeling a bit like a meek human screaming at a tornado to stop turning. "Hey!" he yelled again. His voice rang along the steel railings of the atrium. It was enough to get Basil's attention.

"Just one second, ma—"

"No!" Rhett cut him off. "And I swear to God if you call me *mate* one more time, I'll choke the life . . . or whatever . . . out of you before *she* gets a chance to." He stabbed his index finger at Mak, whose eyes widened ever so slightly. "Someone needs to tell me what the fuck all this is about before I take off and start looking for my own answers." He felt the anger absorb his courage, and he glared up at Theo. "*Capeesh?*"

There was silence among the five of them. Basil and Mak stared at Theo, who was staring at Rhett. Rhett wanted his heart to race, wanted to feel the pounding hooves of adrenaline quiver through his body. He thought about it, focused on it, and a second later felt that lovely, frightening sensation that so often accompanies moments of pure stupidity.

But Theo just looked over at Basil and said, in that mobster drawl, "I like this guy. He's a character." He looked back at Rhett. "You gotta be a New Yorker"—(*New Yawk-ah*)—"with a temper like that."

"Oh Jesus!" Mak hissed. "Enough with this." She stepped up to Basil until they were almost touching noses. "*You* can talk to him, then," she said in his face. And then she stomped away, her boots making hard metallic thumps as she went.

Basil waited, then said, "She's a right pain in the ass sometimes. I swear. Come with us, ma . . . er . . . Rhett. I guess I'm in charge of explaining things to you now. If you're still interested."

Rhett was. For now.

He felt like *he* was the one who was about to be interrogated, instead of the other way around.

The room was as cold and sterile as the rest of the Column, all polished steel and hard edges, a metal table and a couple of chairs, that same icy glow. If it weren't for the subtle shove and tug of the waves, Rhett might have forgotten he was on a ship at all. He wasn't sure if he was one to get seasick, having never been on a cruise or anything before. But when he tried to will himself to feel nauseous, it took a lot more effort than he expected. He decided that getting seasick probably hadn't been a thing for him when he was alive.

Basil, Treeny, and Theo squeezed into the tiny room with him. They stood on the other side of the table, with the glass wall looking out at the rest of the atrium behind them.

"This is one of our workrooms," Basil explained, finally sounding serious. "The crew is made up of teams, usually just a handful of people each. Sometimes we like to have meetings or get-togethers or shindigs or whatever. These rooms are good for that sort of thing."

"I'm glad," Rhett said. "I was beginning to think you tortured people in here."

"No, there's a whole other part of the ship for that. Shackles and chains. The whole bit." Basil grinned.

Rhett crossed his arms and glared. "Tell me everything."

"Everything? Oh God . . . well, I was born in Wales—"

Rhett stood up, shoving his chair into the wall behind him. "It was nice meeting you, but I don't have time for this crap."

"All right, all right, all right!" Basil cried, putting his hands up. "Sheesh. You're just as bad as Mak, aren't you?"

"This is my *life* we're talking about," Rhett said, his teeth grinding together. "Is that funny to you?"

Basil sighed. "Yeah, all right, I get it. And, more accurately, it's your *after*life we're talking about."

Rhett nodded, letting that sink in, feeling the reality of it confirmed.

"Fine," he said, more calmly than he expected. "So then, what is . . . all this?"

"Mak was supposed to be the one to explain everything to you," Basil replied. "She's better at being . . . well, blunt. But I'll do my best. As I said, this ship, the one we're on, is called the *Harbinger*. Its most important function is the transportation of . . . goods."

"What goods?"

"Souls."

Rhett opened his mouth, closed it again.

"Souls," he said. Not asking, just restating. It wasn't really that hard to believe—he had already come to terms with the idea that he was dead, but to hear it out loud . . . "Like, *our* souls? Yours, mine, theirs?" He gestured to Treeny and Theo.

"Well, yes," Basil replied. "But we're different."

"Different how?"

"You see, the *Harbinger* has collected millions upon millions of souls since the beginning of . . . well, forever. And they're all still on board."

"How is that possible?" Rhett asked. The ship was big, but not that big.

"We'll get there. But what's important to understand is that those souls don't just appear on board. They need someone to collect them.

That's us." Basil swept an arm around the room and motioned at the window behind him. *Everybody*, he was trying to say. "And you," he continued, leveling his eyes at Rhett.

Rhett lowered his gaze, trying to absorb the words, letting the pieces fall into place.

"C'mon, mate," Basil said quietly. "You're an intelligent bloke. Do I need to spell it out for you?"

"You're . . . Death," Rhett said, mostly to the hard surface of the table. "As in capital *D*, cloak and scythe, Death." He looked up.

Basil was grinning appreciatively. "That's right. Although, the cloak and scythe are a bit seventeenth century. And not really our style, as you can see." He tugged at the lapels of his blazer. "We go by our original name now—syllektors."

"And . . . I . . . ?" Rhett raised his eyebrows.

"Correct. You're a syllektor. An official member of the club. Don't expect a membership card or anything, though." Basil shrugged.

"I still don't understand," Rhett said, standing because he couldn't help but pace when he was anxious, even when his body felt nothing of the anxiety itself. "Why am I so different? Why are *you*? I mean, if every soul ends up on the *Harbinger*, what makes someone a . . . you know?" He didn't want to say it. The word would have felt funny in his mouth, like trying to pick up a foreign dialect. And there was something even more concerning about the way this conversation was headed, something else he couldn't quite muster the courage to speak out loud.

"Trauma."

The voice was so tiny that Rhett almost didn't hear it. It was

Treeny, speaking for the first time. Her face was still glued to whatever she was working on, but her eyes flicked toward Rhett just long enough to confirm that he had heard her. Rhett waited for her to explain, but she wouldn't elaborate.

Rhett turned back to Basil, who was nodding solemnly.

"What does she mean?" Rhett said.

"There's no definitive algorithm," Basil started, "but the ones who become syllektors when they die are usually the ones who die as a result of some sort of traumatic event. Murder, war, plane crash . . ."

Then all three of them—Basil, Theo, Treeny—spoke at the same time, all of them staring at points in the distance that could have been a foot away or a mile away.

"Gunfight," Theo said.

"Train accident," Basil said.

"Drowning," Treeny said.

Rhett could only stare, trying to absorb their meaning. "So . . . all of you . . . ?"

Basil nodded again. "Mak, too. In her own way, of course."

Rhett sank back into his seat, emptying his lungs with a *shew* sound. What he was releasing, he didn't know. It could have been air, it could have been nothing at all. But it felt good to let it out. He looked around at the other three. Kids, like him. That's all they were. And all of them were dead because of something stupid and horrible and pointless.

And now that he understood why they were all here, he had to ask the question that he'd been avoiding.

"And . . . what about my parents?" Rhett asked slowly, bracing himself.

"They're here." Treeny again, still staring into the washed-out glow of her tablet. "But they're not syllektors. They're not like us."

Rhett put his hands over his face, resisting the urge to scream, to grab the chair he was sitting in and toss it through the window and down the spiraling stairs of the atrium beyond.

"But . . . *why?*" he groaned. His brain felt like it was breaking apart and putting itself back together over and over again. But the tears that he expected weren't there. Of course not. The only way he could truly feel anything anymore was when he made the conscious effort to do so. And he had no interest in showing his grief to these people.

"Like I said, mate," Basil continued, "it's not an exact science. Plenty of people die in horrible ways, but only a fraction of them turn into syllektors."

The room was full of a bloated quiet, heavy with Rhett's silent mourning and Basil's discomforting calm.

After a moment Basil went on: "Our job now is to go out and collect souls. Thousands of syllektors on board, grouped into teams, tasked with bringing the dead back to the *Harbinger* until it reaches its destination."

"Which is where?" Rhett asked, finally looking up again.

Basil lifted his shoulders, then let them drop heavily. "That's a question that no one here can answer for you, mate. Even if they wanted to."

Rhett's mind wandered back to his spot in the driver's seat of his parents' car, his hands gripping the steering wheel until his knuckles were the color of steam, the world twisting around them, filled with glass and rubber and occasionally a beautiful sky. What had he been thinking then? Did he expect to die? Had he been prepared for his life to be stamped out, for the last shreds of his existence to be flung out into blackness, into silence?

Maybe. But no matter what he had been thinking while the car was still in the air, he could never have imagined the *Harbinger* or its crew.

"So now we get put to work," he said. "Is that it? We all die in terrible, horrifying ways and our compensation for that is a job? I'm not even sure you can call it a job. It's . . . it's a punishment."

"It's a second chance." A new voice. Rhett started at the sound of it and looked up.

He stood in the doorway, tall and broad-shouldered, almost as big as Theo but not quite. He was dressed in a dark uniform that was pristine, angular, creased to perfection. It was more like a geometric shape than an article of clothing. The skin of his face was coated in a gray beard and lined with age. There was a captain's hat on his head that matched the rest of his uniform, straight and true, not a speck of dirt or dust anywhere. His eyes were alert, smoldering into Rhett with the intensity of the sun.

"Captain Trier," Basil said, stepping back, immediately handing the room over to the newcomer.

"Mr. Winthrop," the man—the apparent captain—said. His voice was gravelly, yet dense with power. "How's our new arrival?"

"Acclimating," Basil replied. He shot Rhett an uncertain look.

Rhett's outburst probably hadn't done much for Basil's confidence, but Rhett was far from concerned about that.

"So this thing does have a captain," Rhett said. "Who'd you have to kill to get that job?" All at once, the fire and the petulance that had so plagued Rhett during the last few years was back in full force. It was this same challenging attitude that had landed him—and his parents—here. But once he got going, it was nearly impossible to stop, like a snowball that eventually rolls itself into a full-fledged avalanche.

Captain Trier only smirked. "I know this is all pretty overwhelming, Mr. Snyder. But—"

"Overwhelming?" Rhett said, his voice cracking. "We passed overwhelming the second I didn't just poof out of existence. Where we're at now is . . . unreal."

There was another long span of quiet in the room, with Theo and Basil watching Trier nervously and Treeny seeming unfazed.

Trier maintained his slanted smirk, though. It seemed his calm was unshakable.

"So you think that being on this ship is some kind of purgatory," Trier said. His hands were clasped behind his back, his shoulders jutting like perfectly straight shore cliffs.

Rhett thought about that word—*purgatory*. He'd used it earlier with Basil on the rock. He'd cracked a joke about being stuck there with Basil forever, and Basil had genuinely smiled. Rhett's stubbornness dimmed. What kind of purgatory was it when someone could crack a smile like that?

"I . . . I don't know," Rhett said, feeling defeated. "Maybe *purgatory* is an overstatement. But having to work as a spiritual tour guide for the rest of eternity definitely sounds like a punishment to me."

"Punishment for what?" Trier asked.

Rhett didn't want to think about the answer to that. He knew what his punishment was for. The rest of them didn't need to know. He said nothing.

"Punishment from whom?" Trier pushed. "Certainly not me. I only give punishments to crew members who have made vastly unwise decisions aboard this ship."

Rhett could only look at him, his body unable to provide a response to the emotions that thrashed and gnawed at his mind.

"The question, Rhett," Trier continued, "is whether or not you think you *deserve* a punishment."

The words hit the room like an anvil into dirt, thumping into the heart that Rhett now knew he could feel beating in his chest. The rest of his body was inept at feeling anything, but the heart was there. Rhett hated it more and more with every squeeze of its pulse.

"You don't have to answer that right now, Rhett. You don't have to answer it at all. Because either way, we're not here to punish you." Trier turned to the glass wall, hands still held together behind his back, as if addressing the ship as a whole. "Basil, how about you? Do you feel like your time on the *Harbinger* has been a punishment?"

"No, sir," Basil replied without hesitation.

"Oh wow," Rhett said. "Now I'm convinced."

Trier chuckled. "You and Basil will get along very well, I think."

"I apologize, Captain," Basil said through the side of his mouth. "I didn't realize he was such a cheeky bastard until just now."

"Rhett," Trier went on, waving Basil off, "the syllektors aboard this ship are doing the most important work there is. They are a guiding light. Without them, the souls of the dead would be left to wander the world. Alone. Afraid. Confused. You know how it felt right after your death. Imagine feeling that way forever."

Rhett had no reply for that, either.

"You can be angry, Rhett. You can be sad. You can be whatever you want to be. But you have a chance to shape your death into something meaningful. This *is* a second chance. Use it."

Heavy silence again, as if all the oxygen in the room had been replaced with damp gauze.

Finally, Rhett shook his head.

"I'm not interested," he said. He stood, unsure of what was going to happen next. Were they going to make him walk the plank or something? Lock him up somewhere? Strangely, he was more afraid now than he had been at the prospect of having to collect souls forever. He started for the door, hoping that he could slip out and find a way back to New York before Trier started offering him the consolation prize.

Trier sighed. Not impatiently, but with a certain amount of flustered surrender. The words *I didn't want to have to do this* seemed locked behind his lips somewhere.

"What about Roger and Ilene?" he said.

Rhett stopped, head down, chest heaving. If he opened his mouth, nothing but a haunted, horrified scream would come out. So he kept it clamped shut.

"They're on board," Trier said. "Not in this form, unfortunately—they're not syllektors. But they are on the ship, Rhett. I could help you find them. I could help you communicate with them. If you help us, if you perform the duties that you were obviously chosen to perform, I can help you."

Rhett looked back at the captain, who stood in that same insanely rigid position, waiting. Rhett searched for the sincerity in his eyes. He couldn't find sincerity, exactly, but he found no deceit, either. His eyes flitted over to Basil, looking anxious and confused. Apparently, Trier's proposition was something that he hadn't expected.

Roger and Ilene, Rhett thought. His parents. The words repeated themselves, running through his head on a constant loop, like a radio station tuned to static or an orchestra perpetually caught in those first few seconds when they're warming up their instruments. Eventually the names would go from having actual meaning to just being noise, a scream slicing into him like a piece of glass. If he let them.

Rhett stood up straight, taking in a deep breath of whatever passed for air around here, and tried to think with some version of clarity.

"Okay," he said after a moment. "I'm in."

They stepped out of the room, back into the tumult of the complex, seemingly unnoticed. There were a few brief glances in their direction, specifically aimed at Rhett, of course—the new and strange face among them. But otherwise, the crew appeared to keep to themselves.

Captain Trier gave Rhett and the others a stiff little bow, hands still behind his back as if they had been glued together, then went to a spiral staircase at the other end of the floor. He ascended into some other darker part of the ship, consumed partly by shadow, and then vanished completely.

"That's the bridge," Basil murmured in Rhett's ear. He must have caught him staring. "You'll have to check it out sometime. Great view."

"Huh" was all Rhett could think to say. His brain felt like an avocado that had just had its pit gouged out. He wondered faintly if he might be going into shock. His body would never respond to such a thing. But his head felt empty and light, as if someone had just taken him by the neck and shook him until all of the gray, wormy matter that made up who he was had come spilling out of his ears. In fact, this whole thing felt a lot like having hands around his throat.

"Anyway, you'll probably want to eat and get some rest," Basil said. "Allow me to show you to your quarters. Since it appears that I'm also now your bellboy as well as your orientation trainer." He was watching Theo and Treeny, who had given cringe-y smiles and curt waves before retreating toward the lower decks of the ship. It was just Rhett and Basil again.

"Wait, wait, wait," Rhett said, putting his hands in a T shape like an NFL referee. "Back in New York you said it . . . it's all sensation and no feeling. I'm not hungry *or* tired. And I could probably jog two hundred laps around this ship without ever needing to catch my breath."

Basil chuckled. "That's true. You don't *have* to do anything. None of us do. We don't need food. We don't need sleep. But we do those things anyway."

"Why?"

"Sanity, mate. It helps keep you feeling normal. You've already figured out how to sort of *make* your body react, yes?"

Rhett's mouth dropped open slightly.

Basil laughed again. "Don't look so shocked. You didn't think you were the only one who figured out that little trick, did you? You've only been dead for, like, five minutes. There's plenty left for you to understand."

"So even though you don't have to, you still eat," Rhett said, trying to redirect the conversation back to its starting point. "And sleep and everything else to . . . what? Keep from totally cracking up?"

Basil cocked a finger at him.

"You got it, chap," he said. "Imagine another three or four days of just sitting in your room, trapped in your own head without any desire to do *anything*. You'd tear your own eyes out before a week was up."

They were moving down the staircase now, descending through the middle of the Column, with Basil subtly leading the way. Rhett wasn't sure what time it was—there didn't appear to be any windows to the outside—but the number of crew members milling about the atrium seemed to be thinning out. How could anyone tell when they were supposed to do anything?

"And what exactly would that do?" Rhett asked, reeling himself back in.

"What would what do?" Basil said over his shoulder.

"What would tearing my own eyes out do? Would a new pair just appear? Would they grow back over time?"

Now Basil was actually laughing out loud in short, barklike yips. "You would just go bloody blind, mate," he said. He ditched the stairs three or four decks down and made his way to another pair of doors.

"What do you mean? I thought we were . . . invincible or whatever." Rhett was genuinely curious.

Basil stopped and turned to face him.

"Listen, man," he said, letting his chuckles die off. "It's obvious you watched waaaayyyy too much TV as a living person. But that's not how it works. You might not feel the pain, but this version of yourself—this vessel that's mostly made up of your soul—operates under the same principles as your living body did. If I were to rip your arm off right now, you might not be all that bothered by it mentally. Physically, though? You'd be down an arm."

Rhett was trying to make sense of it. If they were invisible to the living and were no longer made up of any kind of physical matter, how could they still be hurt the same way?

"So . . . what happens if this *vessel* were to be destroyed completely?" he asked.

"Ugh! You ask a lot of bloody questions." Basil threw his hands up and pinched the bridge of his nose. "I am not cut out for this part of the process," he murmured under his breath. "Listen, how about

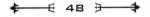

we table this for now, okay? The bottom line is this: Don't get hurt. Your spirit body heals itself the same way your physical body did. Period. And if your head gets lobbed off?" He shrugged.

"Got it," Rhett replied. There was poison in the way he said it. Why would Basil bring him here if he wasn't willing to answer any of his questions? Basil wasn't hiding his annoyance, and neither was Mak. Treeny and Theo seemed indifferent, but still, the only one who seemed to want him here was the one person who had genuinely gotten under Rhett's skin: Captain Trier. But it wasn't even that Trier just got under his skin; he had probed into the most sensitive part of Rhett's life, and then he'd used it against him.

Basil could sense the irritation in Rhett's voice, could probably see it in his eyes, too.

"Don't be sour, mate," Basil said. "It's just been a while since we've had a new recruit. They used to come in all the time. We're a little out of practice at the whole 'welcome to the team' thing. That's all."

Rhett nodded, clamping his mouth shut to keep more of his questions stifled.

They moved on.

Basil showed him the mess hall, which was weirdly reminiscent of the cafeteria at Rhett's high school. It was all the same steel furnishings and chilly lighting, but there was actual hot food lined up at a buffet-style counter, steaming under the warm yellow beams of the heating lamps. Rhett didn't know if any of the food was real and at first couldn't smell it. But he willed his nose to take in the aromas. And then he willed his stomach to growl longingly. It was weird having to force himself to do the things that used to happen on their own, especially his hunger. But the perks were obvious. You could choose when to want food, when to want sleep. You could filter your emotions in a way that even the most apathetic sociopath among the living could not. In a strange way, it was kind of freeing.

Rhett and Basil made heaping plates for themselves, eating in silence, focused only on the task at hand, which was to wreck the hell out of all that food.

And despite everything that he had seen and experienced since the moment of his death, Rhett was still surprised when, after two plates of food, he still wasn't full. He had stopped sending the signals to his stomach to *act* hungry a long time ago. He had eaten way past his normal, *living* capacity for intake. He was also afraid that if he forced his stomach into experiencing the sensation of all that food he'd just stuffed down his throat, he'd yack it all back up. Then again . . . if the food wasn't actually there in the first place, if it was just some trick of the spiritual world, then had he really eaten anything at all?

He decided that line of thinking would only send him right down the rabbit hole into insanity.

After dinner, Basil showed Rhett a few of the *Harbinger*'s other amenities.

There was a gym, a café, a library, a movie theater. None of them were advertised in any grand fashion, only with metal plaques above their entrances. Yet it still made Rhett feel like he was taking a tour of a shopping mall.

"Who knew that turning into a grim reaper would be so . . . lavish," he said to Basil.

"Lucky for you," Basil said gravely, "we're not even close to grim reapers."

There was something weird about the way he said it, and Rhett wanted to hear more. But Basil didn't offer an explanation.

The final stop on the tour, obviously way past what qualified as bedtime since the hallways were all but deserted, was the living quarters. They were down on one of the lower decks of the Column, where hallways fanned out from every side and were lined with numbered doors.

Basil led Rhett down to the very end of one of the halls, to a door at its throat marked with the number 0312.

"Anyway, here you are," Basil said. "I'll deposit you here for now and . . . uh . . . meet me in the mess hall in the morning?"

"How am I supposed to know when it's morning?"

"Well, most of us try to get on the same schedule. Every eight hours, give or take. When you can hear people moving around out here, you're probably safe to head up."

Rhett glanced at the door, suddenly nervous. He was about to be left here alone.

"Seriously, mate," Basil said, putting a reassuring hand on Rhett's shoulder. "Try to sleep. You might not feel like you need it. But up here?" He pointed at Rhett's forehead. "You definitely do."

With that, Basil turned on his heel and headed back down the hall.

Rhett watched him go for a moment, until he was out of sight. And then the silence fell in like a flood of water. He couldn't even hear anyone snoring or talking in their sleep. And why would he? Death was not a translator of those strange quirks of the living.

He opened the door to his cabin and stepped inside.

At first he was delighted to see a porthole window, a thick eye staring out at the gray world. But then he could see the waves and the sky, still bubbling and frothing like a witch's brew. Lightning chiseled down from the sky not too far away, illuminating the water . . . and the enormous creature turning over just beneath the surface. It was mostly just a shadow, but it was at least half as big as the *Harbinger*, with a long, serpentine tail that seemed barbed and jagged on the end. Rhett could just barely make out the shape of it. And then, with the lightning, it disappeared back into the dark.

He forced his attention toward the little room again, glad now that he had opted not to traverse the deadly ocean, and pushed the monster from his thoughts (as much as he could, anyway).

There was a little sink and mirror near the door, a narrow closet (for what, he didn't know—he hadn't brought anything with him), a couple of shelves by the window, and a solitary bunk with a neatly folded blanket and pillow waiting to be used, all dimly lit by a single light in the center of the ceiling.

The empty closet reminded Rhett of something. He slipped a hand into his jeans pocket and dug around. He was looking for his phone, but it wasn't there. A lot of good it would have done him anyway. There couldn't possibly be any decent cell reception in the afterlife. He thought there might have been a picture of his parents on there somewhere, though. Maybe that's what he'd really been look-ing for.

He stood at the sink, looking into the tiny mirror. He appeared the same, as far as he could tell—his dark hair darting out in all directions, his brown eyes. It was all there. And yet he could tell that it wasn't really him. It was a projection, a suspect sketch of who he used to be. Close . . . but not quite right.

Clear, cold water came out of the faucet when he turned it on. He cupped his hands under it, telling his fingers to feel the numb-ing power of the water as it trickled over them. He splashed some on his face and sent the same signals there. He shivered, and it almost felt like he hadn't forced himself to do so.

When he turned off the faucet, he could still hear water drip-ping, a lot of it, as if something had sprung a leak somewhere. Ac-tually, it sounded as if the water was splashing onto the floor right behind him. He turned around, expecting to see a puddle on the floor and some sort of burst pipe above his head . . .

But there was nothing there, and the sound of dripping water had faded. He shook his head. It was probably just the sink draining.

When he lay down on the bunk, he was just below the window and thankfully couldn't see out into the uneasy shadows. There was no moon, no sun, nothing to judge the time by. Just that constantly roiling gray sky.

Eventually he willed his eyes to shut, willed his shouting mind to quiet down to a whisper, and willed his body to sleep.

FOUR

For a moment, just a fraction of the space between seconds, there was the car again, falling. His arms and legs stiff against the wheel, against the pedals, instinctively trying to find purchase, even as the sky and the earth kept switching places outside the windows. The cracked, blistered asphalt rushing up to pulverize him. The world was a concussion of noise: horns and cries and whispering machine parts.

And there was also . . .

. . . the ocean.

Rhett could hear it sloshing against the side of the ship in a hollow, metallic way, as if he were hearing it from the bottom of a tin can. Which, he supposed, he kind of was. The *Harbinger* was as big of a tin can as they came, one full of nonperishable souls.

He sat up in his bunk, steadying himself against the gentle wobble of the sea. There was no change in atmosphere; the room was still just as gloomy and depressing as it had been the night (day?) before. Outside, the turbulent cloud cover was as dreary as ever. Only now there was some scenery: another one of those craggy rock formations, like the one that Rhett and Basil had arrived on, this one a little less welcoming. It curled up out of the frothing ocean like a gnarled finger, tall and slender, layered in jagged outcroppings. It looked as if it were pointing the way.

But to where?

Somebody knocked on the door then, banging against it with what must have been their fist.

"Hey new guy!" A muffled voice from the other side, with a heavy New York accent. Theo. "You up?"

"Uh . . . yeah," Rhett called. He stood and gave himself a once-over in the mirror. His reflection was the same as it had been the night before, except . . . He squinted at the mirror, making sure he was seeing what he thought he was seeing. His face and hair all seemed to be unmarred by his sleep, which he supposed was a tiny bit weird considering he had always been notorious for his bed head. But the really weird part was the fact that his clothes, the same jeans and plaid button-down shirt he'd been wearing, appeared to be a shade or two darker, as if they were losing their vibrancy.

He thought about the crew members he'd seen last night. All their clothing had been dark, too. Maybe it was some kind of effect of the atmosphere? Or of the ship itself?

"You comin' or not, new guy? I ain't got all day to wait for yous." The words were impatient, but Theo's tone sounded playful.

"Coming," Rhett said. His eyes lingered on the new hue of his outfit for just a second longer.

A few minutes later, Rhett and Theo were back at the mess hall. Theo had sauntered there beside Rhett without saying a single word.

Rhett noticed Theo's clothes were the same as the day before: a dark T-shirt and slacks held up by suspenders. His black shoes were polished so that when Rhett looked down at them, he saw a narrow reflection of himself looking back up. All Theo was missing was a fedora. Then his Untouchables vibe would be complete.

The mess hall was crowded with people. It was a sea of dark clothing, the chatter among the crew like the shushing of the tide.

Across the room, Basil, Treeny, and Mak were sitting together. Rhett was surprised to see Mak and felt like he was back at high school, nervous now because he had somehow been lumped together with the cool kids. He got some food and headed their way.

As he wormed around the tables, leaving Theo to debate his breakfast options, he noticed Basil and Mak with their heads together, talking in that conspiratorial way that almost ensures someone is talking about you. When Rhett approached the table, the pair sat up as casually as they could, but Rhett had seen enough.

"Good morning, chap!" Basil said, smacking Rhett on the shoulder as he sat down.

Rhett nearly dropped his tray. "Morning," he grumbled.

"Not much of a morning person, are you?"

"Not exactly."

Rhett started eating, allowing his taste buds to open up and enjoy the flavors again. He looked up and realized Treeny was sitting right across from him, staring. There was no tablet today, just her freckle-spotted hands folded neatly in front of her.

"Good morning," she said, and her voice was so clear and so sweet, even in the din of the hall, that Rhett did a double take. She had only said a few words to him the night before, and it had not been part of a pleasant conversation.

"Good . . . morning," he said around a mouthful of scrambled eggs.

In the meantime, Theo had lumbered over with two trays and squeezed himself into a chair.

"Looks like the whole team's here," Basil said with a grin. Mak shot him a nasty look.

"The . . . whole team?" Rhett asked. He was eyeing Mak with a mixture of contempt and nervousness. "Including me?"

"Well of course!" Basil leaned in. "The captain thought it would be a good idea. Seeing as we're all young and adventurous and . . . well, stubborn."

Rhett hadn't taken his eyes off Mak, who was staring intently at the mediocre lump of oatmeal on her plate, obviously trying to avoid the conversation.

"So," Basil went on, "any ideas for team names?"

Rhett waited to see if he was serious. But when nobody started throwing out options, Basil's cheer deflated.

"No offense," Rhett murmured, "but you guys don't . . . seem like much of a team."

Mak slammed both of her fists onto the table, sending a geyser of Theo's eggs and potatoes shooting into the air. Theo shot her an annoyed look, and she rolled her eyes at him before glaring at Rhett.

"Listen," she hissed. "I don't approve of any of this. Got it? I'm supposed to be leading this team, and I got overruled. As far as I'm concerned, you can park your ass down in the engine room and shovel coal for the rest of eternity. If not, then this is your one and only warning—you get in my way, and I'll make sure you become someone else's problem."

For a split second, at the beginning of Mak's tirade, Rhett almost panicked. He caught himself, though. Captain Trier was right—this was a second chance. To be the person he knew he truly was.

He sat up straight, leveled his eyes at Mak as she threatened to cast him out, and raised his eyebrows. When she was done, he said, "Anything else? Any other disclaimers you'd like to share? Because I guess I missed the one warning me about your bad attitude."

Mak's face grew dark, her lips pursing together until they were a thin pale line. Rhett thought she might lunge across the table and literally attack him. He tensed himself for a physical fight, which was something he was sure he would lose, especially to her.

But Mak just stood and stomped out of the hall, leaving behind her tray and the mess of exploded eggs, which Theo had started eating off the table anyway. There was a strange, intense beauty to Mak, especially when she was angry. Rhett couldn't help but notice it. And he was at least a little sorry. He hadn't intended to be dropped into her lap, to be forced onto her team, and to disrupt whatever dynamic they already had.

He mostly felt good, though. It had been a while since he'd had the courage to stand up for himself like that.

"Oh-ho-ho, that was unwise, mate," Basil said. But he was laughing.

"Sorry," Rhett mumbled. "She's just . . ."

"Strong-willed?" It was Treeny, offering up a better word than any of the ill-fated alternatives that Rhett could have used.

"Yeah," he said. "Something like that. Am I still too new to ask what that's all about? I don't think I did anything wrong. Did I?" He looked around at the other three, searching their faces. But they all just looked down at their food in stiff, weighted silence. Even Theo, who had practically been gorging himself, quit shoving food in his mouth and swallowed hard.

There was an uncomfortable moment when it seemed like the quiet would just keep spinning out like that forever. And then Basil finally spoke up.

"Mak has a certain . . . aversion to new teammates," he said, poking at a syrup-logged pancake and looking genuinely unsettled. "It's been just the four of us for a long time now."

Basil stopped there, but the implication was clear.

"But it hasn't always been just the four of you," Rhett said. It wasn't a question. He looked over at Treeny, who was staring at her hands, scratching at the quicks of her fingernails. Her eyes were wide and fearful and pained.

"No," Basil replied.

Treeny squeezed her eyes shut, and Rhett decided that was enough prodding for one breakfast.

The four of them went back to eating. The mess hall began to clear, with groups of people—teams of syllektors—abandoning their tables and heading back out into the Column. There was a team breaking down the buffet, removing the still-steaming pans of food and switching off the heat lamps. Rhett wasn't sure if he wanted to know where the food came from or where it went. He wasn't sure it mattered much, though—it tasted wonderful.

Another few minutes passed and then Treeny's head perked up, cocked to one side, as if she were listening for something. Rhett took a bite, chewing slowly, wondering what was up. Then Theo stopped with a fork that had impaled a sausage link halfway to his mouth. Basil leaned back, scratching his chin and looking around. He looked like he was waiting for something.

Treeny, in a tiny, heartbreaking voice, said, "Someone's dying."

Rhett nearly choked on his last bite of breakfast.

"What?" he said, except it sounded more like *wad* with the pancake lodged in the back of his throat. He swallowed. "Now?"

"Yeah," Basil said. "Happens all the time. Didn't we go over the job description last night? All those other teams that took off out of here? Where do you think they were going? Death is a full-time job, mate."

He and Theo and Treeny stood and waited for Rhett.

"I'm going with you?" he asked.

Basil looked around. "Uh . . . obviously. You just braved the raging tempest over the fact that you're now a part of our team, remember? Are you sure you don't have some sort of memory . . . thing?"

"I just thought there'd be some kind of . . . I don't know . . . training or something," Rhett said.

Basil laughed, and Rhett had a flashback to the night before. Laughing was Basil's standard response to what he must have thought were stupid questions.

"Not for this, there won't be," Basil said. "Collecting souls is something you have to learn firsthand. Let's go."

They led him up the stairs to a new level of the Column, where there was a glass wall with a set of doors in the middle. Everything behind the wall was sleek and metallic and coated in light. Weapons. Blades and swords, armor, arrows, whips, shields, axes, knives, all hung on rows of metal shelving. It was like a department store for the zombie apocalypse. Rhett didn't see any guns, but there was practically everything else.

"What is this?" Rhett asked breathlessly.

"The armory," Basil said, and his tone was unusually serious. He turned to Treeny. "Where's—"

But then she came storming down the steps, glaring straight ahead at no one. Mak didn't even glance at Rhett as she walked past. Her boots thumped hard against the floor, as if she were slamming them down on purpose. Rhett wouldn't have ruled that out.

They followed Mak into the armory, where she, Theo, Treeny, and Basil all began selecting a set of weapons. Theo took down an ax that was at least half his size. It made him look a bit like Paul Bunyan when he rested it on his shoulder. Treeny, the sweet, silent little kid that she was, had about a dozen throwing knives in her hands, fanning them out and examining them like some kind of ninja. Mak was strapping a long bow knife to her leg. She pulled angrily at the ties, keeping her eyes down.

It was Basil that finally broke Rhett's shocked silence. Basil was spinning a pair of short-handled scythes on his fingers like they were drumsticks, making gleaming circles in the air. Scythes. Literal scythes.

"I thought you said the cloak-and-scythe thing wasn't your style," Rhett said, eyeing the four of them as if they were bombs about to go off.

Basil grinned.

"Yeah, well, I'm a traditionalist, I suppose." He gave the scythes one last admiring look and then crossed them on his back, where they slipped into some sort of specialized holsters.

It looked as if they were preparing to go to war, one fought with only these medieval-looking tools.

"What the hell is all this for?" Rhett was stunned by the immensity of the armory. But the need for it was suddenly clear. "What else is out there?"

Basil sighed and gave Mak a hard look. He was waiting for her to explain. When she finally made eye contact with Basil, his eyes widened and he just barely tipped his head in Rhett's direction.

Mak rolled her eyes and sighed.

"Psychons," she said.

"*Psychos?*" Rhett cried.

"No, psy-*chons*."

"What . . . what are they?" Rhett asked.

"They're monsters," Treeny answered in her wavering voice, a voice that made her sound like she was constantly on the verge of tears. The word *monsters* made her sound even more like a little kid having a nightmare.

Basil chimed in. "They're the more literal inspiration for the Grim Reaper as the world knows him today: the skeletal specter who comes in the night to take your soul away. Except psychons don't need scythes. They are their own weapons. And they don't transport souls. They eat them."

Rhett gave the idea of a skeleton monster a chance to settle into his head, then said, "What do they look like?"

"You might just find out," Basil said, giving himself a pat down to make sure he had everything he needed. "Or maybe not. We don't run into them very often. In truth, we're always kind of on the run from them. But we've managed to keep our distance. I'll give you the whole history lesson another time. Right now you need to pick something out and we need to get our asses in gear."

Mak was already stomping out the way they had come in.

"Hey, boss!" Theo called to her. She stopped and turned back, eyebrows raised. "Yous forgot this." Theo tossed something else at her, something large and lethal-looking: a machete. Mak caught it deftly by the handle . . . and actually grinned.

"Thanks, Theo," she said, and continued out the door.

Theo followed her out, leaving Rhett with Basil and Treeny, who were just about ready to go, it seemed.

Rhett gave the rows of weapons an uncertain glance. Once, he'd nearly cut two of his fingers off with a kitchen knife trying to slice a pineapple. How was he supposed to handle a sword that was as long as his arm? Or something even bigger?

"Do any of these come with instruction manuals?" he asked.

Basil chuckled and gave Rhett a pat on the shoulder.

"I said there wouldn't be training for collecting souls," he said. "But I promise there'll be formal training on weapons handling and combat. If we *do* run into any of the creepies out there, we all have to be ready." He glanced back at Treeny, who had at some point picked up her tablet again. She was poking at it impatiently. "For now, just find something that you're comfortable with."

"Do you have any potato peelers?" Rhett said.

Basil only grinned and followed Treeny back out to the stairs.

All of a sudden Rhett was alone with the world's biggest assortment of dismembering utensils. He didn't have much time to choose. He had to catch up with the group if he (a) wanted to tag along on his first . . . whatever it was they were going to do and (b) wanted to avoid getting lost on this ridiculous ship.

He scanned a few rows of items, noting knives and spears and even a flail. But there was something else . . .

It looked like a far more violent pair of brass knuckles. It had a dark wood handle and metal rings for his fingers. From the sides of the knuckles were two smaller blades that curved out and up, and from the tops of the knuckles were two longer blades that went straight-out, shrinking to deadly points. He picked it up. He didn't even know what to call it but internally thought of it as a knuckle blade. It was easy to hold on to and looked like it could do a lot of damage—it even had a sheath of its own, one that Rhett could strap to his leg. He weighed it in his hand, gave it a pathetically dull test-swipe through the empty air, and decided this was the one.

Rhett took the weapon, dreading the idea of having to use it, and went after the others.

When he caught up with the other four, they were already a few decks down and still descending. Rhett noticed that the farther down they went, the older the levels of the Column looked. It was still polished metal and gloomy blue light, but the steps and the railing were worn, shining in a smooth, almost-bronze color. And the metalwork was more ornate, with the railing sporting swirls and curves and whorled designs.

Rhett looked up and saw all the upper decks of the Column stretching away in a spiraling tunnel. To think that this was the heart of the same ship he'd seen cutting through black ocean waves only a day before. That reminded him of something else.

"We're not getting off the ship?" he asked the group as a whole.

"Why would we get *off* the ship?" Mak snapped over her shoulder.

"That was a special assignment, mate," Basil said quickly, before an argument had a chance to spark. "Had to use a . . . back door of sorts. I'll explain when you're older."

"The *Harbinger* has her own access points," Treeny nearly whispered. Rhett had to strain to hear her.

As Treeny spoke, Mak stepped off the stairs only a deck or two up from what appeared to be the very bottom of the Column. From here, Rhett could hear a thunderous growling—the engines—and the heavy *whump-whump-whump* of the propellers beneath the ship.

This level opened up to a high-ceilinged, diamond-shaped room, with old, splintered wooden doors lining every lengthy wall, about seven of them on each side. There were no signs, no numbers on or above the doors. They just stood there like unanswered questions, ready to collapse into heaps of sawdust, propped up only by the toughness of their frames.

As the five of them stepped into the room, Rhett caught Basil eyeing the knuckle blade that he'd strapped to his thigh. Basil rolled his eyes.

"What are you? Wolverine?" he said in a tone of disgust, and shook his head. But his eyes were smiling.

Meanwhile, Mak was standing in the middle of the room, her head down and her eyes shut. Theo, Treeny, and Basil were eerily quiet. Rhett did his best to do the same but was highly aware of the rustling of his clothes as he rocked from foot to foot in an anxious dance.

After another moment, Mak lifted her head. She immediately stepped to the left and closed the distance between herself and the second door from the right on that wall. She gripped the worn-out brass knob . . . and turned.

Rhett wasn't sure what he expected—or wanted—to see. But when Mak opened the door and a wedge of brilliant sunlight appeared on the floor in front of him, he felt a weird sensation of relief. He hadn't known he missed the sun until it was there in front of him again.

Through the door, Rhett could make out a swatch of prickly desert, wisps of dust doing circles through a tangle of dead, crackling weeds, the white dirt challenging the sun with its hot shine.

Without a word, Mak stepped through the door. Rhett could hear her boots crunching into the brittle earth.

The rest of them followed her through.

FIVE

The light would have been blinding had it not been for Rhett's new existence as Death personified. But it was still bright.

The sun hammered itself into everything, and as the five of them stepped through the doorway onto the gouged, scorched dirt, Rhett didn't even need to force his senses to feel the heat.

They were in the middle of nowhere. Desert stretched out around them like the ugly underside of a painter's canvas, with jagged rocks spiking up here and there, bristling with weeds and a few bulbous cacti. Low mountains warbled along the horizon like flexing muscles.

Ahead there was a cluster of squat brick buildings crowded around a single road, where the heat was baking off the pavement in watery shimmers. It looked like the main drag of some little town.

The five of them looked absurd standing there, surrounded by the dirt and the blue, cloudless sky, in their shadow-colored clothes and armed to the teeth with weapons that were better suited for serial killers and trained assassins than a bunch of dead teenagers.

Rhett glanced behind him, at where they had come from.

Half-buried in the ground was a battered Airstream trailer, coated with rust and textured with dents. The windows were caved in, and a ragged hole grinned wide, showing tufts of insulation and the swirling galaxies of dust and bugs inside the trailer. It looked like a mouth chewing on a wad of cotton candy. The door stood open, but within it, where the filthy guts of the trailer were supposed to be, was instead the room of doors inside the *Harbinger*. It was crooked now, trapped inside the confines of the slanted trailer, but there was nothing different about it. It was like an optical illusion—such a big space behind such a tiny door.

"Theo," Mak said. Her voice was different now without all the high ceilings and wide rooms to amplify it. Out here in the badlands, she was far less intimidating.

Without needing further instruction, Theo stepped past Rhett and Treeny and swung the Airstream's door shut. It clacked against the trailer with a plastic-y smack, and when it bounced back again, the view of the inside of the *Harbinger* was gone. The doorway between worlds was closed.

Somewhere far off, an eagle screamed.

"Now what?" Rhett said, reflexively squinting against the sun. He wasn't a huge fan of the desert. "How are we supposed to know where we're going?"

Mak whirled around, a look of pure curiosity on her face.

"You can't feel it?" she asked. Her tone was suspicious, accusatory. The others looked at Rhett, their faces more interested than anything.

"Feel . . . what?"

There was silence, and the stifling tension ramped back up again. There was a part of Rhett that wished he could crawl back through the trailer door to the ship and go hide out in his cabin. He had no idea what she was talking about.

Then Theo spoke, saving him.

"It's like . . . uh . . . like my Nana's blueberry pie," he said. He was grinning from ear to ear, proud of this profound explanation.

"I . . . I'm not sure what you mean, buddy," Rhett said, afraid of pissing off the behemoth.

Theo thought, drumming his fingers against his lips. "It's just a warm feeling in ya gut. Makes ya feel full and happy. Ya know? It's . . . it's . . . what's the word?"

"Instinct," Treeny murmured.

Theo snapped his fingers and pointed at her. "Instinct."

Basil chuckled, and Rhett just barely caught the fading afterimage of a smile on Mak's face.

"You just need to focus," she said, her voice back to that prosecuting tone. "You should feel it if you try not to think about it."

"I don't even know what you guys are talking about," Rhett responded. "Maybe I'm really not supposed to be—"

"Oh, will you just shut up?" Basil cried. "Close your eyes. Forget about blueberry pie and think about a lasso. Should be easy, considering our current environs."

Rhett gave him a skeptical look but did as he was told. He closed his eyes.

"Now imagine the lasso is around your waist. Imagine it pulling you gently."

Rhett did. He thought about the time his dad had taken him to an indoor rodeo upstate. Along with the bull riding, there had also been riders lassoing calves. He thought about the loop circling around in the air above his head and then coming down around him and cinching tight at his waist. And he imagined some invisible hand tugging on it, nudging him, and . . .

He felt it. Really felt it. Some sort of force—like a wind or a vacuum—pushing and pulling him. He remembered the way the others had reacted back at the mess hall. Surely this is what they had been feeling. Already he knew there was no other choice but to follow it.

"I feel it," he said. His voice was low, excited. "I seriously feel it."

"Show us," Mak said challengingly. "Take us where we need to go."

Rhett glared at her, but he was also smiling. "No problem."

He marched past them, following that unseen guide, confident for the first time since arriving aboard the *Harbinger*. The thought that they were going to find a dying person at the other end of that invisible lasso hadn't even crossed his mind yet.

The town crept closer, and Rhett was sure that their destination was somewhere within it—the shapeless push was leading him straight there.

It was a sleepy-looking place, with a handful of cars parked along the sidewalks. The buildings themselves were mostly businesses, or what used to be businesses. They had boarded-up doors and big sheets of brown paper taped up in the windows, squares of poster board with OUT OF BUSINESS or CLOSED FOR GOOD scribbled across them. The few remaining ventures were the usual staples: a bank on one corner, a decrepit realtor's office halfway down the street, a McDonald's at the far end. This was a town—one of many—that had been left behind.

As Rhett led the group onto the broiling asphalt, focusing on the push, on where it was taking him, he caught sight of a faded, weather-beaten sign just at the edge of where the town began: WELCOME TO TURNSTILE, ARIZONA—POP. 743.

"Quaint, isn't it?" Basil murmured. Mak shushed him.

The group paced down Main Street with Rhett still in the lead, feeling the invisible guide growing stronger. They were getting closer.

As they passed the bank, Rhett glanced over and saw the lone teller with her pinky jabbed up her nose, digging around. He grinned. He felt like he was in the old west, part of a gang of outlaws about to hold up the entire town. Their feet clopped against the hot road and he could almost hear the sound of spurs rattling.

They walked on, with the defunct shells of Turnstile's businesses rolling past them, until they got to the end of the street, where the McDonald's sat on one side. On the other, sitting in an oversize, rock-strewn, weed-littered lot, was a diner.

It was a relic, a long cylinder of metal, like a bullet with windows, propped up on cinder blocks and reflecting the sun in slippery glints. There were tubes of cracked or broken neon lining its edges, and the few signs that were hanging in the windows (OPEN, TODAY'S SPECIALS, ASK ABOUT GIFT CERTIFICATES) were barely legible, the words blasted out by the sun over the span of who knew how many years.

Rhett stopped in front of the diner. The push, now almost overpowering him, propelled him closer to it.

"This is the place," he said. And without waiting for anybody to doubt him, he took the steps up to the door and let himself in.

A bell over the door jingled as he stepped inside, but nobody looked up or glanced in Rhett's direction. He wasn't even sure if he'd heard the bell himself. It had sounded more like a clacking sound than a jingle, the way a bell sounds when you cup it in your hand and shake it. And had the door really opened? Or had his mind fabricated that so he wouldn't have to deal with the wild concept of walking through walls? He could ask himself these questions until his ears bled, but he doubted that the answers would ever get any easier to hear.

While he glanced around at the tacky 1950s décor, the bell did its weird *clack-clack-clack* a few more times. The other four hadn't doubted him after all.

There were only a couple of small groups in the diner. A foursome of teenagers in the back corner, cracking jokes at one another and trying to stifle their laughter for the sake of the atmosphere— they just had glasses of water in front of them. Near the window, there was a group of older folks still nursing their coffees, chatting quietly, occasionally darting annoyed glances at the teenagers. There was a single waitress. Her pretty brown hair fell to her shoulders, and her peach-colored uniform hugged her curves. She might have been just out of high school. Maybe the teenagers in the corner were some of her friends. Rhett doubted it.

The waitress was helping an older gentleman with touches of

gray in his hair who was sitting by himself at the bar. She was leaning close, trying to hear his order.

Rhett felt the push nudge him in that direction.

"There," he said, pointing at the man.

What would it be? Rhett thought. Heart attack? Stroke? Would
he accidentally choke on a mouthful of steak and eggs? Would the
guy just keel over for no . . .

But then the waitress was done jotting down the man's order,
and she had tucked her little notepad back into the pocket of her
uniform as she stepped away from where the man sat, to pass his
order along to the cook. When she moved away, the push moved
with her.

"Wait . . ." Rhett said. But Basil was patting him on the shoulder in that infuriatingly patient, parental way.

"Good work," he said into Rhett's ear. "We'll take it from here.
Just watch and learn."

"But . . . that wasn't . . ." He was stammering, trying to make
sense of what was about to happen.

Mak, Treeny, Theo, and Basil all moved toward the young waitress, who was pouring a cup of coffee for the man she'd just taken
the order from. She was whistling along with Ritchie Valens playing "La Bamba" out of speakers in the ceiling. She finished pouring
the coffee and turned to put the pot back on the burner, her hips
swaying with the song now.

Before Rhett could even imagine what might happen next, the
girl stopped. She was standing between the bar and the back counter,
where the coffeemaker was waiting to receive its steaming pot. But

the pot was still in her hands. And then it wasn't. The coffee pot slipped out of her fingers and dropped to the linoleum, where it shattered and sprayed hot liquid in every direction. The sound was like an enormous egg cracking.

Mak stepped behind the bar, casually, slowly, while Basil, Theo, and Treeny took up positions around her, creating a blockade. Mak moved closer to the girl, who was now just standing there, facing the back wall, steam from the spilled coffee curling around her legs. The older guy, the one the waitress had helped just before, was looking at her, obviously concerned. He was saying something that Rhett couldn't quite make out—"Hey, hun, you all right?" maybe.

Then the girl collapsed.

She sank to the ground, folding in on herself like an accordion, right into the spreading puddle of coffee, right into the waiting field of glass shards.

In some kind of trance, Rhett stepped up to the bar and peered over it. Beside him, the older guy was shouting something, yelling for help, but Rhett could barely hear him. His voice was lost in something else. It sounded like static. But buried in the white noise, Rhett could hear another sound. Something like a heartbeat, slowing . . . slowing.

The waitress lay on her side in a pool that was now equal parts coffee and her own blood. Sharp triangles of glass stabbed into her. Her eyes were open, darting around, panicking. Rhett could almost hear her thoughts: *What's happening to me?* She looked terrified.

Mak knelt beside the girl, her knee dipping into the coffee, and Rhett had a flash of his own death, of the men trying to pull his body out of the car, hunting for a pulse. But Mak didn't look for a pulse. She reached over and took the girl's hand. Immediately the girl's eyes focused, finding Mak and locking on to her, asking a hundred questions without speaking.

"It's okay," Mak whispered. Her face was all at once devoid of its rigid, bitter tension. Now her eyes were kind. She smiled a sad smile at the girl. Mak could have been an entirely different person. "You're dying," she said. "I don't know why exactly. Something in your brain. It's failing. But it's okay. You can follow me. I'll carry you over the threshold, to the clearing. We'll be each other's anchors. You are my weight and I am yours. I will find your way. And you will find mine. There is no emptiness on this side. There is no pain. This is not the end." Mak leaned in closer until her nose was almost touching the girl's. A tear ran out of the girl's eye and rolled down her cheek. "This is not the end," Mak whispered again.

Around them there was all kinds of commotion. The teenagers were standing in their booth, stretching their necks, trying to see what was happening. The elderly folks by the window were trying to get out of their seats, trying to come over and help. One of them was on the phone. But to Rhett, none of this was happening fast enough. It had the quality of a record playing on the slowest setting. Voices were long, moaning howls, and movements stuttered as if broken down into individual seconds.

Rhett sensed all this but never took his eyes off the dying waitress. He had been so eager to get here, to prove himself. For what? For this?

The girl's head seemed to get heavier, sinking down into the soft cushion of her arm. Her eyes found some far-off point, and the light dwindled out of them. She was still.

Rhett wanted to tear his gaze away from the awful sight. But something else was happening. A wisp of thin, almost invisible white smoke crept out of the girl's mouth and floated toward the ceiling. At first, Rhett thought it was more steam from the spilled coffee. He could see the tendrils of swirling mist stretching down into her throat, though. It was like a snake made out of fog, roping itself through the air as if coaxed by a song.

Mak leaned in again, with her lips nearly kissing the roiling smoke, and inhaled. What had escaped the dead girl's mouth was captured by Mak's. The pale smoke swirled down into Mak's throat and vanished. Then she stood, giving the girl's body one last sad look.

"All right," Mak said. "Time to go."

The world around Rhett returned to its normal speed and vividness, snapping back like an elastic string. Suddenly people were shouting for the cook to call 911. The guy who had been the last person served by the girl was clambering over the bar toward her body, knocking over saltshakers and napkin holders, trying to look brave but seeming more petrified. *What is he going to do?* Rhett thought. Surely this guy knew what Rhett knew, that this young woman, who had probably been stuck in this tiny town her entire life, had poured her last cup of coffee.

The guy hopped off the bar anyway, splattering into the brown, crimson-swirled lake, standing over the girl's body, staring at it with a kind of rapt horror. The body lay on its side, soaking up one liquid and dispelling another, its eyes open, staring at nothing, staring at everything. There was no touching that. Not unless you wanted it to haunt you forever. And maybe it would anyway.

"Oy!" Basil yelled.

Rhett looked up and saw him and the other three standing in an archway under a handwritten sign that said RESTROOMS, and beneath that: LADIES FIRST.

"Snap out of it, mate," Basil continued, though his voice was gentle. "The longer we hang around, the better chance we have of running into the you-know-whats. They'll have sensed it by now, so it's time to boogey."

Rhett glanced out the window at the unyieldingly bright desert spread out around Turnstile, trying to make out any hooded figures that might be coming this way. There was nothing. But what reason did he have not to believe the others? This morning he'd been on a boat in the middle of an unknown ocean. He had taken one step through a door and now he was here, in a failing diner in a washed-up town on a great big slab of hot, rocky nothing. And something told him that they were about to step through another door and end up right back on that boat again.

Could he walk away?

Could he just ignore Basil and walk back out through the front door and leave them and the *Harbinger* and Captain Wise-Ass Trier behind? Would he always feel the push? Would he always feel the need to scoop up souls as they were thrust out of dying bodies? Probably. He had a feeling that it would eat away at him until his mind—the only thing that was truly his anymore—was a liquefied pool sloshing around in his pretend skull. Not to mention that he'd be alone. Completely alone.

"Mate!" Basil cried again over the commotion of diners still panicking, trying to make sense of the scene that had played out in front of them.

Rhett let go of the thought of running away and turned back, following the other four into the little alcove. Theo had to hunch over just to fit.

There were three doors back here. The one closest to the dining area was obviously the women's room, and another farther down was for men. The third door had yet another handwritten sign that said EMPLOYEES ONLY.

"Treeny," Mak said. "Little ladies, little boys, or employees only?"

Treeny stepped out from behind Theo, her rail-thin frame making her look like a tiny bug buzzing out from behind a tree. She was holding her tablet and glancing down at it, then up at the doors. Rhett didn't know what kind of underworld Wi-Fi signal she got on that thing, but it must have been magical.

"Little . . . boys," Treeny squeaked after a moment.

"You sure?" Mak asked, leveling her gaze at the tiny girl.

Treeny lowered her eyes and nodded as if she were embarrassed or ashamed. "I'm sure," she said in, impossibly, an even smaller voice.

Mak nodded at Basil, who stepped over to the men's room door and gripped the knob. He held it for a second, leaning close to the door as if trying to hear something. Then he jiggled the knob, turned it, and pushed the door open.

The sign on the door—the little stick man with the giant circle

head—swung away from them, revealing the room of doors in the belly of the *Harbinger*. The hydraulic piston at the top of the door hissed and then popped, and then it began to smoke. It was trying to push the door shut against the force of another dimension.

Basil glanced up at this and said, "The connection's not great. Everybody in."

Theo went first, then Treeny, then Mak. Basil did a melodramatic bow and gestured for Rhett to go ahead of him, so Rhett did. He stepped through the door, imagining that if his body had been able to react to such things, his ears would probably have popped the way the hydraulics on the door had.

He glanced back just as Basil stepped through. There was a barely perceptible warble in the air around him as he did, and the image of the diner wavered slightly. Basil casually kicked the door shut with his heel, like a man who's just gotten a snack out of the refrigerator. It slammed into its frame with a thudding finality, silencing the wailing sirens of an ambulance as it approached the diner.

"Mak," Basil said. "Why don't you show Rhett the steam room?" He waggled his eyebrows at her.

Behind him, Rhett could see other groups of dark-clothed syllektors moving around the room, coming in from some doors, going out through others. He caught sight of cities and forests, hallways and bedrooms, fields and highways, even what looked (and sounded) like a dense jungle. The place was like Grand Central Station but with direct access to any place on Earth.

Mak sighed and rolled her eyes, and that brought Rhett back to the moment.

"Yeah, sure," she said. "Why not? He's earned it, I guess."

"Precisely. Good work indeed, mate. Not many people come to grips with the lasso thing that quickly. I know I didn't."

"Uh . . . thanks," Rhett replied, his voice distant even to himself.

"Not really great at taking compliments, are you?"

"What? No! I'm sorry. I'm just . . . I guess I'm still trying to wrap my head around everything. That girl, she was so young, she . . ." He trailed off. What he wanted to say was *She wasn't ready*. He thought about the way it sounded and then he said it anyway. "I don't think she was ready to go."

The others stared at him with a mixture of pity and some species of annoyance. It's the kind of look an employee gets at a job when they're new and still excited to be there. Except Rhett wasn't excited—he was completely overwhelmed.

"That's not our call to make," Basil said, a slightly bitter tinge hanging in his voice. "We don't get to decide who lives and who dies. We just have to be there to collect the soul. And protect it. That's all."

"Are you coming or not?" Mak said. She was walking away, obviously tired of the conversation.

"Go on," Basil said.

"Have fuuun," Theo called, his deep voice toying and playful, the way it had been before breakfast.

Rhett went after Mak.

He caught up with her when she was already halfway up the

steps to the next deck of the Column. She didn't seem bothered by his presence, but she didn't acknowledge him, either.

"Where are we going?" he asked. He struggled to keep up with her double-step strides, avoiding other syllektors as they meandered past them.

"Steam room," she said. She didn't offer any further explanation.

"I . . . I don't know what that is."

"Well then maybe you should wait and see," she said through gritted teeth.

Two decks up from where the group had transported themselves to the Arizona desert and back, Mak got off the stairs and headed down a long hallway that was more like a tunnel. It was empty. Their footsteps rattled off the walls.

As they walked, Rhett noticed the walls changing, shifting to other versions of the ship's decorum, the same stuff that he'd seen when Basil first brought him aboard. Here was the ornate carpet and the delicate woodwork, followed by the length of metal bulkheads bathed in their unhealthy yellow light, then the warped, twisted wooden floorboards and the flickering torches, tucked at the very end. The hall—the tunnel—came to a dead end at a wall of gray, moldy wood with a single torch hanging from it, the fire huffing from the breeze of their movement.

"Could you move?" Mak snapped.

"What?" Rhett looked at her. She was pointing at his feet. He looked down sharply. There was a trapdoor beneath him, with a metal ring to open it right between his shoes. "Oh," he murmured. "Sorry." He stepped back.

Mak sighed, reached down to yank on the handle. The trapdoor yawned open, groaning like the mouth it resembled. Mak let it fall open with a bang that swept back down the hall like a shock wave, then climbed in, using a ladder to descend into blackness.

"Grab the torch!" she called up.

Rhett mumbled, mostly to himself, "How the hell am I supposed to climb down there with a torch in my hand?"

"Then don't grab it!" Mak yelled from the hole in the floor.

Rhett rolled his eyes and decided to leave the torch. He gripped the rungs of the ladder and started down, letting the shadows consume him. It didn't take long for complete darkness to settle in around him. Above his head, the opening was a wavering orange square.

A few moments later, the darkness was washed out.

The dark walls around Rhett opened up. The ladder fed into a massive chamber at least the size of a small baseball stadium, which seemed to tilt to one side. It was made up of the same bowing wooden walls and floor. Ancient mold crept out of the corners, and the crossbeams were no longer straight but curved, in some places rising and falling in permanent squiggles.

What got Rhett's attention, though, wasn't the sad state of the chamber itself but what the chamber contained.

Settled into the middle of the floor, sitting more level than any other part of the room, was a glass cube. It had to be as tall and wide as a New York apartment building, with metal framework, making it look like some ultramodern living space. There was an extension jutting out from one side of the cube, with the same metal frame and glass walls, like a square tube, stretching away from the cube and disappearing into the wall. Behind the glass, glowing a silvery blue like the moon, was a cloud of mist that looked exactly like what had come from the dead waitress's throat. Only this one was four stories tall and lit the chamber with the same watery, ethereal glow as an aquarium.

Rhett could only stare, and Mak didn't speak. They finished descending the ladder, stepping off one after the other onto the slanted wooden boards. Mak approached the cube while Rhett stood gaping up at it, mouth hanging open, wondering how, after all he had seen just today, he was still in awe.

There was an average-size door cut into the bottom of the cube, sealed by more glinting metal framework. Mak stepped up to it and placed her hand on the glass. When she took it away, a foggy imprint of her splayed fingers and palm remained. It faded slowly, then the door clicked open.

The moment it did, the room was flooded with the sound of whispering voices. The noise was such that you couldn't make out any individual words, but the tangle of them was maddening. Rhett wanted to cover his ears. But he wouldn't look like a coward in front of Mak. Not after he'd just started to prove his worth.

He watched Mak pull the door open and get as close to the cube as she could. She leaned in, opened her mouth, and exhaled. The mist, the soul of the girl from Arizona, came pluming out of Mak's mouth as if it were her breath on a frigid day, and it was gathered up by the gently swirling cloud inside the cube. Mak stared inside for a moment, with the incessant whispers of the dead echoing around them, until a satisfied look spread across her face. She pushed the door shut. The room went quiet again, and Rhett could barely contain his relief.

"I don't have to explain what this is to you, right?" Mak asked, walking back to where Rhett stood.

"It's . . . incredible," he said in response, staring up at the luminescent storm in the box.

She looked with him. She crossed her arms, admiring what was at least partially her own handiwork. "It is."

"It protects them?"

"From everything. Not even a psychon could get inside that thing. If the ship goes down, the souls are safe. No matter what."

Rhett pointed at the off-shooting tube. "Where does that go?"

"It circulates throughout the ship. The *Harbinger* is meant to carry and protect the souls, but the souls also help to power it . . . to power us. Without the *Harbinger* there would be no souls . . ."

". . . and without the souls there would be no *Harbinger*." Rhett thought about his first journey inside the ship and the glass staircase with what he had thought was a big aquarium under it. What he'd actually been looking at were more souls.

"You ready for another go?" Mak asked.

That snapped Rhett back to attention. "Wait . . . what?"

"You can't feel it?" she said, echoing the same question she'd asked when they'd first arrived in Turnstile.

And, as a matter-of-fact, Rhett *did* feel it this time. The push was back. Somebody else's time was up.

"Another one?" he asked, his voice low.

"Another one," Mak said.

They went again.

And again.

All they had to do was follow the push. The push gave them a door through which they would turn up at any seemingly random location. The push guided them to a person, a person who was about to lose hold of their soul, sending it thin and vulnerable into the open air as they died. After that, Rhett realized, the push was always gone. Once the soul was collected, they were on their own to find a way out of there. But Treeny always found a second door somewhere close by that would get them back on board the *Harbinger*.

Rhett wasn't ready for any soul-gathering just yet. He was more than happy to follow the push and guide the others to where they needed to be—which Mak made him do every time, anyway. But the idea of pulling another soul into himself, of carrying that burden even for the brief journey from the living world back to the *Harbinger*, was more than he was ready to commit to.

So Basil and Theo both had their turns.

After Arizona, there was Tokyo, a smear of throbbing lights with arteries of pedestrians flowing through it. Basil collected the soul of a man who had been hit by a car. He lay on the street, with a huge screen announcing some kind of juice product flashing above him, while others paced around him, maybe not realizing what was happening, maybe not caring. He was bleeding out of his ears and his shoes were missing. Basil was as delicate with the man as Mak had been with the waitress, using essentially the same words to ease the process of death.

This is not the end.

Then it was Theo's turn. And the big guy was about as good at being gentle as a rhinoceros would be. In fact, he seemed more nervous than anything—his interests were obviously more in the realm of security. The soul he collected belonged to a woman in northern Canada, in the mountains, where she'd gotten lost and was freezing to death. Theo fumbled some of what he was trying to say, but he got the job done. He pulled the woman's soul into his lungs and left behind the blue, frostbitten shell.

That one had been a bit of a trek, and at one point Mak was sure that Rhett had lost the push and had resorted to leading them around aimlessly. She couldn't quite hide her surprise when the poor woman finally turned up.

After that, Mak went again. Rhett was curious why Treeny wasn't taking a turn but decided it was best not to ask.

They were in Brazil, in a shimmering patch of rain forest, where someone had built a small house and was living on their own, maybe doing research, maybe just enjoying the beauty of the enormous trees and the dapples of sun falling on the forest floor. Inside the house that was really more of a hut, they found a boy. There was a picture on the table of the kid with who must have been his father, and there were things that belonged to the father, like clothes and books. But the boy was alone, lying on a cot, shivering, dripping sweat, curled up under a blanket that he had bunched up under his chin. Rhett noticed a pot still dripping in a strainer. Wherever the dad was, he hadn't been gone very long. And when Mak knelt down beside the boy and took his hand, she told him that she didn't know why exactly he was dying, but that she thought he might have been poisoned by something.

All of it must have happened so quickly, Rhett thought. The dad was going to come back to find his son dead in his cot. What would that look like? Rhett didn't want to know. Mak was gentler than any of them had been all day.

Over the course of the day, they intersected with other teams, passing through the room of doors, passing through the steam room. Groups of five or six each were spending their day doing the same thing Rhett and his teammates were doing. Rhett was so overwhelmed by it all, by the sheer vastness of the operation, that he was almost impressed. Was every day like this? Were there slower days? He hoped so. He hoped against his better nature that every now and then there was a day when not a single door was opened and not a single soul collected.

But he knew better.

Rhett insisted on following everybody to the steam room as they went. He couldn't quite get enough of it. It was brilliant and beautiful. It was life and death at the same time, the essence of humanity but without all the bodies. He could have spent entire days in there, watching it, imagining that lovely fantasy of a day when it wouldn't have to be opened.

As Rhett and Mak made their way down to the steam room for

the last time that day, they passed several groups heading back. The tunnel was crowded with syllektors who had finished dropping off their last . . . what? Deliveries? Deposits? What do you call the most important cargo ever?

"Last one out as usual, Mak?" someone called. It was a lanky guy with tattoos scrawled up and down his arms, images that might have once had color to them but were now completely black—they were just shapes. Rhett couldn't tell if the guy was being sarcastic or not. Either way, Mak ignored him.

They did their business. Mak transferred the soul of the little boy into the cube, and Rhett watched, already trying to mentally prepare himself for the moment when he'd have to do the transferring.

When it was done, they climbed back up the ladder to the trapdoor. Mak swung it shut with another vicious bang. They walked together down the tunnel toward the stairs.

"Heading to the mess hall for dinner?" Mak asked.

At first Rhett didn't even realize she had said something to him. Some still-wonky part of his brain interpreted the sound as his own thought, a question to himself.

"Are you . . . actually speaking to me?" he said. "Like, with words?"

She rolled her eyes. "The captain told me I should try to give you a break."

"When did you talk to the captain?"

"Last night." She had her hands behind her back, walking with the same impenetrable purpose. But her voice was softer, more casual.

"It took you all day to warm up to me?" Rhett asked.

She shrugged. "I needed to see you. Out there, I mean. Anyone can come onto this ship and claim to be okay with what goes on here. It takes a certain kind of person to be able to stomach the actual work."

"Yeah, well, I wasn't exactly an easy sell." In fact, he still wasn't entirely convinced.

"That's what the captain said," Mak replied. "I just needed to see you respect it."

"Respect what?"

"The fact that it's not a choice. It's not a system. It's random. And it's cruel. That little kid back there . . . he probably just ate some random berry or something. Perfectly innocent. And that was all it took for his life to be over." She was focusing hard on her feet as they moved below her, leading them out of the tunnel. "Us. You. Your parents. Nobody sees it coming."

Now Rhett reached out and stopped her, grabbing her forearm. He didn't think she'd allow herself to be turned, but she surprised him. She spun, her eyes wide, not quite angry, not quite sad.

"My parents?" Rhett said, his voice rough. He searched her eyes. "Which one did you bring back? My dad?"

She broke his gaze and took a small step away from him, pointing herself back down the tunnel toward the steam room.

"Theo got your dad," she barely whispered.

"So my mom, then. My mom . . ." He wanted to be angry. He wanted to scream and shake her. But she'd wanted this. She'd brought it up so that he would know. And somehow he was grateful.

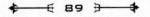

The image was just too much, though. "You watched her die," he said. "You let it happen even though she wasn't ready."

"That's my point, Rhett. You heard Basil. It's not up to us. *None* of us are ready. And that's what I need you to understand." She was still facing away from him, arms folded across her chest now.

"Is that why you didn't want me on the team?" Rhett said. "Or was it because of what happened to your old teammate?"

Mak whirled around. She buried her gaze into him like a sword.

"Don't ask me that question again," she said. "Ever."

Rhett nearly stumbled back. "O-okay. I'm sorry," he stammered. She tried to step around him, but he blocked her. "And thank you," he said quietly. "For taking care of my mom."

Mak stared back at him for the briefest of seconds and then gave him a stiff nod.

With that she kept walking in silence, and Rhett had to collect himself before catching up.

"I'm going back to my cabin," she finally said, her voice rough and edgy again.

"You're not hungry?" he asked.

"Are you?"

Rhett thought about it, and of course he wasn't *hungry*. Not in the way he used to be. But the night before and this morning he'd had a desire to eat. Just another formality of the living that helped give him a sense of normalcy. But tonight?

"No," he said. "I'm not. Can I walk you back to your room?"

She looked at him sidelong, slitting her eyes. "You don't have to do that."

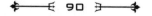

"I know. I just . . . don't want to be totally alone. Not yet."

After a pause, Mak nodded. "Just to my door."

They went on without speaking. There were a million questions that he could have asked. A million things to speculate on and comment on and wonder aloud about, just to get some kind of feedback. But he suspected that once he started, he wouldn't be able to stop. He decided to let the silence be, a weird species of contentedness falling between them.

Her room was down another hall opposite from where Rhett's was. He followed her down it, surprised to see her hands fidgeting behind her back.

Mak turned to say good-bye, reached behind her, and pushed her door open a crack. From within, a voice called out.

"It's about bloody time, love!" Basil said. "How long does it take to drop off a single soul?"

Mak had her eyes shut, grimacing. Rhett was still struggling to comprehend.

When Mak pushed the door open all the way, Rhett got a full view of Basil lying in her bunk, a blanket covering his lower half . . . and nothing covering the upper half. Basil and Rhett locked eyes.

"Oh . . . 'allo, mate!" Basil said, exaggerating his accent either on purpose or from his surprise.

"I'm sorry," Rhett said quickly. "I didn't mean to—"

"Don't worry about it," Mak cut in. "Just . . . don't make a big deal. Okay? And keep it to yourself."

"I . . . yes, I can do that." For one horrible second, Rhett thought he was going to pantomime locking his mouth shut and throwing away the key. He caught himself just in time.

"Training tomorrow," she said. "Someone has to teach you how to use that ridiculous thing." She gestured to Rhett's thigh, where the knuckle blade had rested in its holster all day, unused.

Mak backed into her room, with Basil still looking wide-eyed behind her, and shut the door without another word.

"Good night," Rhett said to no one.

SIX

"Mate, are you sure you don't want to pick something else out?" Basil said. He was referring, again, to Rhett's choice in weaponry.

They were split off into pairs, with Theo and Mak sparring in a far corner of the training room, another wide chamber with high ceilings, padded walls, and big lamps strung up by chains that lit the room with a glow that was almost too warm for the nature of its purpose. They were here to learn to fight. At least, Rhett was. The rest of them all appeared to be able to hold their own, even little Treeny, who was launching her throwing knives into a rubber torso that had seen better days, occasionally having to stop and push her glasses back up onto her nose.

Basil was with Rhett, trying to show him a few basic self-defense moves. Rhett had assumed that Mak would be the one to teach him, but she had avoided him, busying herself with polishing her machete in the corner of the room. And when Rhett was left with the choice of either Basil or Theo to train with, he went with the option that was less likely to leave him maimed.

But they kept coming back to the knuckle blade.

"No," Rhett said. He had the blade in his hand, standing with his feet apart and his arms up, looking like a boxer. He had been practicing with a rubber torso of his own and had gotten the blade lodged in its thick padding no less than five times. "Nobody judges you for your stupid scythes."

"Whoa, whoa, whoa, whoa," Basil cried, throwing his hands up. "First of all . . . my scythes are cool."

"Not really." That was Treeny, of all people, still homing in on the battered, pockmarked abs of her "sparring partner." Rhett couldn't help but admire Treeny's choice in weaponry. The throwing knives kept her as far away from the enemy as possible. His knuckle blade, on the other hand . . .

He wouldn't back down, though. He'd made his choice. And he still liked the way the blade felt gripped in his hand. He liked the heft of it. Even though he had never been in a fight in his life, he could imagine throwing a few pretty nasty uppercuts with the blade.

Basil rolled his eyes at Treeny.

"Yes. They are," he repeated. "But Jack the Ripper over here would look less silly if he was using a toothpick."

Rhett heard Mak snort from across the room.

"Can we please just drop it?" he said. "I need to know how to fight. With this. Will you show me or not?"

"Ugh. Fine," Basil groaned. He was already holding on to one of the twin scythes, spinning it on his fingers absentmindedly. He beckoned for Rhett to join him in the middle of a wide, padded ring.

Rhett gave him a skeptical look but took up a place on the other side of the ring. Treeny had suddenly lost interest in her target, which was now impaled in several places by her knives, like an oversize pincushion. Through the corner of his eye, Rhett could see Mak glancing in their direction also, taking quick peeks in between dodging Theo's swipes with his battle-ax.

"Okay," Basil said, getting into position and finally unsheathing his other blade. He gave them both a quick twirl, and for the first time Rhett noticed how fearsome Basil could really look. "The first thing you need to understand is that the psychons don't care if you're new. They care that they're hungry, and they care that you're in their way. Period."

"So . . . treat them the same way that I would . . . treat a bear?" Rhett said, trying to be funny.

But Basil leveled one of the scythes at him and said, "Exactly! They're animals. Plain and simple."

"Okay," Rhett said. "But to be fair, I'd run away from a bear, not try to have a duel with it."

Treeny actually giggled, still standing beside the ring, watching intently.

"Even if the bear was going to eat your parents?" Basil asked.

Rhett had no response but felt a dark look pass over his face, and he cast it in Mak's direction. She must have heard it, too, because their eyes met for a split second, and she nearly lost her head to another one of Theo's attacks. But she ducked out of the way, rolled, kicked off a nearby support pillar, and slammed her feet into the backs of Theo's knees. He crumpled, losing hold of his ax, and Mak put her machete to his neck, victorious. But she looked frustrated.

"Focus, mate," Basil said. "Psychons equal wild, unpredictable, unhinged animals. Got it?"

"Got it," Rhett said. He shook his head to clear it.

"You have to respect that. You and I can practice combat until our legs give out. But psychons aren't going to fight you. They're going to destroy you."

"Don't you guys have, like, a simulation or something?" Rhett asked. "A hologram, maybe? Just so I can get a grasp on what I'm supposed to be dealing with here?"

"Does this look like the fucking starship *Enterprise*?" Basil cried. And then, without any sort of pause, Basil swiped at Rhett with one of his scythes.

Rhett leaped back, sucking in his gut. Basil's blade passed through the air less than an inch from Rhett's stomach, so close that Rhett could see his own shocked reflection in the polished blade.

"You have to let your instincts take over!" Basil yelled. He swung at Rhett again.

Rhett stumbled back, coming to the edge of the ring, with Basil still advancing. Behind Basil, Rhett could see Mak and Theo, no longer sparring with each other but watching this fight instead. Rhett decided he could learn something from Mak after all.

As Basil brought another scythe down over Rhett's head, Rhett jumped forward, under Basil's arm, and rolled. For just a second he was sure that he was going to stab himself with his own blade. But then he came out of the roll, unharmed, and spun just in time to see Basil coming around with yet another swipe.

Instincts, Basil had said.

Rhett swung his fist, clutching the knuckle blade, upward. The two blades connected with a sharp *krrang* and a spray of glowing sparks. But Basil lost his momentum, and Rhett shot up before he could come in with the other scythe. Rhett stuck his foot out, kicking Basil square in the chest. Basil went sprawling back, nearly losing his footing . . . and stepped outside the ring.

Treeny was applauding, clapping her hands together like the giddy, excited kid she was supposed to be. Even Theo, with his ax tucked under one enormous arm, was clapping. Mak simply stood there, but there was a satisfied look on her face, a look that suggested she might be rethinking her opinions about Rhett. Or maybe that was just wishful thinking.

Basil was grinning. And Rhett was full-on laughing. He couldn't help himself. He was doubled over, cracking up.

"Listen, mate, that was one go-around," Basil said. "Don't get cocky on me yet."

Rhett was still laughing.

"It's not that," he wheezed. "It's just that I had you pegged as a *Doctor Who* guy."

Basil looked confused, but then understanding spread across his face.

"Oh, just because I've got an accent?" he said. "Don't hurt yourself, mate." But he was laughing now, too. Along with Treeny and Theo. And even Mak couldn't fight the miniscule grin on her lips.

When they'd composed themselves, Rhett and Basil reset in the ring.

"Let's try that again," Basil said.

They kept going.

Eventually Mak and Theo were in the ring with Basil and Rhett, offering their own pointers, suggesting different techniques. Rhett gleaned what he could from them, and at some point, the knuckle blade started to feel comfortable in his hand, an extension of his fist as he swung it through the air. He knew that if he switched on his senses, opened his mind and nerves to the exertion he was forcing on his body, he'd probably collapse. But it felt good to know that he was keeping up, that even though he was still very far off from where the others were, he could stand and fight with them if he had to.

As the day went on, Rhett kept expecting the push to interrupt them. He waited to feel it pulsing in his head, guiding him away from the training room and down to the doors, off the ship and into the living world.

But it never came.

For a few minutes around lunchtime, the five of them sat sprawled out on the pads, weapons strewn nearby, not catching their breath (because, really, there was no breath to catch) but taking a mental break. Rhett decided to ask about the push.

"We can't do that every day," Mak responded. "Nobody can."

Treeny had a far-off look in her eyes, her excitement from earlier now long gone.

"We have to keep a certain balance," Basil offered. "Every few days or so, a handful of teams, they . . . get a break, so to speak. From soul-gathering, anyway. And we use those days for training and to take our turns with our 'chores.'" He put his fingers up in air quotes.

"But how?" Rhett asked. "Is there some kind of master switch or something? Because I don't remember turning it off this morning."

"We're not the ones who turn it off," Mak said. She was sitting at the very edge of the ring, her back leaning against a support pillar. She had her machete laid across her lap, its smooth blade reflecting the soft glow from the lamps up onto her face. She could have been lit by the sun. "Remember when I said the souls helped to power the ship *and* us?" she asked.

Rhett nodded.

"Well, the ship controls when we feel the push and when we don't." Mak leaned her head back against the pillar almost lovingly. "The *Harbinger* just knows."

Suddenly Rhett had the unnerving sensation that they were sitting inside the belly of something powerful and alive, something that was using them. Were they really serving a higher purpose? Or were they like tiny fish, picking at the scraps caught in the baleen of a whale's mouth?

He decided to change the subject.

"So, what kind of chores are we talking about?" he asked, mostly kidding.

Theo, who had been suspiciously quiet, piped up.

"You've got your kitchen-cleaning and your cooking and your coal-shoveling . . ." he said in his thick accent. "And your floor-mopping and your weapons-cleaning." He paused, considering something, then went on. "I like peeling potatoes the best."

Mak, Basil, and Treeny couldn't contain their laughter, and Theo just smiled sheepishly.

"Theo enjoys doing chores," Basil said.

"Reminds me of my nana's house," Theo was still holding on to his grin. "That woman . . ." He looked around at them all, eyes wide, as if he were about to tell a deep, dark secret even though his mouth was spread in a huge, goofy smile. "She ran a tight ship." And then he waggled his eyebrows.

"*Pffffft!*" Basil lost it, tipping over onto his side.

Meanwhile Mak and Treeny just rolled their eyes, groaning.

Rhett couldn't help but chuckle along with Basil.

"Maybe you should let me crack the jokes, eh, Theo?" Basil said, fighting against the laughter that was still bubbling up out of him.

"How about nobody makes *any* jokes?" Mak said. She was standing, gripping her machete again. With the smallest tilt of a smile on her lips, it made her look just a touch maniacal. "Let's get back to work."

Treeny hopped up willingly and resumed her knife-throwing. The silly, almost childlike way that Theo had been smiling dropped away and was replaced by the stoic, unreadable exterior again. Basil just hung his head and sighed. He stared at the floor for a moment as if trying to decide if he really wanted to continue.

Rhett was about to stand when Theo surprised him—he came over and stuck his hand out. Rhett took it, and Theo helped him to his feet. The brute's grip was so strong that he stopped just short of throwing Rhett across the room.

"Uh . . . thanks," Rhett said.

Theo only nodded, but it was the first time that Rhett didn't feel like a parasite, latching on to the team and dangling there, holding on for the ride.

For the breadth of a single moment, he felt like part of the team.

SEVEN

After dinner that night, Mak, Theo, and Treeny wandered off to bed, leaving Rhett and Basil in the mess hall. Basil had a cup of coffee and a piece of blueberry pie in front of him. Rhett thought it looked delicious, but he didn't want to risk opening himself up to the exhaustion that his body was surely feeling after ten hours of training. He hadn't eaten much dinner, either. And what he did eat, he hadn't tasted. If he could keep the pain of his sore muscles and weary bones at bay, he was going to do it.

So he just sat there while Basil picked at his pie in a relaxed sort of silence.

"Mak told you about your parents?" Basil asked suddenly, staring down at his plate. "About how she and Theo—"

"Yeah," Rhett said quickly, stopping him. "Yeah."

Basil nodded. "Good. I didn't want you to go too long without knowing. Wouldn't have been right."

Rhett didn't respond, just stared out the big portholes at the blanket of gray clouds rolling across the sky.

A little while later, they were coming off the stairs to the crew quarters. Rhett was absentmindedly walking beside Basil, following him almost, until he realized he was going the wrong way—his room was in the other direction. And he already knew where Basil was headed.

"Well . . . good night," Rhett said awkwardly.

"Good night, mate." Basil had his hands stuffed in his pockets, continuing down the hall toward Mak's room.

Rhett couldn't help himself.

"What's the deal with you two, anyway?" he called, knowing that Basil would understand what he meant.

Basil turned and started walking backward, his hands spread at his sides.

"Your guess is as good as mine," he called back, and then turned and ducked through Mak's door without even knocking.

Rhett got out of there as quickly as he could. Whatever was going to happen behind the door of room number 1026, he definitely did not want to hear any of it.

He went back down to the main room, where all the corridors branched away like struts on a wheel. He looked down the hall to where his own cabin was. The idea of going back there and sitting alone, with nothing to do, made him sad and uneasy. But where would he go?

There were probably other syllektors who were still up, hanging out in the rec area. But the idea of mingling with members of other teams wasn't very appealing, either. That would mean having to introduce himself, having to try and integrate himself into another melting pot of personalities, which just seemed exhausting. Plus, he'd finally seemed to gain Mak's trust—sort of. He didn't want to risk losing it.

What, then?

As he stood there contemplating, his brain already leaning toward the inevitable decision of trudging back to his room and listening to the ocean for the rest of the night, he heard something else—dripping water. It was coming from behind him, the same sound from his first night on board, like big, globular raindrops smacking onto the hard floor.

Rhett turned around . . . to nothing. The floor behind him was completely dry. He glanced around, peering down some of the other corridors. There had to be a leak somewhere. The sound must have been echoing down the halls. How ancient was this ship that it could not have a single leak?

With that thought still fresh in his mind, Rhett realized where he wanted to go and who he wanted to talk to.

He made his way back up to the top deck of the Column, where he'd first come in with Basil. As he went, he passed others who were heading down to their quarters for the night. Nobody looked tired physically or seemed worn out from the day. But they all gave him serious, questioning looks. Their eyes said enough, and again Rhett thought of the little boy in Brazil, of the waitress in Arizona. He thought about what Mak had said coming back from the steam room. This was heartbreak, day in and day out. The ending of lives, over and over and over. And even if the syllektors weren't responsible for causing those deaths, how much of that could one person realistically take?

He was suddenly glad for the knowledge that he wouldn't have to do it every day.

When he made it to the top of the Column, Rhett stood and stared at the spiral staircase leading up to the bridge. Basil had told him that he would want to check it out sometime.

He went over to it and looked up. It circled up into the ceiling, disappearing into darkness.

"Come on up, Mr. Snyder!" It was Captain Trier's voice.

Rhett took an instinctive step back. Had the captain seen him? He shook his head. His nerves were still jangled from yesterday and he was starting to get paranoid.

He climbed the steps, listening to them creak and whine with age. There were a lot of them. At the top, he realized why. He stepped out into a wide, circular room with walls that were made entirely of glass. The room sat on top of a short tower—from the window, Rhett could see the steep drop down to the *Harbinger*'s uppermost deck. He had a three-hundred-and-sixty-degree view of the choppy gray ocean and black, boiling sky. Ahead, the front of the *Harbinger* jutted out and came to a point, the length of at least a few city blocks, covering up the waves in a dark mass and pointing ahead with immense purpose. Behind, the rest of the ship stretched away, with the smokestacks looming over the bridge like behemoth cigars stuck into the ship's hull, always smoldering. Everywhere else, the ocean ran away with the clouds.

"Impressive, isn't it?" the captain said. He was standing at the starboard side, hands behind his back as always, staring at the fuzzy line of the horizon.

"More than impressive," Rhett said. "It's unbelievable."

"You've probably seen a lot of that the past couple of days." Trier turned and looked at Rhett, who could only nod. "It's a lot to take in."

Rhett stepped farther into the room, noticing for the first time the steering wheel and the lever near it that must have controlled the ship's speed. The steering wheel was almost as big as Rhett, made from a dark wood, with handles dotting the outside. In front of it was something else—a lantern set on a pedestal, with a single flame burning inside it, the orange point leaning toward the front of the ship.

Trier caught him staring at the lantern.

"That's my compass," he said. "The flame tells me which direction we should be traveling in. Without it . . . well, there wouldn't be much point to all this, would there?"

"Do you know where it's taking us?" Rhett asked.

The captain smiled. "If any of us knew that, we might not be so inclined to do our jobs. We would just go there and let someone else do it. Someone who's supposed to be in charge."

"You're not in charge?"

To that, Trier simply laughed.

Rhett looked out at the waves dancing in jagged formation like saw blades coming through the far side of a tree.

"Is it all just ocean?" he asked.

"Actually, it's a river," Trier replied. "And if you've read any mythology, you'll know why that makes sense."

"I've read the stories," Rhett said, a touch of impatience leaking into his voice. "But is *any* of this really supposed to make sense? I'm on a giant ship that, apparently, is kind of alive, sailing on what you're telling me is a river that's so big, it looks like an ocean. Oh, and I watched someone *inhale* another person's soul yesterday. So there's that."

The captain thought about it, then said, "I don't expect it to feel real, Rhett. Not yet, anyway. Sometimes it doesn't make any sense to me, either. It makes as much sense as a boy and his family dying suddenly and violently on the side of a New York highway." His eyes bore into Rhett, and Rhett could do nothing but look away. He found a darker-than-dark spot in the clouds and focused on it. Lightning zapped the water below it, illuminating the toothy grin of another one of those massive sea creatures. Or maybe it was the same one.

"What am I supposed to say?" Rhett finally muttered.

"Tell me about them. Roger and Ilene," Trier said after a pause. "Your parents."

The words stabbed at the emotions trapped inside Rhett's mind without any outlet through his body.

"What do you need to know?" he asked bitterly. "You know their names. You probably know everything else."

"Their names I just picked up off your consciousness," Trier replied. "You were obviously thinking about them when you first came on board. Worried about them. It was easy for me to see them in your mind. That's a . . . quirk of mine."

Rhett raised his eyebrows. "Like a special power?"

The captain chuckled. "Not at all," he said. "I had a touch of clairvoyance when I was alive. Death just seems to have amplified it. I can only pick up little bits here and there. But it's the reason I became captain of this ship—I always know when someone's lying to me."

"So—"

"Yes." Trier cut him off. "I know about Mak and Basil. That's an ongoing drama that I prefer to avoid. Much like you, it seems, with the subject of your parents."

"Yeah, well . . ."

"Tell me about them," Trier repeated.

Rhett brushed one of the handles on the steering wheel with his finger, feeling its smoothness, letting it help anchor his thoughts.

"What's there to tell?" he said. "Now that they're . . . now that they're gone." He opened his mouth to go on, closed it. The devastation hadn't even had time to break within him yet. The idea that his parents were dead, killed by his own recklessness, hadn't even really hit him. Was now the time to let that happen? Here? In front of the man who used their deaths to keep him on board?

Why not?

"My dad, Roger, used to be a surgeon," Rhett said. "One of the best in the country, I guess. When . . . when we died, he was working in the stock market, but there was a box of awards out in the garage, all kinds of medical stuff. They didn't talk about it much. Mom was . . . uh, she made candles. Calling her a candlemaker makes it sound like she lived in the eighteen hundreds. She just made them at home, mixing scents and colors and wax and stuff, coming up with different smells. Ilene's Illuminations. That's what she called her company, which was really just an Etsy page and her sitting on the living room floor for hours, trying to get the mixtures right. She was always happy doing it, though."

"They sound lovely," Trier said gently.

Rhett continued to stare out at the unhinged world. "You have no idea. There couldn't have been two people who were more different in the entire world. My dad was all facts and numbers and precision. Mom used to say that he had steel-reinforced hands but a heart with a cracked foundation. She was so carefree. She didn't mind being late if it meant getting to spend a few extra minutes with me and Dad. They had things in common, sure. They loved to read. They loved movies. They loved me. But it was all those fundamental differences that made them love each other more. Those things balanced them out. Dad learned that it was okay to be a little late sometimes, and Mom learned that being two whole hours late was a bit much."

A startling yip of laughter escaped Rhett's throat, and he heard the captain chuckling with him.

"Go on," the captain said when the laughter had passed and the bridge had gone quiet again.

"To really understand what they were like as parents, you have to understand one thing," Rhett continued. "I shouldn't have been born in the first place."

Trier came and stood next to Rhett, hands still behind his back, and gave him a curious look.

"When Mom was still pregnant with me," Rhett went on, "they found a tumor. Right here." He put a finger on his abdomen. "It was going to kill me. My parents had the damn thing in a jar somewhere for the longest time, but I haven't seen it in a while."

"So, the tumor was removed?" Trier asked.

Rhett nodded. "My dad took it out. He came up with this ridiculous procedure. Something the board of medical gurus or whatever they are wouldn't let him touch with a ten-foot pole. He had no backing. But he did it anyway." He stopped, his hand subconsciously caressing the spot where, before birth, a malignant growth had threatened to end his life before it ever started. "He cut me out of Mom's womb. Before I'd even gotten all the way through the second trimester. He said I wasn't even as big as the palm of his hand. They removed the tumor, patched me up, and then put me back inside my mom's uterus and patched *her* up. Which makes it sound supereasy, but Dad said it was a fourteen-hour-long procedure. I had to kind of be born once first before I could be born for real. My dad got fired from the hospital he was working at. He lost his medical license. That procedure was . . . not a good idea, to say the least. Right before . . . before the crash, I had seen a couple of news stories about similar procedures. But back then it was unheard of."

The captain whispered something that Rhett didn't quite catch.

"Huh?" Rhett said.

"A Twice-Born Son," Trier said.

"What's that?"

"That's you. It used to refer to reincarnation. But in your case the term seems to be a bit more literal."

"What does it mean?"

"I don't know. Maybe nothing. It's legend, mostly. Bits of lore that you can find in some of the oldest books in the ship's library.

Regardless of what it means to me, what it means to you is that your life was very precious."

Rhett looked back out at the water clashing with the ship, with the sky. He could feel the emotions inside his head, bottled up, held back by the dam of his body's numbness. He had the power to let them run through him, and so he did. Rhett switched on his body like someone fumbling in a dark basement for the chain that clicks on the hanging lightbulb. He found it and pulled.

His arms and legs tingled, sore from all the training. His eyes burned from the pressure behind them. He could smell burning coal and hot metal. He tasted copper. His stomach tumbled and clenched. It was awful and relieving at the same time.

He nodded in response to Trier. "It was precious because they made it that way. They loved each other until it was gross to look at, but the way they loved me . . ." The pressure became too much, and he felt the warm touch of tears running down his face.

"Tell me about the crash," Trier prodded gently.

Rhett hitched in a shuddering breath. "They made me wait a year to get my driver's license," he said. "We lived in the city, they said. It wasn't that important for me to have it. But I pushed for it. I pushed hard. And then, when they finally let me get it—just a few months ago—I was such an ass about it. I started insisting that I drive any time we needed to take the car somewhere. Mom always let me, but Dad usually wouldn't. I don't know if he was afraid of me growing up too fast or just afraid of my driving. Probably both." He laughed to himself. "We were going upstate. Some sort of party.

The company that Dad worked for was having some kind of swanky thing at a country club. Dad didn't want to go, but Mom made him. To make a good impression, you know?"

Trier nodded. Behind him, the sky lit up with a stutter of blue lightning.

"Anyway," Rhett said, "I made them let me drive. Dad said I definitely wasn't ready for that kind of a trip. Mom . . . she always defended me against him. She always fought him off when he was being too . . . fatherly."

"They let you drive," Trier said.

"*She* let me drive. Dad sat in the backseat with his arms crossed and stared out the window the whole time. He was wearing a new suit. Cornflower-blue tie. I kept trying to tell him he looked nice. He just kept telling me to keep my eyes on the road. I did keep my eyes on the road . . . but it didn't matter." His throat clicked and his voice caught.

"I think I understand, Rhett," Trier said. "You don't have to—"

"Yes I do," Rhett snapped. "You wanted to hear it. I have to tell it to the end."

"Okay," Trier replied quietly.

Rhett took barely a second to pick up the thread again. "We kept driving, and I kept trying to lighten the mood. Dad wouldn't have it. Every time I tried to talk about something else—baseball or something—he'd just bark at me to watch the road. And he'd mumble something about how I shouldn't be driving that far. Mom was irritated, I was irritated. He was just cranky because he didn't want to go to that stupid goddamn party. It got so tense that Mom finally told me to pull over so Dad could drive. I told her no. I was angry at him. Not because he had tried to keep me from driving, but because he was being such a damn baby about it. I was just being a brat."

Rhett stopped. He tore his eyes away from the horizon and forced them to find Captain Trier's face. Rhett wasn't angry at him for guilting him into staying on the ship, not anymore. The souls of his parents were on board, just a few decks below where he stood right now, trapped in a box with probably a trillion other souls. But they were there. He was closer to his parents than he might ever have gotten the chance to be. Short of being trapped in the box with them.

"I don't know what happened," Rhett went on. "I honestly don't. I got so angry at both of them. We were in the left lane, and I just . . . I swerved as hard and fast as I could into the right lane. I think I was trying to get to the shoulder so I could pull over like they asked me to, but . . . I don't know," he repeated. "I didn't check my mirrors before I swerved . . . and there was this big FedEx truck right there. It was *right there* when I pulled into the right lane. I didn't see it until our back end smashed against it. I heard the truck's horn going off, and I could kind of see the truck jackknifing behind us. We were going almost eighty. The car spun in front of the truck and then, I don't know how, but we were in the air. We flipped a couple of times. It was so fast, but it was *so* slow. All I remember seeing is that cornflower-blue tie snapping back and forth in the rearview mirror."

Tears were spilling down his face now. His lower lip shuddered, but Rhett kept talking. "There was all this glass and screeching metal. I could see the sky, and then the ground, and then the sky again. Then we hit the ground, and we finally stopped moving. I . . . I was already dead. I could see myself still in the car. The car was crumpled in around me, and my parents . . ." He choked on the words, his body giving in to the sobs that he'd allowed it to have. He sucked in a ragged breath. "My parents were gone. They *are* gone. They saved my life before I was even born. Both of them. They risked everything for me before I was even really theirs. And the *second* their lives were in my hands . . . the *second* . . ."

His words broke down. Sobs overtook him, and he put his back against the window and slid down until he was sitting with his knees up against his chest. The gentle lift and fall of the ship as it cut through the waves soothed him while he cried. He could feel Trier watching him, but he didn't care. He was content to just be there with his sorrow. It was a strange thing to have missed about being alive, but he missed it just the same.

"Tell me what I'm thinking," Rhett said after the worst of the tears had gone through him. "Tell me what you see."

"I can't read your mind," the captain said. "I can only pick up on certain things. Images, mostly."

"What are you picking up right now, then?"

Trier paused, with his head down and his eyes vacant, as if trying to remember where he'd left something important. Then he said, "You're thinking about the cube. The steam room."

Rhett nodded.

"I have one more question," he said, forgetting about all the other questions he'd had rolling over in his head while coming up here.

"I'm listening," the captain replied, not unkindly. It was obvious he could already tell what Rhett was going to ask.

"What comes after this? I mean . . . can syllektors die . . . again?"

Trier smiled wanly. "That's a pretty simple one, actually. Syllektors obviously can't be killed. We're already dead. We have certain control over our faculties, as you've already found out. We can manifest and show ourselves to the living if we absolutely need to—though, that's a bit trickier. We can be injured in much the same way as we could when we were alive. The only difference is that most injuries that would be considered fatal to the living won't do anything to a syllektor but land them in the medical bay. There's only one sure way to destroy a syllektor."

"How?" Rhett asked.

"By destroying their heart," Trier said.

"Is that what happened to the fifth teammate? The one that I replaced?"

Trier sighed, and for the first time his eyes looked weary.

"That's not for me to tell," he said. "But I will say this—what you're thinking is . . . an impossibility. Syllektors are not meant to join with the souls in the cube."

"So, what happens to them? To us? When our hearts are destroyed do we just . . . go away?"

"Not exactly. The working theory is that syllektors who are 'killed,' so to speak, become . . . ghosts."

"Ghosts?" Rhett said, raising his eyebrows. "Like white-sheet-with-holes-in-it ghosts?"

"Something like that," Trier answered, grinning. "Whatever

part of the soul that's still tethered to the mortal world finds its way back there, to whatever place is most meaningful to the person that was. Usually the place where they died, but not always. You don't normally hear of a house being haunted by the ghost of a person that died under typical circumstances. It's because that ghost probably passed through this ship first. As a syllektor."

Rhett let that sink in, feeling his brain throb under the stress of all the wild, unbelievable knowledge it had been taking in. With that, he turned his physical reactions off, squashing the headache but not the stress, stifling the tears but not the grief.

"I assure you that your parents' souls are on board this ship," Trier said, reaching out a hand to help Rhett to his feet. "It might not be easy to find them, but I can tell you that they are here."

"I know," Rhett replied, taking the hand and allowing himself to be pulled up.

The captain gave him a questioning look.

"Down in the steam room," Rhett said. "When they open the door. All those voices come spilling out. And at first it's hard to hear anything but this weird static. But after a second, I swear I can hear their voices. They're just saying my name, calling out to me, maybe trying to find me. I don't know. But I know I've heard them."

Trier was nodding, stroking his beard, his face as serious as ever.

"Can we really talk to them?" Rhett finally asked. "Is there any way to say good-bye?"

It took a long time for Trier to speak again. When he finally did, his voice was quiet but confident.

"We're going to find out," he said.

EIGHT

The first time Rhett collected a soul, only two weeks after his own death, it was at the throat of an alley, with the sun dipping down below the skyline of the surrounding city—Boston.

They had come through a door that was tucked between two stalls at Quincy Market. It was busy, crowded with tourists and locals. The five of them stood amid the foot traffic as people subconsciously avoided them, the subtle force of their presence enough to guide the passersby around them, giving them a moment to catch their bearings.

Treeny looked especially uncomfortable, standing close to Rhett's side, clutching her tablet to her chest. Basil took a big sniff of the air and gave his stomach a melodramatic rub. Mak and Theo were . . . Mak and Theo, standing stoic and on guard, ever-prepared for some kind of attack.

Rhett closed his eyes and focused on the push, trying to drown out the noise. He'd been here once before, when he and his parents had been in Boston to visit his aunt Lorraine, but could scarcely remember anything about it—just that he'd eaten a lot of really good food. He took a fraction of a second to wonder how Aunt Lorraine was doing, how she'd handled the news . . .

But then the push was beckoning, and he knew where he needed to go.

He guided the group through the masses of incoming and outgoing people, some of them stopped in front of different booths, yelling over the din to order their food. They passed through the dining area, under the great height of the old building's domed ceiling, yellowish and brightly lit and echoing with voices.

A moment later they were out in the streets, breaking free of the orbit of the market and leaving the crowds behind. The sun winked at them between high-rises and skyscrapers.

The push nudged, and Rhett followed.

They came around a few corners, letting pedestrians dodge them instead of the other way around. There was no other city like New York, but Rhett still felt a pang of homesickness at the sight of the old architecture and scattered graffiti, honking taxis and hordes of tipsy weekenders stumbling out of bars.

The push got stronger. And stronger. And Rhett felt his apprehension threatening to knock him out of focus. He didn't think he was ready for this. But Mak had insisted that he was. She had certainly warmed up to him (at least to the extent that she was capable of warming up to anybody—which wasn't much). Rhett still felt like she was watching him, though. Maybe because of what he knew about her and Basil. Maybe because he really didn't belong.

He was about to find out.

When the push was at its highest insistence, thrumming inside of Rhett's head like a swarm of insects, he stopped the group in front of an alley, narrow and infected with shadows. High above, the sun was still bright and orange against the facades of the surrounding buildings. But down here, the day had already gone.

At the back of the alley, Rhett could make out a mound of ratty cloth quivering on the pavement. The push leaned toward it.

"What do I say?" he asked, not directing the question to anyone in particular. The other four were behind him, waiting.

"Whatever feels right," Mak said.

Rhett allowed his feet to carry him into the alley, past a couple of empty dumpsters, to the hump that lay among the littered bits of trash.

The man was on his back, a long beard caked with grime and crawling with lice stretched away from his face. His eyes were wide and bloodshot, staring up at the purple sky as if he were seeing an alien spaceship hovering there. His hands trembled at his chest, smudged with grease and mud. The tattered clothes he wore pooled around his starving frame. Those same trembling hands were more like claws, scratching at his rib cage, searching for his heart.

Basil and Mak and Theo and Treeny were there, watching the open end of the alley, and Mak, in her paranoid, overly tactical way, was watching the opening *above* the alley, where the rooftops reached for the darkening sky.

Rhett didn't think. He couldn't—he would lose his nerve if he did. He grabbed one of the man's shaking hands, and immediately those shell-shocked eyes found Rhett and hooked in. He leaned close to the man, feeling the push fade, replaced by something else, some sense that belonged as much to the man as it did to him. There was something wrong with the man's heart—something in it was breaking.

There was no need for Rhett to consult his memory. He spoke the words that he knew and added some of his own.

"It's okay," he said softly. And in the deepest, furthest part of his brain, he could imagine Mak kneeling over his mother, just as he was kneeling over the man now. "It's okay. I'm here to help you. I don't know why this is happening to you. I just know that your heart is giving out. You don't have to be afraid. We'll cross together. We'll hold each other down. You are my weight, and I am yours. There's no pain on the other side. There's no fear. You'll never have to feel this way again. This is not the end." He squeezed the man's hand even as the man's grip slackened. "This is not the end."

When the man died, his head turned away. His open eyes found a brick wall and stared through it. And a moment later his soul came creeping out from between his lips, curling up in a languid spiral. Rhett leaned in, at the same moment turning his senses on, wanting to truly feel this as it happened, and inhaled.

The soul filled him the way an icy breath of winter air does, cold and sharp.

Rhett stood and found Mak staring at him, her eyes fierce but almost apologetic. Was it respect? Had he passed her final test? Or were there more to come? Maybe she would keep at it forever, never really admitting that Rhett was a true member of the team, of the crew even. He didn't care. Right now what he cared about was the soul that he carried.

"Treeny," he said, taking control before Mak could even get her mouth open to speak.

"On it," Treeny responded, poking away at her tablet.

Theo and Basil continued to stand guard.

He left the body behind and took the soul with him, through the back door of a nearby restaurant, into the room of doors aboard the *Harbinger*. He didn't wait for anyone to try and instruct him—he knew what came next. And when he made his way down to the steam room, feeling the weight of the soul inside him, feeling the breezy movement of it circling through his body, when he put his hand on the door of the glass cube, it clicked open for him the same as it did everyone else.

Amid the restless whispers of the other souls, Rhett released the one he carried into the fold. He watched it slip into the cloud and become indistinguishable, just another swirl of luminescent white smoke. Then he pushed the door to the cube shut and put his head against it. His senses were gone again—he'd let them go when he'd released the soul.

But if they had been there, he would have wept with relief.

After that it was easier.

It was easier to fall in line with the others. He could talk more. He could recognize the push when it nudged him, whether it was at breakfast or in the middle of the night. He could go down to the armory in the morning and grab his knuckle blade without feeling that foreboding sense of regret, the idea that maybe he didn't belong here. And without that thought, he found that he didn't need to force himself to fit in. He fit in just fine.

After Rhett's first gathering, Mak laid off him a little bit. And he continued to keep the secret that she had asked him to keep. He didn't much care what she and Basil did behind closed doors, as long as he had their respect. Their friendship.

Basil and Theo turned out to be easy to hang out with. When the team wasn't together gathering souls or training or doing work around the ship, the three guys spent a lot of time just dicking around, catching movies, playing arcade games, utilizing the entertainment that was built into the *Harbinger*. Basil liked to call these get-togethers "bro-downs" in his best American accent.

Rhett learned a remarkable amount about his team, things that he would never have suspected, things that were pretty obvious, things that sometimes broke his heart. But the biggest thing that he learned was that nobody, not a single syllektor aboard the ship filled with dead people, wanted to talk about how they died.

That was okay with him. He didn't want to talk about how he died, either.

He spent time with all of them, either within the group or alone. He integrated himself. And while he was doing so, Captain Trier continued to find a way to track down Rhett's parents.

It was like trying to catch an electric eel with a soup can, he told him. Souls were fragile, sensitive things. You couldn't just dive into the tank in the steam room and start digging through them. Too much disruption could cause the souls turmoil, to possibly break down, which in turn would cause the *Harbinger* to break down. They had to be careful.

Rhett didn't mind waiting. What else was going to happen? At least he had something to wait *for*.

There were deaths, of course. Many, many deaths.

There were hospital rooms. Dozens of them, hundreds of them—he stopped keeping count. Hospital rooms with all their stark, discomforting gray, where elderly men and elderly women who were deflated and liver-spotted sank into their beds, hitched in their last crackling breaths, and became smoke; where there were kids with cancer who were losing their battles, their beds decorated with cards and flowers and toys, balloons floating up near the ceiling, sparkly stickers plastered to the wailing heart rate monitors, where the lines had gone flat; where babies who were mere days old were trapped in incubators, struggling to see, to breathe, to live, and were failing—their souls were the purest white, perfect, milky tendrils of smoke.

There were houses. Houses where husbands lay down next to their wives at night and slipped inexplicably into darkness, casting their souls out into bedrooms that were silvery with moonlight. Houses where kids ran out to play, chasing balls or runaway skateboards into the street and meeting fast, heavy cars. Houses where ceilings collapsed and ovens caught fire and hunks of food got lodged in throats.

There were cities, clogged with traffic and noise, where construction workers came tumbling off scaffolding; where earthquakes and floods brought whole buildings down in cascades of dust and glass; where cars slammed into lampposts and buses tore in two and vans exploded on purpose; where the sky and the sun winked across sparkling metal and cooked the life right out of some people.

There were diseases, pitiless and unbiased, that swept across run-down countries, strangling their victims with their own blood or squashing their lungs like underinflated balloons.

There were hurricanes that swirled onto coastlines with the force of a bomb and erased entire neighborhoods.

There were unforgiving winters in Russia, brutal heat waves in Australia, landslides in India, avalanches in Colorado, war zones in Syria, collapsing ice shelves in Antarctica.

There were guns firing in every place, knocking down bodies and unleashing souls.

There was death everywhere, all the time, and Rhett was never more aware of it than when he was right in front of it, collecting the lives that had been. Death ran rampant, like a ferocious animal, slaughtering, destroying. And he began to realize that the syllektors were not Death itself, but messengers of Death. They were the unseen deliverers of that final peace, that tranquility where acceptance is the only option. Because to fight it is to fight the unstoppable force of nature.

He collected those souls, and in them he felt more life than he ever thought possible, more warmth and purpose and love. There was death, sure, but it never felt as strong as the life that made up the souls that Rhett brought back to the *Harbinger*. In some backward way, he felt like he was actually saving lives instead of waiting around for them to end. And there was peace in the idea that he might exist that way forever.

PART

TWO

NINE

Rhett opened his eyes one day a little over ten months after he'd first set foot on the *Harbinger*.

He was greeted by the same flat gray light and the same *shush* of the ocean as it seethed around the hull of the ship. Thunder grumbled from far off, like the sound of water gurgling down a sink drain. He was also greeted by the push, tugging at him, yanking impatiently at that invisible lasso.

Before he could even flip his feet out of bed, someone was banging on his door.

"You gettin' it, mate?" Basil called from the other side.

"Yeah," Rhett called back. "Be right out."

He got out of his bunk and stared at himself in the mirror, the way he had that first morning. His clothes were now just shadows of their former selves, the plaid pattern faded out of his shirt, and the jeans, which had been blue denim, were now entirely black.

From behind him, there was the sound of water dripping against the floor. No, not just dripping—*splashing*. And he knew that when he turned around, there would be nothing there but the dry floor.

He had never asked about the leak. Every time it might have come up in conversation, he missed his opportunity. It just didn't seem like that big of a deal. Just another quirk of the ship.

When he opened the door, Basil and Mak were there, standing too close together, giving themselves away. Rhett noticed that as time went on, their caution had waned, giving way to something else, something that wasn't quite reckless abandon but was pretty close. Either way, Rhett had kept his mouth shut about what he knew was going on between them, and he never mentioned to them that the captain knew, either.

"Took you long enough," Mak said.

"Well I'm sure you guys had a head start," Rhett shot back, smiling. Mak gave him a pissed-off look.

They hit the armory, where they met Theo and Treeny, and then the five of them followed the push through the quiet, mostly empty ship.

When they got to the room of doors, it was Rhett who stepped out in front of the group and closed his eyes. He had a particular knack for picking up on the push, and the others were happy to let him lead the way, waiting for him to mess it up. The new guy was still proving himself, even after ten months.

He let the push hum around him, plucking the unseen paths to the doors like guitar strings, trying to find the one that was most in tune. When he found it, he pointed it out, went to it, and opened it.

The room filled with a cacophony of blaring car horns and angry shouts. Through the door, Rhett could see headlights and wet asphalt and not much else. There was a dense fog that pushed up against the door. In fact, the fog actually started falling *through* the door into the *Harbinger*. But the push remained, and it would guide them to their soul, fog or no fog.

Rhett stepped through the door with the others close behind.

They came out onto the street. Rhett could barely hear himself think over the honking horns. The line of traffic stretched away in both directions, cars only visible by the pearlescent glow of their headlights in the fog. Farther up on the left, he could see warbling red lights. There was some kind of accident holding up traffic. That must have been their destination.

Rhett looked across the street, trying to get a read on where they were. But the fog was too dense to see more than a foot or so in front of him. He turned around. Maybe they had stepped out of a recognizable building or . . .

His mouth fell open. The door, which had a single word—MAINTENANCE—printed on it, was attached to a towering orange metal arch. The arch reached straight up into the fog, but lights of its own illuminated enough of the shape for Rhett to make it out. Dense cables swooped down and away from the arch, then swooped back up, connecting with another arch down the street, which he was quickly realizing wasn't a street at all. Down the road, near the crash, the other orange arch dug into the cloudy air, splashing the fog with soft yellow light.

"We're on the Golden Gate Bridge," Rhett said, mostly to himself.

"Put that together, did ya?" Basil asked. "Don't be such a bloody tourist, mate."

It was hard not to be, though. Even with three-hundred-some-odd days of soul-gathering under his belt, Rhett was still amazed every time they turned up in a new place. They had been to San Francisco before, but never like this. The last time had been for a stabbing victim in the Tenderloin. Not exactly an exciting encounter with the city.

But the bridge, in the early hours of the morning, with the fog rolling in across the bay, smothering everything except for a smattering of out-of-focus lights, was one of the most beautiful things Rhett had ever seen. He wished he could stay and admire it, but the push wasn't going to allow that.

And neither was Mak, who was snapping her fingers at him.

"You awake over there?" she said, putting as much snark into her voice as she could.

Rhett, Theo, and Treeny followed Mak and Basil down the side of the bridge, with the railing ticking by on their left and the traffic beeping and snarling on their right. As they went, the fog began to recede ever so slightly, exposing a little more of the bridge and the cars that were stretched out across it but not much else. Rhett could see the emptiness beyond the railing, where there was only the drop into the water.

There was an ambulance ahead, its lights dancing off the fog, looking like fire and smoke from a distance. Near the ambulance was a tangle of metal and leather that might have once been a car, but it was hard to tell now. The image jarred Rhett out of his sight-seeing. The car wrecks were the hardest for him.

The mangled car looked like it might have been a Mercedes,

maybe a BMW. It was something luxurious, either way. Gnarled twists of glossy black finish and shreds of tan leather circled each other in a gruesome dance of destruction.

As they got closer, Rhett overheard a conversation between two paramedics—something about how the car had been going over a hundred miles an hour. And once they were closer still, Rhett could make out the blood that was coating some of the jagged points of metal. He followed the blood, finding the places where there seemed to be more of it, until he found an arm dangling from the wreckage. It was pale, with small fingers and manicured nails. There was a diamond the size of a small asteroid on the ring finger. Wrapped up in all that carnage was a woman clinging to life.

Basil and Mak got there first, and Mak was looking for a way to get to the woman. Around the car, there were probably a dozen paramedics and cops but no firefighters. If anybody was going to save the woman, it would be them. But there was no fire truck in sight.

Then, from way off at the other end of the bridge, as if in response to Rhett's thought, there was the sound of an angry, nasally horn. The fire truck was trapped at the other end of the bridge, caught in traffic with everybody else. There was no way this woman was escaping her vehicle without them.

Rhett took up his position, standing near the smoking wad of expensive steel, fingering the knuckle blade at his hip, sensing Treeny and Theo and Basil completing the perimeter behind him. He had yet to see anything out of the ordinary, but on a morning like this, with darkness and fog and chaos surrounding them, putting up their guard was the best thing they could do.

Mak was saying something. It sounded like ". . . can't even get to her . . ." But Rhett wasn't sure. There was a lot of noise. More honking from cars that were inching past the wreck, angry yelling from farther down the bridge, and the fire truck blasting its horn, trying desperately to get through.

He glanced over his shoulder. Mak was climbing on top of the mangled hulk, peering down through what used to be a window. And then Mak was climbing down *inside* the car, squeezing her narrow, muscular figure through the chewed-up gaps.

"Mak!" Rhett called. "Are you sure that's a good idea?" He was practically screaming to be heard over the din, and he wasn't sure she heard him even then. On the other side of the wreck, Basil made eye contact. His face was concerned now. Apparently Rhett wasn't the only one with a bad feeling.

He watched Mak disappear into the carnage. She was out of sight.

Traffic crawled past them, horns screaming to be heard. Slowly, one by one, the dim glow of headlights turned into actual beams that were attached to vehicles morphing out of the fog. Drivers were hanging out of their windows, hollering at one another as everyone tried to squeeze by the wreck. The fire truck horn sounded out of the void, over and over, wailing like a banshee.

Rhett squinted against the darkness and the fog and the lights filling up the fog, trying to see if the fire truck was getting any closer, in some weird way hoping that it would. He knew it was already too late—the push was enough to assure him of that—but at least then no one would be able to say that it had been hopeless, that a few hundred commuters were too impatient and frustrated to give the fire truck enough room to pass, to give it a fair shot.

The horns rang out like an overture of panic. But somewhere in there, Rhett thought he could hear something else . . .

A roar?

An actual scream?

Whatever it was, it didn't sound like it was coming from a machine. It sounded like an animal, something predatory. Something hungry.

Down at the far end of the bridge, where the fire truck was making its desperate crawl toward the wreck, Rhett could see dark shapes. Tall shapes. Shapes that appeared to be climbing the cables of the bridge and moving across the roofs of the gridlocked cars.

All at once, the angry horns and irritated yells started to die down, and there was a sense of movement coming down the bridge, a wave of chaos.

"Oh my God," Basil said, and Rhett heard him clearly now. "Mak, get your ass out of there! Now!"

But Mak was already midgathering. Rhett could hear her murmuring the words from inside the crumpled car. *I will guide you to the clearing.*

"Basil . . . ?" Rhett started to ask. But after a moment, there was no need. They came out of the fog like phantoms, tall and shadowy, grinning like madmen.

Psychons.

Rhett had never seen one. In his months as a syllektor, the worst-case scenario—the thing that all syllektors armed themselves against—had never happened. He had only heard the stories that Basil and Theo told. These were the things that inspired nightmares of skeletons clothed in shadows.

The real thing was so, so much worse.

They were at least twice as big as a normal person, towering over most of the vehicles. The ones that were scaling the structural parts of the bridge looked like giant birds of prey, preparing to swoop down and collect their kills. The psychons were fleshless, arms and legs sinewy with muscle and cartilage, their hands and fingers made of knobby bones that were hooked into claws. Their faces were mostly bare skulls with a few ribbons of connective tissue strung here and there—up their necks, between the two halves of their jaws, deep down in their sunken, cave-like eye sockets, where beady white eyeballs looked out, vacant, starving. They wore cloaks that were tattered, hanging about their grotesque bodies the way algae hangs on to old shipwrecks, in ragged, fluttering tufts. The cloaks came up over their heads, forming hoods that did little to mask the awfulness of their faces.

"Shit, shit, shit," Basil spat, and ran up to where Rhett stood. The two of them and Theo and Treeny formed a line in front of the car wreck, where Mak was still inside, gathering the soul of the driver. "Mak! Hurry it the hell up!" Basil reached over his shoulders and came back with a scythe in each hand. He did his drumstick spin with them. Theo, grinning, removed his battle-ax from its place across his back. And Treeny, trembling, fanned out a handful of her knives. Rhett gripped his knuckle blade, slipped it from its holster.

"How did they find us?" Treeny whimpered.

"I count six, boss," Theo said. Technically, the "boss" was Mak. But he was speaking to Basil.

"Keep it together, Treeny," Basil said. "You too, mate." That last part was directed at Rhett, who was doing his best to process what he was seeing. The monsters, the soul-eaters. They were actually there in front of him.

"I'm good," Rhett said. "I'm good." He was repeating it mostly for his own comfort.

"Two of them are going up the cables, Theo," Basil said. "They're going to try and come down on top of the car. Make sure they don't. Treeny, Rhett, and I will go after the others. Everyone try to divert them from Mak."

"She should be done by now," Rhett said.

"She's stuck," Basil replied quietly. "She's got to be stuck."

The psychons moved in, four of them on the road, weaving around some cars, going over others, all with unsuspecting drivers behind the wheels, drivers who knew nothing of the fight that was about to break out between two factions of the dead. The other two were slinking up the cables of the bridge. They were moving faster now, closing in, their torn cloaks billowing limply behind them. One of them opened its mouth and a peal of vicious noise escaped it, something like a roar and a scream combined, the noise a beast makes right before chomping into its freshly hunted meal.

"Here they come!" Basil called, glancing one last time over his shoulder, the hope in his eyes that Mak would be there. She wasn't.

All six of the psychons cried out, and all six of them rushed forward, their skeletal claws splayed and their mouths spilling some kind of white goop. They were salivating.

Theo took off first and leaped into the air. He caught one of the bridge cables, where a psychon was clawing its way toward the car wreck. For a second, Theo just hung there by one hand, massive feet dangling above the sidewalk and the protective railing. Then he swung his other arm, the one with the ax held at the end of it, and sliced through the cable with a single blow. The whole bridge jerked as the disconnected cable sprung back, colliding with another cable, the one with the other psychon on it. The cable swung through the air and came down on top of the still-unmoving traffic, smashing several cars. Drivers screamed and abandoned their vehicles. To them, a support cable had just inexplicably snapped, possibly as a result of the car crash. The paramedics and cops were running, too, staring up at the bridge cables, preparing for more to come down on top of them. Everyone scattered, fleeing into the dense fog.

The two psychons that had been climbing the bridge plummeted back down. One of them smacked into the asphalt and lay still for a second, then jerked back up, looking angrier than ever. The other one dropped down on the other side of the railing and disappeared, its roar fading rapidly.

Theo landed on his feet, swung his battle-ax around, and went back for more, running at the psychon that had fallen back onto the bridge.

After that, there was no more time to react.

Basil took off sprinting, head down, toward the oncoming psychons on the road. Treeny took a hesitant step back, then gripped the knives in both of her hands and held her ground, waiting for one of them to come to her. There was a fire in her eyes that Rhett had never seen before. He was impressed.

Rhett had a split second before one of the psychons, its eyes homed in on him, cutting through him like lasers, was on top of him. He took that split second to give one more look over his shoulder at the pulverized Mercedes—or whatever it was. The woman's arm still hung limp and pale out of the mess, her ring winking at him with the glow from the headlights.

Then the second was up, and suddenly Rhett was upside down, the psychon's skeleton claw wrapped around one of his legs. The bridge, still mostly obscured by the fog, flipped around in his vision like a pancake. Rhett hung tight to his weapon for as long as he could, with the psychon flinging him around like a human tassel, until the velocity became too much and the blade slipped from his grip. He saw it flip away into the fog.

Rhett tried to kick out of the psychon's claw. He snapped his feet out, pushing and squirming as the world spun around him in a whirlwind of lights. At one point, his face passed right above the pavement, his vision filling up with the black rock and yellow lines.

Then he was looking at the psychon itself, right in the face. But it was shrinking, getting smaller by the second, and Rhett's feet were no longer caught in its grip. The psychon had thrown him.

He smashed into the side of a car, crumpling the door with a metallic crunch. Glass from the shattered window rained down on him. He slumped to the ground, with his back against the severely dented car and his legs stretched out in front of him, one of his pant legs torn and the ankle beneath it gouged. There was very little blood, but Rhett could see the pink muscles, sliced and splayed open, exposing part of the bone.

Something wet plopped into his lap. It was thick and mucus-y. A string of it glistened in front of him, still caught between the glob on his pants and its source. Rhett followed the string up and saw the ugly, grinning face of another psychon perched on top of the car, looking down at him.

"Shit, shit, shit," he murmured, echoing Basil.

There was one above and one across the bridge from him, and Rhett had no weapon to speak of. The one that was across from him, the one that had tossed him like last week's garbage, took a menacing step toward him. At the same time, he heard the one on the car growl above his head, not in a hungry way—they didn't want to eat *him*, after all, they just wanted to get him out of their way, probably in the most violent manner possible.

Rhett tested his legs, pulling them toward him. The one that had been massacred was the right one, and while the left one curled up with no problem, the right one stayed where it was. He couldn't feel any of the pain and wouldn't dare force his senses to feel it. But the leg was no good now. Even if he wanted to make a run for it, he couldn't.

The psychon that stood facing Rhett took two or three more steps in his direction. Meanwhile, farther down the bridge, it looked like Basil had taken the arm off another one, but they were still circling each other, the psychon down an arm and pissed, Basil spinning his scythes cockily, ready to remove more appendages.

Theo was beating one of the monsters with his bare hands, his ax either lost or forgotten. And Treeny was fending one off from inside the backseat of a now-ruined sedan, the psychon clawing at the outside, popping in windows, shrieking in frustration while Treeny kicked at it with her feet and swiped at it with one of her knives.

When Rhett brought his attention back to his own shitstorm, the psychon that had thrown him was still closing the distance between them. And the one above him was crawling down the side of the car, its face unsettlingly close, its cloak hanging down around its pointed cheek bones, drowning most of its features in shadow. Its eyes were still bright, though, staring out of that darkness with raw intensity.

The lights began to flicker. All of them. Even the headlights on the cars. They stuttered on and off in random patterns. The shroud of fog that still hung about the bridge looked like it was performing some sort of light show, the golden sparks dancing around inside it. All up and down the bridge, the lights were seizing, creating a war between the darkness and the light.

The psychons were messing with the lights somehow. Or maybe when Theo cut that cable, something else snapped, causing an electrical malfunction. But that didn't explain the headlights.

And when Rhett glanced back up at the psychon that had been slinking toward him from on top of the car, it was retreating slightly, hesitating. It looked around at the flickering lights, obviously just as confused as Rhett was.

Rhett could still hear the grunts and clangs and angry yells coming from the other three, but they had to be seeing this, too. He looked back down the bridge for them. What caught his eye, though, wasn't their ongoing fights but a wave of darkness that was passing over the bridge. Where the lights at this end were still sputtering and dancing, the ones at that end were going out completely, the fog making it that much more difficult to see.

The shadow rolled toward him.

It fell over Basil and Theo and Treeny and the other psychons, squashing them into blackness, seeming to take the sound of their battles with them. Rhett made eye contact with the psychon standing in front of him. Those bright little eyes were still angry, but now there was something else. Could it be fear? Rhett was sure that it was. And that made him terrified.

Then the lights went out around him. There was an audible click as they did. And darkness descended. The psychons were somewhere in that black abyss, but he couldn't hear them, couldn't hear anything. The rest of the lights across the bridge went out. The dark was complete, impenetrable. Not even the lights from the city were making it through the fog.

Rhett waited. The killing—or, he supposed, the *ghosting*—blow would be coming. If there was anything that was going to work to the psychons' advantage, it was this.

Time stretched out. He didn't know what to do. He was about to try to get to his feet (or at least to his one good foot) when a handful of the lights snapped back on.

Only a few of them came back to life—some of the headlights, a smattering of the bulbs high up on the bridge's arches. It was enough light to see by, but most of the bridge was still obscured by darkness.

And when the light returned, everybody was gone. There were

no psychons, no Basil, no Treeny, no Theo. No drivers who had abandoned their vehicles when the support cable broke. Rhett couldn't see anybody . . . except for the girl standing right in front of him.

Only, she wasn't a girl. Rhett knew that from the start.

She was standing only a few inches away from the soles of his shoes. She was maybe a couple of inches shorter than he was, but from this angle she seemed to tower over him. Her skin was pale, sketched with blue and purple veins that warbled down her arms and legs. The only thing she was wearing was a ratty hospital gown, faded by time—eons of it, probably—and hanging loosely around her. Her neck was ridged, corded and straining, but the face was soft in an intimidating sort of way, like she had nothing to lose. There was dark hair that hung down to her shoulders in knotted clumps. And her eyes . . . her *eyes*. They were entirely black except for tiny white pinpricks for pupils, like distant suns in a vast wasteland of space. Those little white dots stared into Rhett, stabbing into his severely exposed soul. He recognized that stare somehow and pushed himself back against the car, wishing he could go *through* it, trying to get away from her penetrating eyes.

She was also sopping wet. From head to toe. The water dripped down along her arms and came off the hospital gown in fat drops. It splashed to the ground around her feet, making sharp, wet pecking sounds against the asphalt. It was just dripping water, but Rhett knew it was the same as what he'd heard aboard the *Harbinger*, alone in his quarters, all those times that he'd chalked it up to a leaky pipe. This girl, this *thing*, had come to see him before.

Rhett opened his mouth but found no words there. His throat was empty. All the reserve energy he had was now dedicated to fear, a thrumming, panicking knot of it that was locked inside his mind.

He didn't need to speak, anyway. The girl, still staring at him—*into* him—opened her own mouth. And when she spoke, her voice was cataclysmic. It was a gentle young girl's voice but surrounded by others. Not one voice, but a thousand. Like the whispers that came out of the tank in the steam room when the door was open, only amplified—shouting instead of murmuring. It dove into Rhett's mind, flooded all his channels of thought, pulverized his memories, overtook every picture and word and sound. If she spoke for too long, he would surely go insane from it.

"I am the speaker of languages. You are the keeper of souls. The decider of fates. The Twice-Born Son. If you do not heed me, I will obliterate you. If you do not abide, if you choose to act in dignity and courage instead, then the souls of your parents will be forever lost. These are your last days, Soul Keeper. Find your power. Then I will come for it. I will come for you. *Know this—if you fight me, you will fall."*

She stopped speaking, and in the haze of his disorientation, Rhett caught sight of the overturned car behind her. It reminded him so much of the car he'd been driving the night he and his parents died, the way it was crushed, the way it had flipped so easily under the force of someone's carelessness. And yet, staring at the girl-thing on the road, surrounded by the carnage of ruined vehicles, he questioned whether it was carelessness at all . . .

Before he could follow that thought, the few lights that had come back on went out again, blotting out the world. Rhett was left in the shadows, in delicious silence, the memory of her voice echoing through his head, threatening to send him into madness. He could still see those eyes. The sheer black emptiness of them, with just those little white holes for pupils. The only light that seemed to exist within her—within *it*—existed in those holes.

The lights began to flicker again, *all* of them this time. The yellow and white glow stuttered up and down the bridge for a moment, until the lights came back on in full, illuminating the fog and the road and the towering orange structures of the arches.

The psychons that had surrounded Rhett before the blackout were back, one above and one across from him, and when they saw him again, they dove. Their claws were splayed, their boney mouths hung open in mock laughter.

Rhett didn't think, just reacted. He fell to his side, letting his bum leg fall limp while he kicked up with the good one. His foot connected with the jaw of the psychon that had been reaching down for him. The bottom half of the jaw broke off with a sickening crunch and went spinning into the white curtain of fog. Whimpering, the thing fell to the ground beside the car and squirmed there.

The other one was coming for him, its fearsome gait turning into a trot, then a run. Rhett had one option, and that was to keep kicking. He turned himself into position, his mutilated right leg dragging across the asphalt. He tried to imagine what the pain would be like if he could actually feel it, but couldn't. He assumed it would have been astounding.

The psychon was sprinting toward him now, weaving around some of the unmoving cars, vaulting over the tops of a few. Rhett braced himself for the impact, staring deep into the monster's shiny-slick throat.

But there was no impact. The psychon stopped short, skidding to a halt at almost the exact spot where the girl-creature had appeared. It had its head cocked, listening to something. After a few seconds it took a step back, its tiny, buglike eyes boring into Rhett with a knowing glare, a look that seemed to say it would have its chance at ripping Rhett apart soon enough.

Rhett heard something else then, too, coming from the belly of the wrecked car, the thing that had drawn them all here in the first place. It was Mak.

"Hey!" she cried. "Hey assholes! What the hell is going on? I'm stuck! Caught on . . . something!" She grunted, and there was the sound of something metallic being punched or kicked.

The psychon turned toward the sound, eyeing the wreck, its thick saliva oozing through the gaps in its ever-smiling teeth. It was the soul the psychons had come for. And now the soul was inside Mak.

In some far-off reality that existed only in his peripheral vision, Rhett was aware of Theo and Basil dispatching the psychons they had been fighting. Theo finished pummeling his with his fists, leaving a bruised, scraped, dented mound of gross muscle and bone, veiled slightly by its tattered cloak. Basil had left behind a pile of detached limbs, all dripping some sort of black sludge that must have been the psychon's blood.

In the span of a few brief moments, Theo moved on to the psychon that was still going after Treeny. He hopped onto the roof of the car that she was in, ax now somehow returned to his hand, and leveled it at the psychon. It quit lashing at the vehicle and made a bizarre sound, a sound that was full of pleasure, as if to say, *Bring it on.* Then it leaped at Theo, and the pair fell backward together, vanishing behind the car.

The psychon that had made a run at Rhett stormed toward the original car wreck, where Mak was still trapped. Basil caught sight of this and made a noise that Rhett had never heard before. It was somewhere between a howl and a battle cry. He ran at the psychon but wasn't fast enough. It jumped high into the air, bounding over two lanes of traffic at once, and landed next to the smashed, overturned vehicle that Mak was still battling to escape. It took hold of the wreck with both of its powerful hands and *tossed* the entire thing.

The whole balled-up mess flipped through the air. Rhett caught sight of the lifeless arm that still jutted from the confusion of metal and leather and glass. It wobbled from side to side as the car rolled through the air, and it reminded Rhett of his own body, how it had seemed to almost wave good-bye to him back on the highway in New York.

With a booming *crunch*, the car crashed onto the sidewalk and the railing at the edge of the bridge. The railing gave way, breaking off the concrete and bending down into a mangled curve. The car scraped and skidded, one end edging out over the drop to the bay waters. It teetered dangerously. Metal groaned and bits of concrete came crumbling off the smashed sidewalk.

The psychon leaped again and landed near the destruction. But Basil was there to meet it. He had run full force toward the car when it came down and now was barreling toward the psychon. Rhett could see what was about to happen, and from his place on the ground, leg useless, all he could do was scream.

"*Basil, NO!*"

Basil collided with the psychon and sunk the curving blades of his twin scythes into the creature's body. It shrieked, falling backward under the force of Basil's tackle. Basil held on tight as the two of them, a tangle of skeleton limbs and dark clothes and flailing legs, went careening over the side of the bridge. They plummeted into darkness, with the fog quickly dampening the sound of the psychon's screams.

There were only two psychons left now—the one whose jaw Rhett had broken, who was still on the ground nearby, whining and wheezing, clutching at its reduced face, and the one that Theo was still working on. Rhett could hear them brawling behind the car that Treeny had been hiding in. Treeny herself was nowhere in sight.

From the tottering wreck hanging over the side of the bridge came Mak's voice: "*Someone get me out of here!*"

Rhett looked around, hoping Treeny would show herself and at least go help Mak. He was surprised to find that he didn't care if they all left him here as long as Mak got back to the *Harbinger* with that woman's soul still intact.

Treeny wasn't there. Maybe she was helping Theo, but Rhett didn't think so. Wherever she was, she was scared, and he hoped she was okay, almost as much as he hoped—*willed*—for Basil to be okay. But they were about to be down two team members instead of one if someone didn't help Mak.

Ignoring the writhing beast beside him, Rhett gripped the opening in the car he was leaning against, where the window had been. He pulled, heaving himself up and putting all his weight on his good leg. He attempted to distribute some of the pressure to the right one, but he nearly collapsed. The leg would take no weight.

So, using the stopped cars as leverage, Rhett hopped his way back across the bridge. He leaned on hoods and clung to side-view mirrors. What he would have given for a damn crutch.

As he made his slow way across the road, he glanced over to where Theo had taken on the other psychon. They were rolling around on the pavement together, Theo throwing punches and the psychon slashing at his face in return. Theo's face was purple with blooming bruises and covered in angry red claw marks. His ax was buried in the passenger door of a nearby Honda. Rhett wanted to help him. But there was no time—not with only one good leg.

He kept going for Mak.

Finally, after the most cumbersome walk he'd ever taken, Rhett made it to where the car—which was about to be Mak's tomb—sat half on and half off the bridge. He heard Mak screaming in frustration. There were also sounds of her beating and kicking and squirming inside. The car groaned and seemed to tilt slightly toward the drop.

"Hey!" Rhett called. "Mak, stop! You'll send the whole thing over the edge!"

"Rhett?" she yelled back. "What's going on? Where are the psychons? Where's Basil?" Her voice sounded almost frantic at the end.

Rhett peered over what remained of the railing at this section, staring down into the fog-covered black. There was no sign of any movement.

"The psychons are mostly taken care of," he said, loud enough for her to hear. "Basil is . . . gone."

"Don't you tell me that!" she screamed. "Get me *out of here, goddamn it!*" She was flailing again, attacking whatever it was that had her trapped. The car really did tip this time. With a stuttering, metallic groan, it tilted like a seesaw toward the water.

Rhett stood on one foot and stuck his hands into a crease in the metal of the car. He pulled. The car tipped back onto the bridge and nearly crushed the only useable foot Rhett had left. He used that foot to haul himself up to the part of the vehicle that was once the passenger's side but was now the top. He crawled across the length of it, to the warped passenger window. When he looked down inside, he could see Mak, wedged between a shredded leather seat and a jagged shard of metal that had come out of the dashboard and was pointing right at her, aimed like a knife at her rib cage, at her heart. If she moved the wrong way, if that torn piece of metal happened to stab into her . . .

There's only one way to destroy a syllektor, Captain Trier had said.

"Lean up against the seat," Rhett said. Mak looked up at him, startled. She gave him a skeptical look. "Just do it! Suck everything in!"

She took a deep breath and pushed herself as far up against the seat behind her as she could. When she did, Rhett could see behind her, could see an expensive purse and the keys dangling out of the ignition and the lower half of the woman who had died in the crash, her body white. Beneath him, Rhett felt the car leaning back toward the bay again. He took his shot.

Sitting back, letting his injured leg dangle over the front of the car, over the fog and the water below, Rhett stuck his good leg through the window and kicked down as hard as he could. His foot connected with the sharp, angled chunk of car that had blocked Mak's escape. It bent downward, giving her just enough room to pull herself out.

Except she wasn't going to be able to pull herself out. The car was slipping down toward the bay. Metal scraped across metal. Rhett yanked his leg out and reached back in with his arm. He felt Mak grab on to it. He pulled up with all he had, lifting her up and out. He had Mak in his arms without even having to think about it. They rolled together, off the back end of the car, and slammed onto hard concrete. There was one last metallic shriek as the car slid over the broken edge of the bridge . . . and then heavy silence, the car rocketing down into the black water.

Rhett and Mak lay side by side, staring up through the fog, which was beginning to thin out, at a sky of disappearing stars. The sun was rising as the spinning world finally came to a stop around them.

Mak sat up first. She looked around at the aftermath of the battle. Her eyes settled on something and got wide. Rhett sat up and followed her gaze.

It was the psychon with the broken jaw. The jaw was growing

back, bone emerging out of the taut muscles of its throat with an ugly squelching sound, like shoes in mud. The psychon was doubled over, clawing at its own face. The process of growing back missing body parts was obviously painful.

"You didn't kill it?" Mak hissed. Her hand crept over her shoulder, finding the handle of her machete.

"I . . . thought it was injured," Rhett whispered back.

"We have to run now," Mak said, slipping the machete out of its sheath and slowly pushing herself up onto her haunches. She never took her eyes off the psychon. "Can you run?"

"I can try. But why? Can't we just fight it? There's only one of them and two of us."

Mak tapped her chest, not taking her eyes off the psychon, and Rhett understood. She had the soul. The psychon wouldn't stop until it had its meal.

"Get ready to run. NOW!"

She was up in a second, reaching down and yanking Rhett up with her. Any harder and he would have been down an arm, too. They ran together between the lanes of cars, heading toward the city. Rhett moved as fast as he could, using the cars as support again. His right leg still wouldn't take any weight, but he forced it to at least stay up and out of his way.

Ahead, Rhett could see Theo and the other psychon on top of a car farther down from where they had previously been. Their fight had gotten much worse, and both sides looked beat to hell. Rhett watched as Mak approached the car from the front, hopped up onto the hood with one stride of her long legs, and sliced through the psychon's middle. Its two halves went tumbling over the side, smacking onto the road and staying there.

From behind them, the last psychon let out an angry, agonized scream that rattled the cables of the bridge. A couple of car alarms started going off. There was a crash and crunch of metal behind him, but Rhett didn't dare look back. He focused on Mak and Theo in front of him, focused on hopping after them with as much speed as he could muster out of his numb muscles. He was moving, gaining momentum . . . and then he was facedown on the asphalt. He had tripped over something.

Looking back, Rhett flipped over and saw an arm sticking out from under one of the cars. It was pale and dotted with freckles, quivering. Treeny.

Rhett clambered over to where her arm was. He glanced up, hoping not to see the psychon charging at him. There was nothing there. The thing was after Mak now, and it was Mak it was going to chase.

Underneath the car, Treeny was shaking, staring with wide, wet eyes, her glasses close to falling off her face. She was letting her senses through, or maybe she couldn't help it. Rhett put his hand out for her.

"Come on," he said. "Treeny, we have to go. I'm right here with you. You just have to take my hand." She shook her head. Rhett groaned. "Treeny, I'm not going to leave you here, okay? I won't. You have to come with me!"

"It won't be safe," she whimpered.

"It will be safe. I promise. Just take my hand."

She hesitated for another second, then reached out and took Rhett's hand. He helped her out from under the car, and together they sped down the bridge, using each other as support.

There was a roar from above. Rhett looked up and saw the dim shadow of the psychon racing across the uppermost cable that swooped down to the end of the bridge, right where Mak and Theo were running far up ahead. Rhett hobbled faster, leaning on Treeny for support. He could tell she was struggling, but she didn't say anything. They pushed on, closing the distance between themselves and the other two.

They passed the fire truck, with its lights still warbling. There was no horn now. And the truck was empty. Everyone must have evacuated the bridge when the cable broke, apparently not wanting to stick around to see if the bridge would hold.

Up ahead, Mak had stopped running and was looking into the windows of cars, cupping her hands around her eyes. Theo was behind her, eyes locked on the psychon that was rapidly descending toward them.

The sun was rising, casting a blue glow across the bay and the bridge. It was going to break over the horizon soon, and there was a silly part of Rhett that hoped the psychon would burst into a cloud of ash when it did. He didn't think he would get that lucky, though.

Mak found what she was looking for, shouting "Ah-ha!" when she did, and yanked open the driver's-side door of a big SUV. "Get in!" she yelled at Theo and Rhett and Treeny.

Rhett and Treeny were neck and neck with the psychon as it moved down the cable, preparing itself to lunge at the SUV. They rounded the other side of the car, hearing the engine turn over as they went. Treeny pulled open the backseat door on one side while Theo opened it on the other. They jumped inside together. Rhett hopped into the passenger seat. In some recessed part of his mind, he realized that this was the first time he'd been in a car since his own accident.

He pulled the door shut and said to Mak, "Can you drive this thing?"

She eyed his mangled leg. "Can you?" she said.

The psychon smashed onto the roof then, crushing most of it in on top of them, digging its claws into the metal. One talon stopped just short of gouging Rhett's eyeball.

"*Go, go, go!*" he yelled.

Mak threw the car in reverse and slammed on the gas. The tires spun and screeched and protested, spewing smoke. But they found purchase. The car launched backward. The psychon fell over, crashing onto the hood and rolling off onto the street.

There was only one car behind theirs, and Mak swerved the SUV around it, squeezing between two lanes with a shower of sparks and a squawk of collapsing metal. Once they had backed off the bridge, Mak swung the car around, put it in drive, and pushed the pedal down to the floor.

They screeched away, zigzagging between other cars, narrowly missing pedestrians who were still clustered near the bay, watching to see if the bridge was going to collapse. Mak avoided streets that looked crowded with morning commuters, and Rhett kept checking the rearview mirror, trying to see if the psychon had followed them. But there was no sign of it.

He glanced over at Mak. She stared ahead, face blank, betraying nothing of whatever torment was going on inside her.

Basil was missing. They'd all just gotten their asses handed to them by a pack of monstrous beings. And the soul of the dead woman was still inside Mak. They had no way of knowing if there would be more psychons coming after it, especially with one of them left alive.

That was Rhett's fault, along with the fact that he'd lost his knuckle blade back there. He thought of something else. He shifted in his seat so he could look back at Treeny. Theo was holding her hand, tilting his head so he could fit under the crushed-in roof. His face was a disaster of scratches and bruises, but he was watching Rhett, waiting for what he had to say, ready to keep fighting if he had to. Rhett suddenly had a newfound respect for the big lug.

"Treeny, do you have your tablet?" he asked.

She waited a moment before shaking her head. "I lost it back there," she said.

"Shouldn't we go back and get it? I mean, what if one of those things gets a hold of it?"

"It'll destroy itself," Mak said quietly. "And even if it didn't, the psychons aren't smart enough to figure out how to use it. Right now we just need to find a way back to the *Harbinger*."

"What about Basil?" Rhett protested.

"You said it yourself." Her eyes shifted just slightly. "He's gone."

They drove on, the city scrolling by around them. Rhett didn't have time to admire it. His thoughts were back on the Golden Gate, with Basil, with the psychons, with the thing that looked like a girl but was clearly something else. *These are your last days*, she had said. *Find your power. Then I will come for it. For you.*

Even without her tablet, Treeny knew where a door that led back to the *Harbinger* would be. It was one the team had used on a previous outing to San Francisco not long before Rhett had arrived.

They dumped the car where Treeny directed, in a tiny lot on the corner of Mission Street and Eighth. Rhett wondered briefly about what it must have looked like to see a big SUV driving itself. But nobody seemed to notice. The major news, according to the TV that hung just inside the window of a corner deli, was the cable break on the bridge and the damage that was done to hundreds of vehicles (including the one that had inexplicably fallen into the bay). They kept saying it was an earthquake, lacking any better explanation for what had happened.

After they left the car behind, it was slow going for Rhett. He hobbled along in the comforting brilliance of daylight with Theo's arm around him. It almost would have been better if he could feel the pain of his injury. At least then he wouldn't have felt so pathetic.

Treeny led them a block or so up to an abandoned laundromat. The windows were dusty and edged with cobwebs. There was a crooked CLOSED sign that hung against the inside of the door. Through the grimy windows Rhett could see an expanse of dirty blue and white linoleum, broken occasionally by weedy nests of electrical cords and tunnels of vacant pipe that jutted out of the floor and walls.

"This is the place," Treeny said. "Remember, Mak?" Her tone was fraught with sweet, ignorant innocence, like a child looking for the pride of their parents.

Mak nodded. "Yeah. We go inside, right?"

"Yes. It's the supply closet."

Mak pulled the door, and even though Rhett expected it to be locked tight, it opened just as smoothly as if the place had never been closed. Rhett had another one of those mind-warping moments of debate with himself, considering the idea that the door wasn't actually opening at all, that when Mak stepped inside the laundromat, she was passing *through* the door in a splash of ghostly mist. He preferred the alternative reality, where things appeared as they should.

The four of them stepped inside, into a different, dimmer light that gave Rhett the heebie-jeebies. He half expected another psychon to come stepping out of the gloom. Or worse . . . the she-thing.

But there was nothing except the dingy aftermath of a doomed business venture: crumpled receipts, empty soda cans, tiny boxes of detergent, a lone folding cart. There was a mouse nibbling on the bulbous end of a stale Cheeto.

Mak and Rhett and Theo followed Treeny to the back, where two doors faced each other in a cramped nook. One was marked RESTROOM, the other was marked EMPLOYEES. Treeny pointed to the latter.

"That one," she said.

Mak took hold of the doorknob, leaned into the splintered surface, listening. She jiggled the doorknob a couple of times. The sound was enormous in the empty space, like gunfire. Then she finally turned the knob and pushed the door open.

It swung away, revealing the room of doors on the *Harbinger*, but the room was not the quiet, solitary place it normally was. Rhett had originally thought of the room as Grand Central Station but had come to think of it more as a library, with syllektors passing through mostly silently, taking a moment to find what they needed but ultimately minding their own business. It was a library that literally allowed them to travel the world.

Now, though, the room was more like his original comparison, crammed with people all trying to be heard over one another. Doors on the other side of the room opened onto streets that looked weirdly familiar. And then Rhett caught a glimpse of a cable car jingling past one of the thresholds. The other syllektors were searching San Francisco, for them.

Captain Trier was there, too, bending at the waist to give orders into a young girl's ear. She was nodding, mouth open and eyebrows knitted together in concentration. When the captain was finished, he stood back up and the girl ran off, disappearing through another door. That was when Trier spotted Rhett and the others.

"*Everybody hold it!*" he bellowed, and it was loud enough to come rolling into the laundromat and rattle the front windows. "They're here," Trier said when the noise had faded.

The other syllektors looked in the direction the captain was staring. Then Mak and Treeny and Theo and Rhett were swept through the door. Once on the other side, Rhett allowed himself to fall to the ground, giving in to his mutilated leg and his overwrought mind. Somebody he'd never seen before started examining his injuries.

Mak asked, "How did you know where to look?"

"Treeny's tablet," the captain replied. "It gave off a distress beacon."

"Not bad technology for a ship that's as old as dirt," Rhett said from the floor.

The captain grinned crookedly, but the grin quickly faded. "Basil?" he said.

"Missing," Mak replied, folding her arms, looking away. "He went over the side of the bridge." Then she turned and tried to disappear into the crowd of syllektors that were making their way out of the room.

"Mak," Trier called after her. "Mak! *Makayla!*"

Mak stopped.

Rhett found Treeny and held her gaze. He mouthed a single word at her. *Makayla?* Treeny only shook her head, as if to say that further investigation into the matter was a cautionary tale waiting to happen.

"I know you're hurting, even if your face doesn't show it," the captain said gently. By now the room had mostly cleared. The mumbled conversations of syllektors either going back to other parts of the ship or following the push out through the doors was dying away.

Mak stood with her head down. Her shoulders were hitching, and her hands were balled into tight fists, quietly in need of something to obliterate.

"Blimey, what's all the bloody fuss about?" a voice said from the

far corner of the room, where a door was just snapping shut. He came limping out of the shadows, dripping water into huge puddles that he left in his wake. "That damn bay is a disgusting moat of a thing."

Basil had one scythe in his hand, lathered with black pus. His clothes had been clawed into strips, with long scrapes and slices in his flesh underneath. His left leg hadn't been gouged at all, but it was cocked from the knee at an unpleasant angle. And yet his grin was unaffected, still tilting across his face as if it had been permanently fixed that way.

Mak spun around and found his eyes. Rhett saw her face crumple, the barriers of her bitter facade coming down, her emotions finally allowed to roam free across the landscape they were best suited to exist upon. She ran to him, and they collapsed together in a heap on the floor, her face buried in his shoulder.

The captain looked genuinely relieved. He turned to Treeny. "Very good work setting off the distress signal, Treeny," he said.

Treeny nodded with a thin smile. She still looked shaken, but she exchanged a quick wave with Basil, who gave her a thumbs-up, then she turned and practically ran out of the room.

Theo cocked his finger in Basil's direction, his own crooked grin carving its way across his brutalized face. He took a few steps in Treeny's direction—probably wanting to go after her and make sure she was okay—before losing his balance and sitting down hard, with his arms resting on top of his knees.

Rhett wanted to worry about Treeny. He *really* wanted to worry about Theo. Instead he lay back on the floor, staring up at the high ceiling, at the ornate woodwork that curled like smoke across it. The image of the she-thing's eyes invaded his view. Those black holes with only the tiny specks of light in the middle.

"I don't mean to be a pain," he eventually said. "But can someone get me off the floor?"

TEN

The medical bay was as cold and uninviting as it sounded, coated in that fluorescent, medicinal glow that always meant you were among the sick and dying. In this case, it was just Rhett, Basil, and Theo, all three technically dead already.

The whole place looked overly sterile, without a single smudge on any of the shining steel. But then again, Rhett didn't figure the place got much use. There were glass cabinets with bottles of actual medicine in them—bandages, syringes, slings, empty vials. Plastic curtains hung around empty beds. There was one nice feature: a wall that had three large portholes set into it, giving a spectacular view of the very unspectacular world outside.

Rhett also couldn't help but note the wide glass tube that stood in the very center of the room, connecting the floor to the ceiling like a support column. The tube was filled with souls. They glowed and ebbed and pressed up against the glass, their whispering voices blessedly unheard from the outside.

The boys were all given beds, Rhett and Basil across from each other, Theo near the portholes next to Rhett. Other syllektors, ones who had obviously brought some sort of medical training with them when they died, set Basil's leg and wrapped Rhett's. They did as much as they could for Theo—bandages and gauze and tape—and when they were done, he looked like a horrifying cross between the Mummy and Frankenstein's monster. The poor guy fell asleep almost instantly.

Once all the bandaging and casting were done, they were left to themselves, with Mak sitting next to Basil's bed, holding his hand, resting her face on his chest. Rhett watched them, listened to them.

"I thought we were goners back there," he murmured to her. "Thought we might lose each other."

Rhett was somehow comforted. He thought of his parents, of their beautiful, untarnished love for each other. He thought of how the world seemed to rotate around them, how it could pummel them with constant obstacles and how they always, *always* overcame them together, as one, holding each other and comforting each other and each of them feeding off the other's optimism, like Mak and Basil were doing now. And when, one year on his parents' anniversary, Rhett had asked his father what made their relationship so strong, so impenetrable, his father had told him that there's no such thing as having to work at a marriage, that life might be hard, but love is easy.

Watching Mak and Basil, Rhett heard those words play over and over in his head. That had been one of the best conversations he'd had with his dad. He was glad for it.

He looked out at the churning gray sky and wondered again about the night of the crash. He thought about losing it and swerving the car, yanking the steering wheel, trying to make a scene, to get his dad's attention. He thought about the road in front of the car and how empty it had seemed. He could never have seen the truck behind them when he swerved, but the stretch of highway in front of the car had been completely devoid of traffic, of anything. It had been totally empty.

Hadn't it?

Days went by. The boys healed together. Basil called it "a never-ending bro-down" in his ridiculous college-jock American accent. Treeny came by every now and then, mostly to check up on Theo, who had been her first savior back on the Golden Gate.

Mak was there often, visiting with Basil and mostly ignoring Rhett, which was as it should be. She quickly hardened back into her old prickly self, losing the cuddly nature that had overcome her when Basil turned up alive. Sometimes they nagged at each other, but it was usually in fun, and Rhett loved to listen to them. If the mood was just right, it really was like being in the room with his parents again.

Not long after they'd first been brought down to the medical bay, Basil had told them the story of how he'd survived the psychon and the drop into the bay.

"The bastard broke my fall," he said. "We hit the water and it might as well have been a brick wall. If my scythes didn't kill the damn thing, the hit from that water sure bloody did. And I still managed to break my leg."

Then it was just a matter of getting back to shore, he told them. He had sunk with the psychon, trying to free his blades in case there were more that might come after him but only managed to get the one.

"I took it and doggy-paddled my way to one of the beaches. It was pathetic. After that, I had to limp through half the city to find a door that would get me back aboard the ship."

Basil told the story with the same cocky air of indifference with which he told pretty much any story about himself. But Rhett sensed an underlying tone, something in the neighborhood of uneasiness. Basil had been afraid. Maybe as much for himself as he had been for Mak. It had certainly been a close call. And if Rhett understood anything about what Captain Trier had told him, about the existence of a syllektor after the destruction of their heart, it was that "ghosting out" was the worst possible thing that could happen. An eternity surrounded by memories that you can't touch, can't feel, can't enjoy, haunting the hollow shell of your lost life. It was worse than a horror story. Because it could happen for real.

At night Rhett and Basil would alternate between playing chess and playing Scrabble. Theo tried to play (according to Basil, Theo was actually a fantastic chess player), but his hands and face were too bandaged up. He was content to just sit and watch, though, usually falling asleep halfway through a game.

Chess had been Basil's game of choice. "Back when I was a young little mouthbreather," he said, "I'd play with my sister on a set that we made out of an old crate and some bottlecaps." Scrabble had been a staple in the Snyder household while Rhett and his parents were alive. His parents even began implementing "Tequila Scrabble" on Saturday nights. Sometimes they'd even let Rhett join in . . . but with club soda instead of tequila.

Over those games, Rhett told Basil and Theo about his parents, about the accident, about how guilty he felt for causing it. About how he sometimes hated himself, both for the accident and for the guilt, not knowing which was the right way to feel.

Basil nodded. "The hating yourself part is the hardest thing to get over, isn't it?" he said. "You just feel like you could have been so much better. Ha-ha! Triple Word Score!" And he went on as if he hadn't said anything at all.

One night Mak poked her head through the door, eyebrows raised in question. She found Rhett and held his gaze.

"Basil's asleep," Rhett said quietly. "Although what we're listening to is either his snoring or the mating call of a hippopotamus. It's hard to tell the difference."

She stepped into the room with a tiny smile on her face, and Rhett felt a little firework of pride go off inside him—it wasn't often that he got a smile out of any of them.

"I'm . . . actually here to see you," Mak said, her voice low to keep from waking Basil and Theo, who was also turned over and snoring loudly.

Rhett was sure that he couldn't hide the surprise on his face, but he tried to play it cool.

"Well then, by all means, step into my office," he said.

She picked up a chair and set it next to Rhett's bed. She sat down with her elbows on her knees, as if she was about to give him some kind of pep talk. Maybe she was. He didn't know. He was in uncharted territory.

When she didn't say anything for a while, he asked, "Is everything all right?"

"I never thanked you," she murmured.

"What do you mean?"

"I never thanked you for saving me. On the bridge." She was staring at her hands fiddling with each other.

"Oh. Well, you don't have to thank me," Rhett said. "It was a group effort, anyway." He nodded toward Basil, a growling lump under the sheets across the room.

"I know," she replied. "I just . . . I was afraid. I didn't realize I was stuck right away. Because at first I couldn't move. As soon as I heard that there were psychons out there, I . . . I froze. I failed my team. Again."

Rhett was stunned. He was incapable of finding the words to fill the gap of silence that was stretching out between them.

"Theo looks like crap," she went on. "We almost lost Basil. I think Treeny is completely traumatized. And look at you." She gestured to Rhett's leg. She paused, then said, "You were braver than I was out there. You pulled me out of that car, and because of that, we saved everybody. So . . . thank you."

Mak stood, leaned over Rhett's bed, and put her lips against his cheek. Without thinking, he switched his senses on. The pain in his leg was phenomenal, daggering into him with seething red blades. But the feeling of her kiss against his skin blew the pain right out of him. It wasn't romantic—he wasn't sure he could ever feel anything like that for Mak, especially after having compared her and Basil to his parents. It was the simple act of being soothed by another person that made the agony in his leg worth it. When she pulled away, he let his senses fade again.

Rhett opened his mouth to tell her about what he'd seen in San Francisco, about the girl that had appeared to him and nearly ruined his mind with just her voice, about what she had said (*I am the speaker of languages. You are the keeper of souls*), about the fear that was burning a hole inside him. But what came out instead was "You don't have to thank me, Mak. You're part of my team, and you're my friend. Even if you're a little pushy sometimes." She laughed quietly. "And you didn't fail anybody. We might be dead, but we're still mostly human. In fact, I think I feel more human now than I did when I was alive."

Mak sat back down, cocking her head in a silent question.

"I just mean that before I died, I was so . . . disconnected. High school is . . . the literal worst sometimes. And everybody's always so caught up in their own stuff. It was like being on a different planet from everyone else. Here . . . it feels like I've known you guys forever." Now he was the one fidgeting.

Mak was nodding, her head down.

"Her name was Lana," she said. Rhett looked up at her, startled by her words. "She was around Treeny's age. They were really close. And she was like a little sister to the rest of us." She looked around the room for a moment, seeming uncertain. But she went on. "We were in Austria, picking up the soul of this skier who'd gotten caught in an avalanche. It was taking too long. We all knew it. We were digging through the snow, trying to find the guy. I was about to just call it. Give up and let the psychons find him. I should have. But Lana wanted to keep going. She was never afraid, that kid. Never." She swallowed. "The psychons showed up, of course. We tried to fight, but the snow was so deep and unsteady. They . . . they dragged Lana away. I couldn't figure out why they would do that. But I saw the top half of the skier sticking out of the snow. He was long dead, and I could tell his soul was already gone."

"Jesus . . . ," Rhett whispered.

"Those monsters ripped her apart. They opened her up and took the soul right out of her chest and then they . . . they smashed her heart. For fun, I guess. Or maybe because she got in their way. She was gone. Ghosted. Just like that. We were all broken for a long time. Treeny still is. She was never right after Lana. We fought—hard—to be a team again. That's why when you showed up . . . I just couldn't let history repeat itself."

Rhett let out a long, heavy breath. It hung there between them, like an invisible speech bubble waiting to be filled. Finally, he said, "How do you feel now?"

Mak looked over at the spot where Basil's chest was rising and falling, filling and emptying with the air he didn't need to breathe. She turned back to Rhett and stared at him.

"Now I feel like we're lucky to have you," she said.

Rhett smiled. It was all he could do.

"What about you?" Mak asked.

"What do you mean?"

"Are you still angry you got roped into all this?"

He thought for a moment, listening to the give and take of Basil's and Theo's snores.

"No," Rhett said. "I'm not angry about being here. Sometimes I'm angry because I feel like I got yanked out of a life that I hadn't even figured out yet. But if given the choice between being here or there . . ." He nodded at the tube of souls glowing in the middle of the room. ". . . I'd rather be here. With you. With them." He looked around at where Basil and Theo continued to sleep soundly.

It was Mak's turn to smile.

Rhett took her hand then, and she let him. And they were quiet for a while.

Basil and Rhett were released from the medical bay long before Theo, who continued to look like Frankenstein's Mummy for a solid two weeks.

Rhett and the others got back into the groove of things as best they could—training, gathering, working. Mak pushed the team harder than ever in the training room, including herself. Rhett caught her early one day, alone in a corner of the room, pummeling a rubber torso with her machete, slicing it into foamy wedges, her senses and emotions coursing through her so that she was dripping with sweat and tears. The handle of the machete was slick with blood from blisters on her palms. She may have finally told Rhett what happened to the fifth team member—Lana—but that didn't mean that she had forgiven herself. He left her alone that day and decided not to mention it to anyone.

The first time they had to go out and collect a soul without Theo was nothing short of tense and frightening. Rhett was glad to have a new knuckle blade to replace the one he'd lost on the Golden Gate, but that didn't make it any easier.

They found some poor guy who'd been on a hunting trip and had somehow been shot, either by his own bullet or someone else's. The guy was bleeding out in the middle of a dense forest, where a pack of psychons could have rushed the team at any time, from any direction. They had all agreed ahead of time that Treeny would collect the soul, and Mak and Rhett and Basil would stand guard. But even with the three of them surrounding her, Treeny still seemed terrified as she pulled the hunter's soul into her.

They got out of there as quickly as they could.

After that it was only slightly easier. Every new death brought with it its own set of risks, and without Theo, the team's chance of survival against the psychons was severely damaged. Which is why they were all extremely happy to have him back when he was finally released from the med bay.

And of course he was released on a working day, when the push was nowhere to be found and the five of them were down in one of the cargo holds, hauling crates of food up to the mess hall. Theo was with them, though, working as hard as ever, even with his face still yellow and swollen from the battle on the Golden Gate. Rhett was glad to see the big guy back on his feet, and he said so.

"Thanks, stretch," Theo replied, his New York accent like a kind of music. He tossed a crate of potatoes onto one of his massive shoulders and took a few stiff steps over to where they had a flatbed cart waiting. He set the crate down. "It's good to be out of that stinkin' ward. Never liked those kinds of places."

"Because you don't like hospitals, or because you were such an outstanding citizen in your former life that you never had to visit one?" Basil asked. He and Rhett were in new clothes, pulled from a collection that had accumulated on board over the centuries. Rhett had really only needed some new jeans and found a decent pair right away. He had wanted to ask if there was some kind of Goodwill donation box for the afterlife. Basil, on the other hand, had searched high and low for a new blazer to replace the one that had been ruined by the psychons. Now his new blazer was hanging off the corner of one of the crates, and Blazer Guy himself was dragging crates across the floor to the cart, sleeves rolled up and his normally perfect hair dangling in his face.

Theo only grinned in response to Basil's jab.

The cargo hold seemed to be as long as the *Harbinger* itself, stretching out under hanging yellow lights for as far as Rhett could see. The hold was overtaken by mountainous stacks of crates, which, according to Treeny, never diminished. There was always a supply of food on board, no matter how many syllektors there were or how many meals they ate. The five of them were deep in the labyrinth, schlepping crates onto the cart as quickly as they could, trying to be done with the day's work.

Mak and Treeny were mostly silent, each of them still harboring their guilt from what happened on the bridge in San Francisco. Rhett understood that. Every time he looked at Theo's face he was reminded of all the things he could have done differently. But he'd helped to save Mak, and, in a way, he'd saved Treeny, too. If not for the other thing—the she-thing—he might have considered that day a victory.

"Hey guys?" Rhett said suddenly, surprising even himself. He was going to tell them. The words were there on his tongue, waiting to burst out of him. The eyes of the girl-monster flickered in front of him.

The other four stopped—Mak with a crate resting on her hip, Basil with his arms folded and leaning against one of the stacks, Treeny behind a crate as big as she was that she had been pushing toward the cart, and Theo with his muscular arms wrapped all the way around a crate marked WINE. They were all looking at Rhett, waiting, and he wished that he could pop open the crate Theo was holding and have a drink.

"I just . . . wanted to say . . . thanks," Rhett stammered, losing his nerve. "Thanks for taking me in."

They all smiled at him—even Mak—and for just a moment all thoughts of the she-thing were pushed from his mind. On the worst day of his life—at the *end* of his life—he had lost one family but gained another. They were all standing here in front of him. He trusted them and they trusted him and they were friends. More than that, they were a team. They had conquered the psychons once and, if they had to, they would do it again. But for now they were content to just be together, working, training, gathering. And that was happiness enough for all of them.

"Don't get all sappy on me, mate," Basil said, winking.

"Yeah, you're not allowed to get soft," Mak said playfully. "I need a human shield the next time we run into the *psychos*."

They all laughed, including Treeny, who shook quietly with giggles, covering her face.

"Did Mak just make a joke?" Theo asked, his voice legitimately concerned. And they all cracked up again.

When they had settled down a bit but still weren't inclined to get any work done, Basil glanced over at Theo.

"Here's a thought," he said.

And then they really did crack open the wine. Rhett wasn't sure if there was an age limit for alcohol aboard a ship of the dead, especially when the dead people in question could avoid the effects of getting drunk if they wanted to. But he gladly took a swig from the bottle when it was passed to him and allowed his senses to absorb the flavor—and the alcohol—as it went warm and heavy into his stomach.

They sat among the crates, passing the bottle around, telling stories about life and afterlife and everything in between. When Mak mentioned Lana without any hesitation at one point, the others joined in, telling Rhett about her fearlessness, her passion. Rhett talked about his parents, their apartment in New York. He told them about his high school and the places he used to hang out at in the city.

They ignored the work they were supposed to be doing, enjoying the rare time they had to relax and, who could have thought, just be teenagers. A couple of hours passed. Until they heard someone coming into the cargo hold, their hard-soled shoes clacking against the floor. The five of them scrambled to gather the wine bottles that they'd gone through and get them back into the crate. But Theo fumbled one and it shattered against the floor. Everyone cringed.

Captain Trier stepped into their little alcove of stacked crates, hands behind his back as always. He stood there with one eyebrow cocked.

"I started to get worried when I didn't see any of you in the mess hall for dinner," he said. "I obviously had nothing to worry about. Except maybe for that." He dipped his head in the direction of the broken wine bottle.

"Our apologies, Captain—" Mak started, but Trier cut her off, holding up a hand.

He glanced around the hold with a look of pure interest. Rhett held his breath, waiting for whatever punishment was about to be doled out.

Finally, with a smirk, the captain said, "Don't drink all the wine." And that was it. He turned and disappeared behind the crates, going out the way he had come in.

When he was gone, Rhett and Basil broke down into hysterical laughter, uncontrollable, and the other three joined in, holding on to the edges of crates to keep from falling over.

"We just got straight-up busted," Basil said, nearly weeping.

"Worth it," Rhett replied.

They sat and drank and talked until the *Harbinger* went quiet for the night, their voices echoing above them in the massive hold, replaying the sounds of their laughter.

ELEVEN

He tried to fend off his fear, but it was no use. His mind was still more powerful than he was, and it delivered its messages in the only way it knew how: through his nightmares.

Of psychons swooping down from the tumultuous sky and tearing into him, pulling him apart as he watched, until there was nothing left but a few scraps of flesh and his still-beating heart, *whump-whump*ing on the floor.

Of the she-thing that had come to him with her threats and her warnings, promising vengeance if he defied her. He could hear the water dripping on the floor, could see her black eyes boring into him.

Of his parents, caught in a violent freeze-frame, with the disintegrating car around them, the world outside turned upside down, their eyes squeezed shut, mouths dropped open in screams. And then his father, in that same still-shot, staring at him, his face perfectly calm, saying, *You did this. You did this.*

Of the girl in Arizona, the waitress who had died too young, standing behind the bar at the diner, the pot of coffee in her hand, turning to him and saying, *You did this, too. You did this to us.*

They were swift and vicious. They were the cruelest kind of guilt, the kind that he could not control or stifle or smother. He could have told anyone about the girl from the bridge. He could have told Captain Trier, Basil, Mak. All he had to do was open his mouth. But every time he did, a jolt of fear would rocket through him, paralyzing every empty nerve and muting every imagined sensation.

If you fight me, you will fall.

And he believed her. He didn't want to. But in just hearing her voice, he knew how powerful she was. She would destroy them all if it came down to that. And he was not going to put everyone on the *Harbinger*, and the souls that powered it, in the path of destruction. If there was some kind of power in him that she wanted, she could have it.

The power just needed to show itself.

Basil and Mak sat across from Rhett in the mess hall, their shoulders touching. Mak was trying to look stiff and stubborn as usual, but Basil kept nudging her with his elbow, bumping the food off her fork. Rhett kept waiting for her to get angry, but she kept laughing instead.

Rhett was poking at his lunch, decidedly not hungry after days of keeping what he knew from the others. That, paired with nights of terrifying dreams. He didn't even want to pretend to be hungry, just for the sake of eating—normalcy had lost its glamor, it seemed.

The three of them were sitting there, waiting on Theo and Treeny, when the push slammed into them, hard, threatening to literally drag Rhett down the stairs to where the room of doors waited.

"Whoa," he said, letting his fork clatter onto his plate, knowing all too well what that massive *whump* of the push meant.

Across the table, Mak and Basil exchanged a look. Their touchy-feeliness had vanished in an instant.

"Mass casualties," Mak said, her voice low. "Multiple souls." She stood up, her worried eyes darting around the mess hall. She was looking for something, and she found it over the top of Rhett's head, locking on to it and nodding.

Rhett turned and saw two other groups of syllektors on the other side of the hall that had stood up, rising above the gathered mass. He counted the heads of the syllektors that were now standing—nine in total—all of them waiting while the rest of the crew continued their meal. From the first group, a tallish man with piercing eyes and a baseball cap made out of completely blacked-out fabric nodded in response to Mak. From the other group, a woman who appeared to be about Rhett's mother's age, her blond hair cut short and hanging down to her chin, did the same thing. Then both teams began making their way out of the mess hall.

When Rhett swiveled back around, Mak was already moving around the table to leave as well. She stopped and turned back to him and Basil.

"You guys coming?" she said matter-of-factly, even though her face was scrunched with anxiety.

The boys nodded.

The three of them, plus the two additional teams, moved down to the armory, where they met Treeny and Theo. Treeny looked more shaken than ever, as if she had just seen a psychon in the hall on the way over.

"I've never felt it this strong before," Rhett said to her, trying to comfort himself as much as he was trying to distract her.

She only nodded under her curtain of red bangs.

"It's freaky, isn't it?" she said.

She had that right. After what happened in San Francisco, anything out of the ordinary was cause for alarm. But as Rhett looked around at his team and the other two that were apparently joining them—fifteen syllektors all told—he realized that this wasn't really out of the ordinary at all. *Mass casualties*, Mak had said. Rhett was surprised that even though he had seen this kind of thing before, had even been a part of it before, it still unsettled him.

But he didn't have time to dwell on it—the push was insistent. It was impatient. If he didn't get downstairs right away, he had a feeling that his body would eventually be carried there by invisible hands that would simply toss him through the correct door.

They got moving.

"Anybody else have a bad feeling?" Basil asked as they descended the stairs.

Nobody responded, and that was answer enough.

Rhett headed up the oversize group as they went into the room, and he didn't even need to stop and think about which door they needed. The push was all but carrying him toward it. It was gray wood, slightly crooked in its frame. Even though all the doors in the room looked pretty much the same at first, Rhett had learned that some of them were older than others and some of them were made out of different types of wood. This one appeared to have both of those anomalies.

He opened the door to an inferno.

Rhett was flung back by a blast of heat and flames, a fireball that erupted out of the open door, reaching up toward the high ceiling of the room. Everybody jumped backward, ducking their heads to avoid the blast.

Basil, Mak, Treeny, and Theo helped Rhett to his feet, their faces as concerned as he felt. When he was standing again, he could see the source of the fireball—a living hell caught within the frame of the door.

There was a short hallway with cheap plastered walls and checkered linoleum that cut off at a stairwell. A dark, splintered banister followed the stairs up and down, and another hallway extended away from the stairwell on the other side. There were apartment doors lining both hallways, and all of them were spewing flames, lashing orange tongues that swiped at the hot, empty air, looking for something to scald. Clouds of black, acrid smoke roiled along the ceiling, flickering with the lights of a fire alarm that was still giving off a faint, tinny whine. It looked as if the building had consumed a lightning storm.

People ran in and out of the doors, up and down the stairs,

frantic, smudged with soot and struggling to breathe. Rhett could hear panicked screaming and banging from somewhere. He stood frozen, watching the chaos unfold.

Someone grabbed his arm.

Mak leaned in close and said, "We have to get in there. Now. Before that place sets the whole ship on fire."

She was right, of course. Because even as the three teams of syllektors stood there watching, flames were still licking at the edges of the doorway that led back to the *Harbinger*. If they left the door open much longer, the fire would find its way onto the ship.

Rhett took an unsure step toward the door and then stopped.

In the stairwell at the end of the hall, a flaming hunk of debris went roaring past, falling through the opening. Rhett heard it collide with the bottom of the building in a crash of shattering wood and angry fire. The entire building was ablaze.

Rhett turned back to Mak. Was she really expecting him to lead all these syllektors into that mess? She was the leader of their team. She should be the one to lead this group. He would follow her in, if that was the call she made. But he had no intention of following the push to his ghosting with everyone else in tow.

And for the briefest of seconds, Mak looked just as unsure as he was. Her eyes shifted from the engulfing flames in the apartment building to the calm, smooth floor beneath her. After the smallest of hesitations, though, her resolve hardened across her face.

Mak moved past Rhett and took a stance in front of the open door, ripples of heat wobbling through the air around her head.

"Okay," she called to the group. "Everyone goes in. Everyone comes out. No unnecessary risks. No heroes. Got it?" The group—including Rhett—gave her their acknowledgment. "You find a thread, and you follow it. You get a soul, and you haul ass back to this door." She pointed behind her, where the flames were already dancing near the spot where the *Harbinger* ended and the apartment building began.

"What about the fire?" the man in the baseball cap asked.

"We're not all going to find another door out of there," Mak replied. "We leave this one open." She hesitated again. "For as long as we can."

The group of syllektors didn't look happy, but they did look determined. Basil, Theo, and Treeny exchanged a look with Rhett, who only tipped his head.

"Together," he said.

Then he nodded at Mak, who nodded in return before turning and running through the door. The fire rippled around her, like flickering orange hands trying to grab at her skin, and she was gone.

Rhett took a deep breath, gathering his courage, and followed her.

As soon as he was through, he could feel the heat and smoke weakening his body. He couldn't actually feel it in his nerves, but his movements became sluggish, his body's responses to his brain delayed. And he began to cough involuntarily. Up ahead, from within the haze of smoke that was getting thicker by the second, he could hear Mak doing the same thing. The fire was killing their bodies.

He made his way to the stairwell, giving himself over to the push, letting it guide him. When he got to the banister, he understood what Mak had meant by "find a thread." The push was nudging him in several different directions at once, its lure moving both up and down the stairs and also curling around the open stairwell to the hallway on the other side.

He could just barely see Mak over there, her machete ready at her side as she stepped into one of the apartments. There was a window at the end of that hallway that was blackened by the smoke, letting in just a hint of pale sunlight.

Behind and around Rhett, the other syllektors were falling into the building, following the various threads of the push to different floors. Looking down through the opening of the stairs, Rhett could see at least three more floors below him and six or seven above him. Who knew how many people were still trapped in here with them, doomed to let the flames win?

Basil sidled up next to him, a scythe in each hand reflecting the unruly firelight in their polished steel curves.

"Hell of a way to spend an afternoon, eh?" he said. And then he took off down the stairs. Rhett wanted to call after him, tell him to be careful. But after the Golden Gate Bridge, he knew he didn't have to give that warning. To anyone on *his* team, at least.

Rhett shook his head and mind back into focus and began climbing the stairs.

Flames crawled up the walls, reaching for him. Smoke poured down his throat, and his lungs continued to reject it, sending it back out in heaving, crippling hacks. More flaming debris came crumbling from the ceiling, and he could hear it crashing from other parts of the building. The whole place was ready to buckle.

He climbed one flight, and even through the growl of the fire he could hear the murmuring of syllektors gathering souls. The push nudged him up even farther. He climbed two more flights to a spot where the smoke was unbearably thick, the flames just warbling flickers hidden by shadows. Glowing embers swirled around Rhett, landing on his clothes and singeing holes into them, into *him*. If he turned his senses on now, he'd feel the tiny stabs of heat across his flesh.

The push guided him down the hall, where the only things that were truly visible were the growing glow of the fire and the ugly pattern of the floor. He let it keep him on track, even as he heard other syllektors barreling up the steps behind him, moving upward still.

Rhett came to the apartment at the end of the hall, on the left. The door was open, and inside he could hear the taunting crackle of more flames, like mad laughter. Through the haze, he could make out the shapes of furniture—a couch along one wall, a coffee table, an abandoned easy chair—but they were all just mounds of darkness in the gloom. In one wall, there was a cutout that led to a little kitchenette. The fire had found its way in there, and Rhett could see the jagged angles of flame snapping at the air.

He stepped farther into the apartment, letting the push point him where he needed to go—past the living room furniture and the kitchen, to the alcove where, on the left, there was a bathroom. It had its light on, the porcelain still weirdly white and glistening, as if untouched by fire or smoke, and on the right, there was a bedroom.

There were no lights on in there. No fire. And if there was a window, it must have been covered by curtains. Just outside the door, there was an oxygen tank laying on its side, with a clear tube circling across the carpet, disappearing into the bedroom. Whoever lived here could never even have tried to escape the fire, because they probably never left their apartment in the first place.

Rhett was reminded yet again of just how unfair death could be.

He traced the tube from the oxygen tank with his eyes, moving to go into the bedroom. As soon as he had this soul, he could get back downstairs, make sure everyone else was on their way back to the *Harbinger*, and get the hell out of here. The thin, clear tube slipped into smoky blackness, laying on the carpet for a few inches and then twisting upward . . . to a pair of withered feet that dangled off the floor.

Rhett realized that he had been holding his breath, trying to fend off the smoke as best he could. But now he let it go, gasping at the sight of a massive, hulking shadow that filled up most of the bedroom doorway. It had arms that reached out and held the body of an elderly man—the owner of the oxygen tank—who was unconscious, limp in the shadow's grip, clutched by hands that were mostly bone and shreds of muscle.

At the sound of Rhett's gasp, it turned, still holding the old man, and glowered at Rhett through the wafting smoke with its mostly empty eye sockets and forever grin.

The psychon didn't seem bothered by Rhett's presence. In fact, it seemed to want him to watch as it pulled in a deep breath of smoke-tainted air. From the old man's mouth, a thin wisp of white smoke unfurled, dancing in the air between his mouth and the psychon's.

"NO!" Rhett yelled, and lunged at the psychon. He pulled his knuckle blade from its holster, gripping it as tightly as he could, and swung with it.

The psychon dropped the old man's body, his soul now detached, and came at Rhett with a powerful backhand that carved a clear space through the swirling haze. Rhett ducked, dodging the swipe by just an inch, and lurched upward with his blade. He sank it into the psychon, cutting through its cloak and what little flesh there was hanging from the bones of its chest. It let out an ear-shattering scream.

Rhett yanked the blade out from between the psychon's ribs, but as he did so, the psychon slammed its other fist into him. He came off his feet and flew into the pristine bathroom, smashing into the vanity, cracking it, breaking a pipe open and sending a shower of water arching above his head.

Through the doorway, Rhett could see the psychon step up to the old man's soul, still hovering in the air, twisting and fluttering. The psychon stuck one of its knobby fingers into the white smoke of the soul and twirled it in the air. Something began to happen to the soul—it darkened, turning from white to an unhealthy-looking brown, mingling with the actual smoke that was still filling up the cramped apartment. The psychon kept twirling its finger, letting the soul wrap around it like a piece of fabric.

Rhett pulled himself to his feet, ready for another attack. He spread his legs, remembering that first day of training—and all the other days since—with Basil in the ring. He sprung forward . . .

. . . and without even a glance, the psychon turned and hit him with another devastating backhand. Now Rhett was launched into the living room, slamming into the coffee table. It snapped in two beneath him.

The psychon let out a deep, satisfying grumble, almost like a laugh but ten times as horrifying. It took a step toward Rhett, the ragged ends of its cloak waving around its ankles. It still had the soul caught around its finger, and the soul was getting even darker, withering like the petals of a flower, changing from brown to black and somehow getting thicker, denser.

Rhett watched, helpless, as the soul that had once been weightless and pure now turned into thick, goopy black sludge. It dripped into the psychon's waiting hand, pooling there like oil. And, with another one of those disturbing chuckles, the psychon buried its face in its hands, slurping up the sludge as if it were soup.

It devoured the old man's soul.

There was only one thing for Rhett to do: run.

He clambered to his feet and left the psychon behind in the apartment. But even as he darted back out into the hall, knuckle blade still clutched in his hand, he heard the psychon rush across the living room after him.

Of course there were more. Rhett came running back out to the stairwell and was met by the sounds of screeching psychons, clanging metal blades, and yells from the syllektors, trying to communicate, trying to fight back.

The flames were worse than ever, wrapped around parts of the banister, consuming entire walls. Flaming beams cracked and broke apart, falling through the drywall of the ceiling and landing wherever they may. The whole world was smoke and fire and rain-ing embers.

Rhett needed to find his team.

But first, the *scratch-thump-scratch* of the psychon's boney feet running up behind him. Rhett waited until the sound was right on top of him, then dropped to his knees, spun, and plunged the four deadly-sharp points of his blade into the psychon's gut. He used the creature's momentum to heave it upward. For a moment Rhett could sense its massive weight on top of him, threatening to crush him, but then he gave one last shove with one hand still holding the knuckle blade buried in the psychon's stomach and the other flat against its chest. He threw the psychon across the open, empty stairwell. It flailed in midair before colliding with the banister on the other side, which was coated in angry red fire.

The banister fell apart, but the psychon's cloak ignited immedi-ately, and the flames spread across the fabric as if it were made of gasoline. When the psychon rose to its feet again, it was wearing a cloak made entirely of fire. It began to squeal and flail, dropping to the ground again and rolling. Its bones turned black as they burned.

Rhett didn't wait around to see if the psychon was going to survive—he flew back down the stairs, to the floor just below. There were three more psychons down here, each of them caught in battle with a different syllektor. One of them was Theo.

He was doing his thing with a psychon that was bigger than even he was. Theo deflected swing after swing from the psychon with his ax, holding it high up on its neck—there was little room for fighting in such a cramped space. Theo's broad shoulders slammed against the narrow walls of the hallway, his ax carving gouges into the already disintegrating plaster, as the psychon continued its advance, pushing Theo farther and farther down into the throat of the hall. Rhett could see a tight knot of smoke billowing back there—more fire.

As Rhett descended the last couple of steps to where one of the other syllektors—the woman with the short blond hair—was doing her best to fend off her own psychon attack, Mak was coming up them.

The psychon spotted Rhett immediately, but it never saw Mak coming.

She came off the steps, swinging her machete upward, her face a raging mask. The blade swept through one of the psychon's arms like a knife passing through water. The psychon let out a screech of pain that echoed up and down the stairwell, stumbling back from the blond syllektor. Rhett stepped up to it as it stepped past him, falling against the stairs that he'd just come down. He went in for an uppercut with his knuckle blade, colliding with the underside of the psychon's grotesque jaw. Its remaining arm and legs spasmed briefly and then it was still.

"Do you have one?" Mak was asking the woman as Rhett stepped away from the psychon, his blade covered in the black goop of its blood.

The blonde nodded.

"Then get back to the ship," Mak said. "Now."

The woman looked back at the other two battles that were still going on nearby. Theo continued to spar with his psychon, not backing down. The other syllektor—the lanky guy with the blacked-out tattoos, Rhett realized, the one who'd called out to Mak on Rhett's very first day of collecting souls—wasn't holding up as well.

But the blonde did as Mak said, turning to go down the stairs to where the door back to the *Harbinger* was waiting.

"And Gwen?" Mak said. She had her hand in the crook of the woman's elbow, holding her in place. "Make sure Captain Trier is aware of what's going on. Get as many people on that door as you can. We can't let a single psychon through. You keep it open until everyone from the other teams is back on board."

"What about you?" Gwen asked.

Mak glanced at Rhett. Her eyes were bloodshot and her face was streaked with dark smudges of soot, but she looked more sure of herself than she had at any point during the last few weeks. Rhett gave her a quick nod.

"We'll do what we have to," Mak said to Gwen, and then let her go.

Gwen didn't wait. She ran back down the stairs, carrying her soul with her, to the protection of the *Harbinger*.

Beneath and above them, the structure burned, the sounds of collapsing walls and beams filling the air.

"Where's Treeny?" Rhett asked. He and Mak made their way around the opening of the stairwell to where the tattooed guy was starting to lose his position, falling back, blocking the psychon's claws with a short dagger.

"On the ship," Mak replied. "Basil?"

"Haven't seen him."

"Don't get your panties all in a bunch!" came Basil's voice from behind them.

Mak and Rhett turned to the sound. Basil was coming up the steps with a still-smoldering hole burned into the sleeve of his new blazer and, despite the increasing heat of the fire, his lips looking bluish. Rhett took another glance at Mak and realized that hers were the same way. He put his free hand up, examining his fingers—they were pale, losing what little color they had left after becoming a syllektor. Something else occurred to him: He was no longer coughing—none of them were. After only a second, Rhett understood why—they'd all stopped breathing. The fire had officially eaten up whatever oxygen was left in the building and replaced it with thick, poisonous smoke. It had killed their lungs.

How were they going to fix that?

"Listen," somebody else said. It was Tattooed Guy, still ducking and dodging and blocking swipes from the psychon, who was getting angrier and angrier by the second. He must have gathered a soul as well. "I hate to interrupt, but . . ." He gestured frantically at the psychon, its beady, glaring eyes reflecting the stuttering light of the fire surrounding them.

Mak sighed. She made her way in that direction.

"So," Rhett said to Basil. "Think you're gonna find *another* blazer back on the ship?"

"Don't start with me, mate," Basil replied. Rhett couldn't help but grin.

Mak screamed then, and her body was tossed across the opening of the stairwell. The psychon had gotten a decent punch in some-how. Her machete skittered across the linoleum as she flew through the air. Basil and Rhett were there, on the other side of the opening, to catch her before she could fall into it. She smacked against the banister, dangling however many floors up above the scorching fire below, and the wood nearly broke under all three of their weights. But the boys pulled her up just before it could collapse.

Back on the other side of the building, Tattooed Guy was losing his battle.

The psychon had its gnarly claw around Tattooed Guy's throat, holding him up a foot off the ground. The psychon's face was right up against the syllektor's, its toothy grin spread apart, inhal-ing. Tattooed Guy was flailing, kicking out, grabbing the psy-chon's wrist with both hands, trying to loosen its grip. From between Tattooed Guy's lips, a swirl of white smoke came twist-ing out. It seemed to be fighting against the current, fighting to go back into the peaceful embrace of the syllektor's body. But it was no use.

When the soul had been completely removed from the syllektor, it floated between them like a cloud, waiting to be eaten up by the psychon. In one swift motion, the psychon lifted its skeletal arm in the air, still clutching Tattooed Guy around the neck, and brought it rushing back down over the stairwell's opening. It flung Tattooed Guy down through the center of the building, down into the in-ferno.

Rhett took his chance, while the psychon was still positioned over the drop and the soul was still floating in midair, helpless, vulnerable. He took two running steps . . . and jumped, kicking off the faulty banister, which snapped under his feet. It gave him the leverage he needed, though. He leaped across the open stairwell, glancing down at the uncontrolled flames at the base of the building, and aimed his knuckle blade right at the psychon's face.

The creature roared, loudly, angrily. And then it brought one of its massive fists up in a wide arch. The punch hit Rhett square in his ribs, and he heard the sickening sound of something breaking inside him. His body went limp, hurled into the hallway where the fire had blackened and charred every surface.

Rhett hit the floor. Hard.

"Uh . . . fellas?" It was Theo, from somewhere nearby. Rhett was having trouble getting his bearings. The world felt upside down for a moment. But he could hear the faint edge of panic in Theo's voice. He had to help him. Slowly, Rhett tried to find his way to his feet.

A second later, though, and he could hear the sounds of a scuffle back by the stairs—Mak and Basil and the other psychon, the bastard who had sent Rhett flying. There were hideous noises—bones breaking, metal twanging, tormented screeching. And then the heavy footfalls of the psychon, running, running down the hall toward Rhett.

He braced himself for another blow, one that might end his existence as a syllektor.

But the blow never came. The psychon came sprinting down the fire-choked hallway and leaped over Rhett, completely ignoring him.

Rhett turned over, finding the floor and using it to steady himself as he sat on all fours. His body was weak, breaking down. There was no oxygen in it anymore.

He looked up just in time to see one psychon join the other, both lunging at Theo, who had been backed into a dead end, with the walls and floor engulfed in flame behind him. The psychons tackled Theo, and all three of them fell together into the floor, into the fire. The wood beneath the linoleum caved in, crumbling downward. Theo disappeared with the psychons in a splash of embers and smoke.

"*Theo!*" Rhett cried. But it was more like a croak.

All around him, the walls began to bow and crack. The ceiling began to come down in heavy, flaming clumps. Rhett pulled himself together, denying his body its desire to fall to the floor and wait to be crushed. He got up.

And again, he ran.

The hallway fell apart around Rhett as he ran as fast as he could back to where Mak and Basil were waiting. Mak was leaning against Basil, the side of her shirt torn and the flesh beneath it gouged. The sound of falling debris chased Rhett out into the stairwell, and a cloud of smoke and dust encircled him when he made it. It looked like it was just the single hallway that had collapsed. The stairs were holding strong. For now.

"We have to get out of here," Mak said. Her lips were bluer than ever, and her eyes were bright red, leaking tears.

"What about Theo?" Rhett asked. Their voices were gravelly whispers.

"If he's in one piece, he'll find his way back," Basil replied. "Now let's get back to the bloody ship."

They made their way back down the stairs, Basil helping Mak and Rhett leaning into his damaged side. The building seemed empty now. There were no syllektors down any of the halls and no psychons to speak of. It was just the fire and the dying building and . . .

Rhett stopped a floor above where they needed to be. He had been hoping to himself that the door back to the *Harbinger* would still be open. But now . . . now . . .

The push hummed around him, curling its unseen finger at him to follow it down the nearest hall. It pulsed in his head, heavy as a heartbeat and insistent as a drum. There was still a soul to be taken back there somewhere. He had no choice. He let the push guide him.

"Rhett?" Basil said, calling to him. "Rhett, what the hell? *Mate!*"

Rhett ignored him. The push wouldn't let him go. But even as he moved down the hall, he could sense the other two behind him, there to protect him. Maybe they could feel it, too. Maybe not. It didn't matter.

He found her half in and half out of an open apartment door, lying in a crater formed by the partially collapsed floor. She couldn't have been older than fourteen or fifteen. Her face was calm but also pained. Fire danced around her, mingling with clusters of debris and fluttering across the fallen beam that was on top of one of her legs.

The other two peered over Rhett's shoulders, trying to see what he had brought them here for. There was a feeling of quiet uneasiness among all three of them. How had everyone missed this girl? Why had the psychons left her behind? Maybe they hadn't. Maybe they were going to come back for her soul any second now.

The push did its thing—it pushed. It pushed with the force of a stampede of buffalo. If Rhett didn't get down and collect this girl's soul, it was going to rip him apart.

He fell to his knees beside her. Out of the corner of his eye, he saw Mak and Basil steadying themselves, preparing for a fight should another psychon show up. They watched the open end of the hallway.

Static filled Rhett's ears, and buried within the static: a heartbeat. The girl's heartbeat. She was alive but fading. He was amazed that she was still breathing, although it was hitched and labored, an unsteady wheeze. The soot-smudged window was there at the very end of the hall, open just a couple of inches. It must have been letting in enough oxygen to keep the girl from suffocating.

But her spare time was about to run out.

Rhett slipped his hand into the girl's palm. At once, her eyes opened. They shifted and found Rhett's. They pleaded silently, for comfort, for painlessness, for joy. It was the same as every other soul that Rhett had collected . . . except for one thing.

The push didn't go away.

Normally, the moment that Rhett and the others reached the soul they were intended to take, the push fell away, clicking off like a radio. Now, though, the push persisted with the same intense, unceasing force. It wanted something else from Rhett.

He tried to concentrate, but his ears were filled with the static sound of death and the undercurrent of the girl's slowing heartbeat. He could feel Mak watching him. He stared into the girl's eyes.

"It's okay," he started, and paused. Time yawned open. Rhett's heart gave an unexpected thump in his chest. And then another. It was an involuntary sensation, something that he felt without having to consciously switch on his senses. It thumped again . . . and again. He saw the image of his own limp body hanging upside down in his mother's wrecked car. It flickered in front of his eyes like a bad film reel. He saw the waitress in Arizona and the coffee pot sinking toward the ground in slow motion. He saw the boy in Brazil. He saw the first soul he had ever gathered himself. And then he saw the red, quivering fist of this girl's heart, flexing in her chest, sending whatever life force it could to the rest of her body. There wasn't much left. Rhett's heart beat again, in time with hers.

In some distant world, past all the static and flashing images and synchronized heartbeats, there was the sound of shattering glass. As if from a thousand miles away, a psychon screamed. And Rhett knew it had come for the girl. The force of her death had spread far enough to hold one of them back, it seemed. Or maybe there was something else, something awful, that kept leading the psychons back to them.

Rhett didn't have time to think about it. He knew what he had to do.

"You're going to be okay," he said, and all at once the world around him snapped back into motion. The push broke away, fading like the pressurized cuff of a blood pressure monitor. The psychon roared from some other part of the building, mixing with the sounds of the building as it kept on crumbling. Basil had disappeared, maybe to try and head off the psychon. But Rhett could still see Mak in his peripheral vision, and she was staring at him with her mouth open and her eyes squinted. "You are not going to die today," Rhett continued.

"What are you doing?" Mak said.

He ignored her, gripping the girl's hand even tighter and holding her gaze. "This is not the way your life will end. I am your anchor. To life. To living. Hold on to me. This is not your time."

"Rhett, what the hell are you doing?" Mak yelled.

Around Rhett and the girl, something strange was happening. The little fires that were sprinkled across the debris began to stutter and spark, turning purple. The smoke that plumed in the air was filled with tiny lightning. The beam that was crushing the girl's leg was no longer burning but surrounded by jagged bolts of purplish-blue electricity. The beam cracked in half suddenly, falling away in two pieces, releasing the girl from its trap.

"Oh my God," Mak breathed. "What . . . what are you?"

Rhett paid no attention. "I don't know why you're here," he said to the girl. A single tear fell from her eye and rolled down her cheek, which was blooming with the first faint roses of color again. "But I'm telling you that you're not ready."

The girl's limbs and muscles stiffened, gaining strength. She continued to stare at Rhett, but there was a focus in her eyes now that hadn't been there before. She was seeing him, *really* seeing him. He was glad to have her attention.

"You are not ready to die," Rhett said again.

The girl began to sob.

Rhett let his hand slip from hers, and as he did, the sound of the strengthening heartbeat that was nestled inside her chest dropped away. The girl couldn't see him anymore. She was looking at everything in the hall *but* him.

In that same moment, the window at the end of the hall shattered inward, and a dark, shrouded figure filled up most of its frame, silhouetted by the bright sunshine behind it.

The girl screamed, and Rhett sat back in surprise.

"Ma'am?" the shrouded figure said. And as it leaned into the window, Rhett could see the shape of a helmet and the outline of a gas mask. A firefighter. "Ma'am, can you make it to the window?"

Rhett stood, watching the scene play out, feeling the sense of his own heartbeat dwindle out of him again. Strangely, he was happy to feel it fade.

Mak was there, looking at him with wide eyes. "What—"

One of the other apartment doors behind her exploded, the doorframe buckling and an eruption of plaster and dust filling the hallway. Mak spun, ready for another fight even though her body was completely devoid of color and looked as if it was about to fall over.

The girl on the floor screamed again.

"Ma'am, we need to get you out of there now!" the firefighter yelled from the window.

A psychon stepped out into the hall. It looked colossal in the small space, having to cock its head to keep from putting it through the ceiling. This close and this still, Rhett could see every gross detail of the psychon's body, every pockmark in its bones, every red, twitching thread of muscle. Its tattered cloak hung loose and ratty around its wide shoulders, and the hood—for once—dropped a shadow across its skull face, leaving only the macabre grin of its teeth. Rhett could hear the slow, wheezing sound of the psychon's breathing.

It stepped forward, crushing a spiderweb of cracks into the floor, its claws dancing with excitement. It looked at the girl, who was sitting up now, holding her knees to her chest, frozen with panic. She couldn't see Rhett or the psychon, only the destruction that was raining down around her.

Come on, Rhett thought. *Get up.*

The psychon looked at Rhett, then back to the girl. Rhett squeezed the handle on his knuckle blade, preparing to strike as soon as the ugly-ass thing was close enough. Even though it couldn't exactly make facial expressions, Rhett could still see a certain curiosity on the psychon's face, in its tiny white eyes. It sniffed at the air, looking for a soul to consume . . . but now there was none. The soul that it had come for was no longer available.

Basil came thundering down the hall and pulled up short behind the psychon. The creature gave him a passing glance and then stared hard at Rhett. Rhett stared into the deep craters of its eyes as it tried to figure out what had happened, why the soul that it had smelled was somehow sewn back into the girl's body.

The psychon roared in anger and frustration, the sound of it like a small nuclear bomb going off in the confines of the hall.

Then it turned and charged back through the wrecked doorway

that it had come from. It vanished into smoke and darkness, making crashing sounds as it tore back through the building.

"What in the bloody hell happened here, mate?" Basil said. His voice was laced with suspicion but overcome with panic. They didn't have much time left.

"Don't let that psychon get away!" Mak suddenly yelled from beside Rhett. "It knows what he did! Basil, *it knows what he did*!"

Basil gave them both another confused look and then turned and ran after the psychon, scythes in hand.

Beside them, the girl was slowly pulling herself to her feet, staring with wide, bloodshot eyes and an open mouth at the damage, at the fire that was still crackling and snapping at the building. Rhett glanced at her, willing her to go with the firefighter . . . and she did. Her eyes were still red and wide, and her lower lip shook, but she was gripping the firefighter's gloved hand, letting him help her out of the rubble and ruin of the collapsing building.

Rhett turned back to Mak, and she took a step away from him.

"Mak, I—" he started, moving toward her again.

"Don't," she said. And again she stepped back from him, this time with her machete held out in front of her.

Rhett stared at the weapon. "Mak . . ."

She hesitated. "I . . . We just have to get back to the ship."

"Please, Mak," Rhett tried. "You have to know I'm just as freaked out as you are."

"Trust me," she said. "I don't think you are." She took a couple more steps backward, indicating that she was heading back to the *Harbinger*, with or without him.

Before he followed her, Rhett looked over his shoulder again, at the open window where the girl and the firefighter had already disappeared.

"She'll probably spend the rest of her life thinking she's crazy," he murmured.

He didn't think Mak had heard him, but she said bitterly, "The rest of her life was supposed to be five minutes ago. Let's move. Now."

The building echoed and shuddered with the sounds of its collapse. The fire on the bottom floor was completely out of control, burning with an intensity that sent heat waves warbling up the stairwell.

Mak tried to keep up the prisoner routine with Rhett, but as the building grew less stable, she gave up and ran beside him. She held on to her machete, though.

The steps buckled and cracked under Rhett's feet as they ran down them. At some point, Rhett realized that Basil was on the other side of him, chasing the steps down to the next floor, where the doorway back to the ship was still hopefully open.

"Bastard got away," Basil mumbled, answering the unasked question.

The three of them dove off the steps and onto the landing just as something fell apart beneath them and the flight of stairs broke away from the wall, tilting sideways. From above, massive hunks of fiery debris came plummeting down. The sound was enormous and terrifying.

Rhett was sure that when they rounded the corner to the door, it would be closed. But as they entered the hall, he could see the open door and the inside of the *Harbinger* behind it. The hallway was coated in fire, licking at them as they sprinted down the hall, with the building coming down behind them.

Treeny was just inside the door, waving them on.

"Come on!" she yelled. "*Run!*"

Rhett heard the building roaring and whining like some kind of animal. He pushed his poor, weakened body to run faster.

He and Basil and Mak tripped over one another as they fell through the door. They hit the polished floor of the room of doors and slid.

Within the doorway, the building was collapsing in a rush of wood and plaster and dust and furniture, sending bits of debris and dust through to the ship. As the entire thing came down on top of the doorway, Treeny swung the door shut. It slammed into its frame, cutting them off from the destruction.

Everything was quiet.

Looking around the room, Rhett saw most of the other syllektors that had gone in with them. Gwen was there, and the man in the baseball cap. All of them were coated in soot and battle-ravaged. But there was no Theo.

Basil stood first. Then he helped Mak to her feet. And as soon as she was up, she brought the end of her machete down and set it at Rhett's throat, holding him to the floor. Basil stared at her in disbelief.

"Is someone going to tell me what in the bloody hell happened back there?" he said.

Mak wouldn't look at him, wouldn't take her eyes off Rhett.

"Oh, I am not gonna like this, am I?" Basil said.

"You need to explain yourself," Mak said, her voice unnervingly calm, her eyes locked on Rhett's. "I don't want to have to do anything either of us is going to regret, but . . . I can't trust you. Not after what I just saw."

"Mak, I swear, I have no idea what happened," Rhett said. "The push . . . it did something. It . . . it was just different this time. I can't explain it."

"Well you better figure it out." She kept the machete aimed at his neck.

Captain Trier stepped in then, weaving through the waiting party to get to where Mak was holding Rhett. There was a shadow over the captain's face, one that seemed to apply his true age to his ageless features. When he took in the sight of Mak holding the machete at Rhett's throat, his face fell even more. Something was wrong.

Mak stepped back and let Rhett get on his feet. Treeny joined the three of them but stood with Basil and Mak. Rhett was their prisoner now. But he didn't wait for any of them to approach the captain.

"What's wrong?" Rhett asked.

Trier looked at him, eyes slightly wider than usual, probably trying to pick up on signals from Rhett's mind. "I might ask you the same thing," he said.

"Captain, we have a problem," Mak said, still holding the machete between her and Rhett.

"We have much more than a problem," Trier replied.

"What do you mean?" The machete dropped away a couple of inches.

"It's the lantern." Trier grabbed at his beard, his eyes troubled.

Rhett remembered the lantern from his first visit to the ship's bridge. It was the compass, the captain had said, the thing that guided the *Harbinger* to whatever its destination was supposed to be.

"What about it?" Basil asked, his voice frail, hesitant.

The captain swept his eyes across the group.

"It's gone out," he said.

TWELVE

Mak put her machete away long enough for the four of them and the captain to make their way up to the main deck. The captain had told her it wouldn't be necessary even before she had a chance to explain why she thought she needed it. Rhett was relieved to have at least one person who would give him a chance to explain himself.

The other syllektors who had gone into the now-destroyed apartment building were all following them up the stairs, and when they reached the tunnel that led to the steam room, everybody except for Rhett and the captain went down it to deposit the souls they had collected. Rhett couldn't quite shake the image of the psychon holding the cancerous-looking black ooze that had once been a weightless soul and gulping it down in just a couple of greedy swigs.

After that, the biggest portion of the group were sent by the captain to the medical bay, leaving Mak, Basil, Treeny, and Rhett to follow the captain up the last few flights of stairs to the main deck. When they arrived, Captain Trier led them into one of the small workrooms, one that was similar to the room where Rhett was first told about the syllektors. That moment now felt like it had happened on some other planet, to some other person, on some other time line. But Rhett could still feel the shock of it and the strange comfort in knowing that he hadn't been suffering from brain damage or losing his mind.

Now he was looking for that same reassurance. He needed someone to tell him that what he had done back there—to that girl—was normal. Maybe not normal. But at least understood. He could still see that girl's confused and frightened stare, the knowledge in her eyes that she should have been dead—that she had been *sure* she was going to die—even as she escaped the building. Rhett had made that happen; he'd broken that certainty. He had conquered the absolution of death, without even knowing that he was going to do it.

How?

When the door was shut, Mak used her machete to point at a chair.

"Sit," she said to Rhett, the way she might order a dog around. "And don't move. Don't even speak."

Rhett sank into the chair willingly, happy to be able to sit and allow his body—scraped and bruised and covered in singe marks (not to mention the possibility of his broken ribs)—to rest.

Captain Trier put out a steady hand and pushed the machete down, getting it out of Rhett's face. Mak looked frustrated, but she didn't raise the blade again.

"You first," the captain said. "And you can start by telling me what happened to Theo." He fixed his eyes on Rhett, who had to look away as he simply shook his head. The captain let out a rush of air that was somewhere between a sigh and a sob, and said, "Okay. Now the rest."

Mak explained it all to him, her way. She told him that Rhett had given the girl's life back, that he had made the choice for her to live, that he had healed her.

"He's not a syllektor," Mak said. "He's . . . something else."

There was quiet then, ominous and smothering. Rhett thought that he would suffocate under the weight of it, even though suffocating was apparently not possible. The captain was staring at him, maybe trying to assess the validity of what Mak had said. He raised his eyebrows in question. Rhett had no choice but to nod—Mak may have spun it into something that sounded terrible, but all of the major details had been true.

Rhett took a quick glance in Basil's direction. He was standing against the wall in his ruined blazer, arms folded, eyes enormous and shocked and afraid. He didn't look like Basil at all.

"How?" the captain asked, regaining Rhett's attention.

"I have no idea," Rhett said.

"Enough about this bollocks with Rhett," Basil suddenly burst out. "No offense, mate. But I want to hear about the bloody lantern."

Captain Trier looked around at them, his eyes searching theirs, possibly for the best way to tell them what had happened and why. He opened his mouth, but before he could speak, there was a knock at the door.

Everyone lifted their heads, the unspoken hope hanging between them that Theo was the one knocking, that he really had found his way back, just as Basil said he would.

The captain nodded at Treeny, who opened the door slowly, gingerly, as if the steel had been superheated and was going to burn her.

A man with almost no hair and round spectacles stepped in. He had on a shirt and tie and slacks, all black as night. He matched the captain's military stance, hands behind his back, feet apart. He was a syllektor, but he definitely wasn't Theo, and he was also all business.

"Captain, I'm sorry to interrupt," the new guy said.

"That's okay, Henry," Trier replied. "What is it? Please tell me the lantern's come back on."

"I'm afraid not, sir," Henry replied, his face falling. "There's something else you need to see."

The captain followed Henry out of the room without question and without finishing his story about the lantern, and the others followed the captain. Mak didn't even try to stop Rhett when he got up and trailed behind. The unspoken question hung around all of them, like a piano about to drop from the sky: *What now?*

Henry led them all up the spiral staircase to the bridge. It was a percussion line of feet on metal as all six of them made their way up, with Rhett bringing up the rear. He pulled himself onto the bridge, where the others were all standing together, looking out over the front of the ship.

A few miles ahead, hanging above the water like a living shadow, was a gargantuan mass of clouds. They were so black that not even the nearly constant jabs of brilliant, blue lightning could illuminate them. A sheet of rain fell from the bottom of the clouds, swaying like the hem of a dress in the wind. More lightning stabbed at the waves. Thunder grumbled and cracked.

Nobody said a word.

"Sir?" Henry said.

Trier stepped closer to the window.

"Prepare the ship for an attack," he said, his voice low. "Alert the crew."

Henry's eyes got wide. He took a few steps backward, as if retreating from the oncoming storm. "Aye, Captain. Right away," he said, and then ran back down the stairs.

"Captain," Basil said. "Are you . . . are you sure there's going to be an attack? I mean, that's just a storm. Isn't it? We're used to this kind of thing. I mean, I am. I don't know about you guys . . ." His voice trailed away, getting small and helpless as the bubbling knot of black storm clouds expanded across the horizon.

"I've been on this ship for more than three hundred years, Mr. Winthrop," Trier responded, almost in a whisper. "And I have never seen anything like this before."

Rhett stepped up next to the captain, maybe to get a better view, maybe to get away from Mak and her machete for what he was going to say next.

"I think I need to tell you guys something," he said, turning to face them all.

Mak narrowed her eyes, squeezing the handle of her machete with both hands as if trying to choke it to death. Basil and Treeny were still only capable of gaping, except now they were gaping at Rhett instead of the storm.

"Go on, Mr. Snyder," the captain said without taking his eyes off the sky. Rhett had a suspicion that the captain had known about the she-thing for a long time, had probably picked it up from Rhett's defenseless thoughts the moment they had returned from San Francisco. He felt stupid for not realizing it earlier.

But he told the others. He told them about the flickering lights and how the world had seemed to cease its existence in those few moments that the girl in the hospital gown had shown herself to Rhett. He told them what she had said while she stood there, dripping water that came from nowhere onto the road. *These are your last days*, she had told him. And she had been nothing if not truthful. If she had anything to do with the storm that was about to overtake the *Harbinger*—and of course she did—then she was coming for him. As she had promised.

Find your power. Then I will come for it.

I will come for you.

When Rhett was finished, the captain spoke first.

"Her name is Urcena," he said casually, like it was the most logical thing to say at that moment.

"Wait . . . what? How do you know?" Mak asked, her voice implying that she had lost her trust in everybody, not just Rhett.

"When you got back from San Francisco, it was all over Rhett's mind. He was afraid." Trier glanced at Rhett. Rhett felt ashamed and relieved all at once.

"Well shit, I'd be afraid, too," Basil nearly yelled. "That bitch sounds like a bloody nightmare. What does she want with us?"

"It's not any of you she wants," Rhett said quietly, running a hand through his hair. He looked at Basil and saw the understanding that bloomed on his face.

"Back there . . . in the building . . ." Basil began.

"Yeah."

"What is she?" Mak interjected, directing the question at Captain Trier.

"It's hard to say. After I saw her in Rhett's thoughts, I did some research. I had to go pretty deep into the library just to find anything remotely like her. But I came across that name, and it seemed to match up. Most of what I found claims that she's some kind of demon."

"Great," Basil said. "Bloody great."

"It's not a coincidence that all of this is happening at the same time," the captain continued. "The demon—Urcena—has the power to bring this entire ship to its knees. But not alone."

"The psychons," Rhett said, realizing what he should have already.

"She's using them," Mak whispered. "That's how they keep finding us."

"In the physical plane, yes," the captain said, turning back to the storm. "But I believe that the psychons' ship is in that storm somewhere. And there's no way that either they or Urcena could have found us here."

"Wait, did you say the psychons have a *ship*?" Rhett asked. "Here?"

The captain nodded. "I'm afraid so. The psychons interact with the physical plane the same way that we do. Their ship is an abomination. But its formidability is nearly as strong as the *Harbinger*'s. I've only ever encountered it one other time, and that day was . . . unfortunate."

The room fell silent for a moment. The gray clouds and water were behind them and beside them. But ahead of them, the storm was advancing, its blackness eating away at the sky little by little, spitting daggers of lightning that lit the waves . . . and everything below the surface. Rhett caught sight of a monstrous shadow—an enormous creature that seemed to be moving with the storm, heading for the *Harbinger*. There was at least one giant, lobsterlike claw and the familiar curl of tentacles. Rhett's mind raced with panic.

"So how did the psychons—and this Urcena . . . thing—find us?" Mak asked.

The captain waited, pondering the question. "Someone told them where to find us," he said finally.

Mak's eyes widened into huge, angry discs. She aimed them at Rhett. "You did this," she seethed. "You and that stupid, unnatural thing you can do."

"Mak, listen—" Rhett started.

"There's nothing to listen to!" she cried. She stepped forward, her machete held out in front of her. Basil moved to stand between her and Rhett.

"Mak, love," Basil said. "Let's just take a second—"

"Makayla—" the captain tried.

"Don't you call me that!" she snapped. "Don't you *dare* call me that! It's not fair."

Basil took a step toward her, hands up. "Sweetheart . . ."

Captain Trier stood by, apparently letting the accusations run their course. Treeny had shuffled closer to him. She had her tablet held at her chest and her arms wrapped around it like a schoolgirl. Her eyes were closed and her mouth was moving. Maybe she was whispering to herself, trying to drown out the fighting. Maybe she was praying.

While Mak and Basil had it out and Rhett stood there, with the storm drawing nearer behind him, Treeny turned and stepped in front of Captain Trier. He was following the argument between Basil and Mak, concern growing on his face. Treeny's tablet slipped from her hands and hit the floor with a dull, plastic-y *crack*. She stood facing the captain.

And then she plunged her hand into his chest.

Captain Trier's face went dark as Treeny's arm disappeared into him with a sound like some vegetable being split open. Her hand dove through his uniform and through his flesh as if they were no denser than tissue paper. The captain's mouth fell open, and the veins that wormed their way up his neck and across his face turned a deep, deep blue.

Treeny rummaged around in the hole she had created, her arm wedged between two of the captain's ribs, and when her hand re-emerged, it held a still-beating heart. She tossed it in the air once and then caught it like it was a baseball.

"CAPTAIN!" Mak screamed. She ran at Treeny, machete held above her with both hands.

Treeny lifted her leg up and kicked the captain right in the center of his chest, just to the right of the empty, exposed cavity she had left in him, where there was nothing but some hollow, dangling tubes and red, shining flaps. He flew backward, slamming against the window that encased the bridge, shattering the glass.

Rhett moved as quickly as he could, sprinting toward the captain as Mak brought her machete down on top of Treeny. There was a clang of metal on metal as Treeny met the machete with one of her own knives. Rhett caught the captain before he could fall to the floor.

Lightning struck the water near the *Harbinger*'s front end and the world went blindingly white. Thunder cracked so loud above their heads that Rhett thought the universe itself was being ripped in two. And when the bellow of the thunder and the overwhelming brilliance of the lightning faded, the rain started, a curtain of it that swept across the ship from bow to stern, coming down in sheets and pouring inside the bridge through the broken window.

Mak—and now Basil—went after Treeny for the captain's heart. But Captain Trier seemed to know how things were going to turn out. Because he looked at Rhett, his face turned up to the clouds and being pummeled by raindrops.

"Remember . . . what I said . . . Twice-Born Son," he said. His voice was low, little more than a harsh whisper. "This is a second chance."

"Hang on, Captain," Rhett said. He was fighting against the rain. It was whipping into the bridge from the wind, making the floor slippery. His body was weak and injured. He was losing his grip.

Behind him, Treeny was holding the other two off but barely.

She was working with only the single knife in one hand. Her other hand still held the captain's heart. And yet the ferocity in her movements didn't waver. She was faster and stronger than Rhett had ever seen her, clearly pulling strength from the other thing that must have been lingering inside her all along.

She ducked below Basil's scythes as he swung them at her one after another, metal singing as it cut through the air above her, and then she shot back up and swung her foot around. It collided with the side of Basil's head. He went down, scythes skittering away across the slick floor. And in the same fluid motion, Treeny turned, gripping the hilt of her knife in her fist, and got Mak right under her chin. Mak went down, too.

Rhett was helpless. He couldn't let Captain Trier fall.

Treeny held the heart up. It flexed in her hand, squeezing itself, pumping its empty life force. Treeny wrapped her fingers around the dense red muscle. It pushed out against her grip, but she squeezed tighter . . . and tighter . . .

When the heart broke, it turned to ash almost instantly. One second it was red and beating strongly. In the next second it fell apart into specks of black, as if it had only ever been an illusion.

Rhett heard himself scream. He turned back to the captain, who had still been clinging to Rhett's arm. But there was no weight there anymore. For a moment Rhett could still see the shape of the captain's face, made of those same little particles of darkness. And then they were washed away by the rain and the wind. The captain's hand disintegrated in Rhett's, and soon there was nothing but the rain patting against his empty palm.

The storm raged on around them.

Mak fell to her knees, face buried in her hands. Basil was still down for the count, slumped in a heap over by the lantern, which was dark and useless. Rhett sank to the wet floor, dripping from head to toe and still being slapped with rain.

"Treeny," he said. "What did you do?"

She turned to him, and there was a flicker of the old Treeny there—timid and nervous. Her eyes were red and leaking tears.

"She's beautiful, isn't she?" Treeny asked, speaking directly to Rhett. For the first time, her voice was full and, in a strange way, lovely. "When she first came to me, I thought she was here to save me. From all . . . *this*." She spat the last word, gesturing around her, at the ship, at her broken team. "But she didn't care about me. She doesn't care about anything." Now she was openly weeping. Tears dripped from her eyes and plunked into the rainwater on the floor.

"We . . . we can help you, Treeny," Rhett said.

She scoffed. "Don't be so naive, Rhett. It's not a good look for you." She stopped. She was shaking. When she spoke again, her voice was soft, full of pain. "She makes you hurt. All the time she makes you hurt. She makes you remember things you want to forget and forget things you want to remember. She makes you afraid to eat, to sleep. So you just sit there and wait for her to come back. And every time you think she won't, that maybe you're finally rid of her, she turns up again. She makes you do shit like this." She motioned around her again.

"You're a traitor," Mak said from behind Treeny.

"Right back at you," Treeny said, turning around to face Mak, the pain suddenly absent from her voice, replaced by spit and fire. "You don't care about this team, Mak. Not anymore. Oh, and for the record, psychons are definitely smart enough to operate my tablet. As long as I've disabled the self-destruct feature and left it behind for them. It's got a navigation system that led them right to us."

She was talking about San Francisco, the Golden Gate. She had lost her tablet on purpose, and that's how the psychons—and Urcena—found the *Harbinger*. Rhett suddenly wished that he'd left Treeny inside that car. *It won't be safe*, she had said. She hadn't been talking about safety for herself.

While her back was turned to him, Rhett lunged, pulling his knuckle blade free of its holster. He kept his mouth shut to stifle the cry of rage that welled up in his throat, but his feet splashed in the puddle that had formed from the incoming rain. Treeny turned at the last second. Rhett had a brief image of her slicing his head off in one swift motion. But she couldn't do that, could she? Not if she wanted him in one piece.

He charged on, slamming into her tiny body with all the force he had. They hit the floor together and slid. Rhett climbed on top and pinned her, holding the pointed ends of the four blades that extended from his weapon just an inch from her throat.

"They have Theo," Treeny said at once, before Rhett could even begin to think about cutting into her. Rhett's face must have melted from fury into surprise, because Treeny gave him a smile that made her face look all wrong. "You didn't think I'd just come up here and ghost the captain without having a decent escape plan, did you?" And when Rhett didn't reply, she said, "You really are as ignorant as Mak says you are."

Out of the corner of his eye, Rhett caught movement—Basil, crawling for the lantern.

Distracted, Rhett felt Treeny get her feet under him. She kicked out. He tumbled backward, splashing back into the puddle. She was a lot stronger than she looked. But maybe she was getting help.

Treeny was on her feet between blinks, diving for the flameless lantern. But Basil was quicker. He reached up, grabbed it off its pedestal, and sent it skidding across the floor toward Mak. It rattled and sparked but made it all the way. Mak reached for it, yanking on its thin metal handle, and tossed it over her head. It was like some bizarre basketball game. The lantern bounced off the floor once with a harsh metallic scrape and then fell down the spiral staircase to the main deck. The stairs shook, clanging over and over. Then they went still.

Mak gave Treeny a satisfied grin, knowing that Treeny would have to fight her way through all of them to get down the steps. Treeny sneered back at her.

"It doesn't make any difference," she growled. "Urcena isn't after the lantern. When Rhett is ours, we'll have control of something much more valuable than a glorified paperweight." She glared at Rhett, backing up toward the shattered opening in the window. "Keep your friends away, Soul Keeper," she said, and there was a touch of the she-thing in her voice now. Treeny was not entirely Treeny anymore. "You were warned. Defiance will end in disaster.

When the time comes, you will give yourself up. Or be taken along with your precious cargo."

She fell silent, turning away. She broke into a run, took three long strides, and jumped through the opening and into the downpour. Her body fell away, disappearing into the shroud of rain.

Rhett and Mak ran to the window, where thunder and lightning were warring for control of the sky and thick droplets of rain wept from the sharp points of broken glass. They peered over the edge, trying to glimpse any sign of Treeny. It wasn't a terribly far drop but enough that someone's legs would probably be broken from the impact. The shadows cast by the storm clouds were too dense, though, and the light was too chaotic. If she was down there, she was well hidden.

Basil lumbered up behind them, and they all three stared out across the acres-long bow of the ship, toward the spot where something was emerging from the strings of unyielding rain, something almost as big as the *Harbinger*, something dark and jagged and ferocious-looking.

"Is that . . . ?" Rhett breathed.

"Yeah," Mak replied. "The psychons' ship."

It really was an abomination.

Like the *Harbinger*, the psychons' ship appeared to be made up of several different sailing vessels that had probably been brought together over the course of centuries. Unlike the *Harbinger*, the psychons' ship had no rhyme or reason to the way it was constructed. It was lopsided, angled strangely, with ships and boats jutting out of it from all directions. In the unkind light, it looked more like a malformed geode. Rhett could see the bows of ships hanging over the waves, propellers spinning in the open air, several wooden masts poking out of one side like an array of toothpicks, torn and blackened sails shaking in the wind. There was a collection of smokestacks all shoved together into one area, making them look like organ pipes that spewed an acrid, lightless fog of smoke. He could see smears of black ooze streaked across the sides like rogue paint strokes. Whole skeletons dangled from ropes tied to poles and wooden crossbeams and propeller shafts. Rhett didn't think that what he was looking at could even be called a ship. It was more like a raft, composed of various salvaged wrecks from a millennium of sailing through this world.

As it got closer, Rhett noticed the angular front end of a smaller ship sticking straight up out of a confusion of other parts. There was a single word printed high up on the starboard side: CYCLOPS.

"What do we do?" Rhett asked, practically yelling against the static torrent of the rain.

Nobody spoke.

From somewhere aboard the *Harbinger*, a siren began to wail.

THIRTEEN

"Welp," Basil said. "I say we just call it. What do you think? We knock off for the day and start over fresh tomorrow?"

From deep within the ship, the siren continued to cry out. Mak had turned her back to the psychons' ship—what Rhett now thought of as the *Cyclops*. She had her head down, pinching the bridge of her nose.

"You heard Treeny," Rhett said. "I have to give myself up."

"I don't think it's that easy, mate," Basil replied, seriousness deflating his sarcasm.

"He's right," Mak said. "Why would they be threatening an attack if all they want is you?"

Rhett finally tore his eyes away from the tangle of maimed and butchered ships that made up the *Cyclops*. For probably the millionth time, he thought about what Urcena had said to him on the Golden Gate: *Find your power.*

He closed his eyes and saw the purple fire and the color returning to the girl's cheeks back at the apartment building. Was that really all Urcena was after? Did she want him to use his "power," which he had only just discovered and had absolutely zero control over, to heal her somehow? To give her life? He didn't even really know what Urcena was, but he was sure that she had never truly been alive. If not that, then what?

"They could have taken you any time," Mak went on. "In San Francisco. Today, in that building. Why did they go through so much trouble to find the *Harbinger* if they just wanted you? Treeny even left the lantern behind. Why?"

"Because they're out of their bloody fucking minds, that's why!" Basil cried.

Rhett saw the hallway, broiling in the flames, and the electric sparks dancing in the air as the girl's life siphoned back into her. He opened his eyes.

"The souls," he said as it hit him. What he could do. What he could create.

"What?" Mak and Basil said at the same time.

"She wants the souls, too. The tank in the steam room. She must think that I can bring them all back to life or something."

"Can you?" Mak asked.

"I . . . I don't know. She already has an army of psychons. But maybe she wants an army of the living, too." Rhett thought it sounded ridiculous even to himself. But he could think of no other conclusion.

"Why would she want an army of living people?" Basil asked.

"Why would anybody?" Rhett responded. "Leverage. Power. She could use the souls that we have to get control of somebody who's still alive, somebody she can't touch. Government officials, presidents, kings. And think about how many souls are in that tank. If I'm able to bring one back, I'm probably able to bring them all back. She'd have an army of the resurrected. An army that could die and come back to life over and over again. They'd be unstoppable."

"You seem to have thought a lot about this." Mak folded her arms.

"Oh Jesus, will you give it a rest already?" Rhett yelled. She took an involuntary step back. He realized that he had never yelled at her before. "I don't know what's going on! I don't know what this is inside me. What I did back there to that girl . . . it was unbelievable. But I swear to you that I had no idea until then that I could even do it."

"So then why didn't you tell us when you saw Urcena in San Francisco?" she spat back.

"Because I could have just been losing my mind! You have no idea how fucking stressful all this is. I may not always be able to feel anything here"—he pointed to his chest—"but it's always, always up here." He pointed at his head.

"*I have no idea how stressful this is?*" Mak roared. "You haven't even been here a year. Do you know what it's like to stand in the middle of a battlefield and take the souls of an entire squadron of soldiers? Do you know what it's like to watch towers fall with thousands of people inside them and then have to bring those souls back with you, one at a time, and stuff them into a giant fish bowl? There are no words that make those moments easier. Nothing we say or do is going to fix the hurt and the loss. And yeah, sure, some of them get turned because the trauma is too much. You, me, Basil, Treeny, Theo"—her voice broke slightly as she said that last name—"everyone on this ship. We have to carry that trauma with us and then we get to add to it. Over and over and over—" She cut herself off, turning away. When she turned back, she had composed herself somewhat. "Then one day the pieces fall apart," she whispered. "And you end up like that." She pointed out through the hole in the window. Rhett didn't have to hear it to understand that she was talking about Treeny.

"I'm sorry," Rhett said with a sigh. "You're right. I don't know what any of that is like. But I do know what it's like to watch my friends get taken, just like you watched Lana get taken. I know that I'm telling the truth. And I know that I want to help you stop whatever it is that's about to happen."

Basil stepped up and put a hand on Rhett's shoulder.

"Mak," he said. "I believe him."

"Yeah? Why?" she asked. She was trying to sound accusatory again, but the fight had gone out of her.

"Because Captain Trier sent me to collect him. And I trusted the captain to the end."

Rhett looked at Basil, shocked. Mak stared, her eyes curious.

"What are you talking about?" Rhett asked.

"It's my job to collect new syllektors in the first place," Basil explained. "But the captain knew something was going to go down in New York the night of your . . . well, you know." Rhett nodded. "So he sent me to check it out. But he wouldn't tell me what was going to happen. Maybe because he didn't know. That's why we had to go through the back door. To stay undetected by prying eyes." He nodded out at the dark shape of the *Cyclops* as it moved ever closer. Then he turned to Mak. "And why I couldn't tell you where I was going, love."

"So, when you collected me . . . you didn't think anything was strange?" Rhett asked.

Basil turned back. "I thought it was strange that the captain wanted to be so secretive about it. But otherwise . . . no. When I saw you just sitting there in the middle of the road, staring at your own corpse, I knew what I had to do. The captain knew there was something important about you. I just don't think anyone understood what it was until today."

They were quiet. Rhett turned back to the storm. The *Cyclops* was right on top of them now, its crooked, pointing shadow falling onto the hull of the *Harbinger.*

From behind him, Mak sighed.

"Okay," she said. "Fine. If you believe him, then . . . I guess I believe him, too. But what now?"

Rhett bent down and picked up his weapon, fitting the knuckle blade onto his hand and closing his fist around the grip. He turned back to the other two.

"If Urcena wants me and the souls together, she's going to attack the ship no matter what," he said.

"I always did peg you as a glass-half-full kind of guy," Basil murmured through the corner of his mouth.

"The only thing we can do now," Rhett continued, "is fight. It doesn't matter if they take me. We just have to keep the souls safe." The memory of his parents' faint, echoing whispers coming out of the tank in the steam room filled his ears. They were in there, too.

But he had to let the words settle in. What was he suggesting? A fight to the . . . ghost? How many other syllektors would suffer that fate by the time the fight was done?

"All right, mate," Basil said. "I'm with you. Together, remember? What's the plan?"

Rhett blinked at him. "Um . . . well, I . . . uh . . ."

"Oh, come on! Don't tell me you haven't got a plan. You just dumped a truckload of all this heavy shit on us and you don't even have a plan?"

"Oh . . . well, I thought . . ." Rhett turned to Mak.

"Don't look at me," she said. For the first time since that morning in the mess hall, the flicker of a smile danced across her lips. "This is your rodeo, cowboy."

The spiral staircase rattled angrily. Mak and Basil grabbed their weapons off the floor, and all three of them stood ready, unsure of what was coming up the steps.

A bald head appeared out of the floor. It was Henry. They let out a sigh.

Rhett stiffened again when Henry fully emerged from the staircase and saw the mess. He was holding the fallen lantern in one of his hands.

"I think you . . . lost . . . something," Henry said slowly, eyeing the room.

Mak went over and took the lantern. She slipped the handle under the strap for her machete sheath and attached it. It dangled from her side.

"Henry, listen to me," she said. "Captain Trier has been . . . ghosted."

Henry's face drew out in shock. "What? What happened? I was gone for ten minutes!"

"I know. Just pay attention, okay? Treeny ghosted the captain. She might still be on board somewhere."

Henry looked around at them, disbelief flooding his features.

"Treeny?" he said. "Are . . . are you sure?"

The three of them exchanged glances.

"We're sure," Basil said.

"I'll . . . gather a search party—" Henry started.

Mak grabbed him by the shoulders and held him where he was.

"No, Henry," she said, trying to be gentle but failing. "You're the *Harbinger*'s first mate. That makes you in charge of the crew now. We have to focus on the attack. Look."

She turned Henry to face out the shattered window, where the *Cyclops* had all but consumed the view with its ugly, pointed features. Henry's eyes got wide.

"Make sure we're ready," Mak said. "Protect the *Harbinger*. And if anybody sees Treeny . . ." Her eyes flicked to the big wooden steering wheel, where she had probably seen the captain maneuvering the ship thousands of times. "They're to ghost her on sight," she finished savagely.

Henry was nodding frantically. "Okay. Okay. I understand." He seemed to be reassuring himself more than he was reassuring them. "Where will you three be?"

"The steam room," Rhett said, hoping that he was understanding the plan that Mak was putting together. She nodded at him in confirmation.

"Got it," Henry said. "But you should hurry."

"What for?" Basil asked.

Henry lifted a hand that shook ever so slightly, his senses breaking through, the fear taking over. He pointed toward the window and the storm and the psychons' frightening ship.

"We're under attack," he whispered.

Basil, Rhett, and Mak whirled around.

Rhett expected cannonballs. He expected psychons swarming the *Harbinger* in insectlike hordes. He expected the storm to throw the ship off-kilter and for the whole world to seem like it was falling over. All of that *was* happening. But what he didn't expect— what he had forgotten about—was the sea monster.

When he was fully turned and seeing what Henry was seeing, the first thing that caught Rhett's attention was the massive tentacle curling up out of the chopping waves, swinging like a baseball bat toward the bridge tower. It was mammoth and slimy-looking, dwindling to a rounded point like a serpentine tongue. It cut through the torrential rain, gaining momentum. Lightning flashed, and in the brief light, Rhett saw that where there would normally have been suction cups on a regular octopus's tentacle, this tentacle had circles of creeping, spindly legs. They looked like crab legs, hundreds of them, reaching and clawing at nothing, eagerly awaiting the chance to grab something and pull it apart piece by piece.

And behind the tentacle: everything else. The cannonballs, the psychons, the storm. There was barely a second to process everything before the tentacle had filled up the space just outside the bridge windows.

"KYMAKER!" Henry screamed.

All four of the syllektors in the bridge dropped down, flattening out with their faces in the puddles of water.

The tentacle smashed into the roof and the windows. The whole tower that the bridge sat on jerked to the side, leaning. Glass and metal rained down around Rhett. He instinctively covered his head, knowing that even if he wouldn't feel the pain of something falling on top of him, it would surely crush him anyway.

He felt the rush of air as the tentacle passed just above him, and, in the panic of the moment, he allowed his senses to come on for just a second, flooding his nose with the sickening smell of rotting fish.

The sea monster—Henry had called it a kymaker—swung its tentacle away. Metal screeched somewhere, and the bridge tower lurched again, going completely crooked, like a broken limb. Without the roof to shield them, the syllektors were washed over with the driving, relentless rain. Rhett felt it flooding his mouth and his nose, felt it soaking him in an instant. The floor of the bridge was now smooth, wet, and leaning. Rhett and the others slid down it as if it were made of ice.

As he struggled to find a grip, Rhett looked up just in time to see the top half of the now-pulverized steering wheel flipping toward him. He rolled onto his back and let it hurtle past him.

"*Look out!*" he screamed down at the others.

The wheel missed Mak and Basil by a margin, but Henry looked up too late. The splintered half-sun shape of the wheel slammed into him. Henry grunted, lost his grip, and fell backward over the opening to the upper deck, off the edge of the misshapen platform that had been the bridge only moments before. He vanished.

Rhett heard Mak curse.

The *Harbinger*'s siren continued to wail.

"*Where is it?*" Basil yelled over the storm. "*Where did the bloody thing go?*"

Rhett was still sliding, trying to aim for the opening to the spiral staircase, hoping to get down to the main deck. If they could just get inside the ship, they might have a chance at preparing the crew and protecting the steam room.

But, as if in answer to Basil's question, Rhett caught sight of the kymaker again, its tentacle snapping into the air like a whip, preparing for another swing. And from somewhere down below the bridge, on top of the ship, he could hear the sound of hundreds of running feet and the *gong* sound of something smacking iron. The psychons were on board, trying to make their way down into the lower decks.

Above them, the tentacle swung, moving like a wrecking ball toward the base of one of the smokestacks. When it hit, the entire ship seemed to move backward in the water. The smokestack buckled at the spot where the tentacle connected, bending forward as if bowing to them. It was going to fall right on top of the bridge, where Rhett and Mak and Basil were still trying to hold on.

The dark metal of the smokestack loomed, continuing to cast out its enormous plume of black smoke. Rhett caught blue lightning zapping across the inside of the plume, as if it were just another storm cloud. Metal groaned and shrieked. The stack fell.

"*Everybody jump!*" Mak screamed.

She and Basil leaped off the side of the crooked platform in the same spot that Henry had fallen. Rhett let go and allowed himself to slide full force toward the edge. The smokestack rushed down to meet him. He planted his feet on the broken edge where the window had been and jumped.

The rain obscured pretty much everything, but when the lightning uncoiled into the growing waves, Rhett could see the onslaught of psychons flooding the ship, looking like packs of grotesque bats with their cloaks billowing out around them. There were too many of them to count.

He smashed into the black iron hull of the ship and rolled, hoping to avoid a broken leg. Or two broken legs. The last time he'd been in the presence of psychons with an injured limb, it had almost been the end of him.

Luckily, when he sprang to his feet and sprinted to the railing at the edge of the ship, everything seemed to be intact.

The smokestack crashed into the bridge tower with an almighty roar of tearing metal and collapsing supports. The base of the tower stabbed into the *Harbinger*'s hull, and the smokestack split apart into sections, turning into something that looked more like a spring than a cylinder. More smoke erupted from the breaks in the stack. It swept across the top deck, engulfing the rest of the ship.

Rhett stumbled away from the destruction. He came to the port-side railing and gripped it, searching for something solid to hold on to. He looked around for Basil and Mak, but there was no sign of them. He glanced over the railing and saw what was waiting in the water below.

The kymaker had broken the surface, showing its horrid face. Really, there *was* no face. Just a gaping mouth, a funnel that was lined with a spiral of teeth that seemed to lead the way down into its throat. There were more than a dozen tentacles, some smaller, some bigger, flipping and snapping in the air, all of them equipped with those circles of weird crab legs. The monster also had two jointed arms that extended from the top of what Rhett assumed was both its head and its body. There were giant, unshapely lobster claws at the ends of the arms, one of which was currently buried in the side of the *Harbinger*.

All of this Rhett saw from the height of at least one New York high-rise, but some of the monster's tentacles still whipped danger-ously close to his face, spraying him with even more water. The monster let out a pathetic-sounding moan, something akin to a whale call, and the *Harbinger* listed to port, leaning down toward the monster's terrifying maw.

Rhett held on to the railing as the ship tilted and the water (and the monster) came closer. Tentacles smacked and clanged off the railing. Rhett looked back, hoping to see a way to climb away from the edge, and saw another tentacle curled up over the starboard side of the ship. The monster had wrapped one of its ap-pendages all the way around the ship and was pulling it down, trying to sink it.

Loose pieces of metal and broken sections of the smokestack and bridge dislodged and tumbled across the angled deck of the ship. Rhett rolled around on the port railing like the lone survivor in a game of dodgeball, barely avoiding pieces of debris as they whistled past him. Some of them crashed into the railing itself, sending the whole thing into teeth-chattering vibrations.

"RrrrrrrheeeeeeeeeeeeEEEEEEEEEEETT!"

He looked up. Mak and Basil were sliding toward him, hands clasped, kicking and flailing, trying to slow themselves down. Rhett didn't know where they had come from, but behind them, a portion of the already mangled smokestack was rolling toward the edge.

Rhett put out both of his arms, steadying himself on the narrow bars of the railing. Basil and Mak smacked into the crooks of his arms, and all three of them tipped over the side of the ship. Mak caught one of the bars and dangled there, Basil caught another with one hand and, with the other, caught Rhett, who had lost his grip altogether, before he could plummet down into the kymaker's hungry mouth. They hung there, suspended over the writhing tentacles and gnashing teeth, as the *Harbinger* listed further and further. Rain sloshed over the side of the deck. Rhett looked down at the front of the crooked ship and saw a few psychons go tumbling into the water.

"Is this not just, like, the worst day ever?" Basil said.

A few seconds later, the unmoored chunk of smokestack that had followed Basil and Mak down rolled over them with a crunch, leaving a trail of falling bits and pieces in its wake. It was a piece probably the size of a large house, and it flipped end over end toward the water, toward the toothy pit of the sea monster's mouth.

The debris barreled into the kymaker's throat, breaking off a few pointed teeth as it went. The monster pulled away, loosening the tentacle that it had wrapped around the ship and yanking out the claw that had punched a hole in the riveted iron hull. Instantly, the *Harbinger* righted itself in the water, rocking back and forth for a moment as it regained its balance. The kymaker sank down below the surface, using its claws to try and pull the giant circle of metal out of its mouth. It let out an agonized wail of pain that seemed to synchronize with the *Harbinger*'s siren.

Rhett, Mak, and Basil heaved themselves back over the railing, sopping wet and mentally exhausted.

"Yep," Basil said. "Definitely the worst day ever."

"Come on," Mak said, getting to her feet. "We just got lucky. That's not going to happen again. If we don't get back inside the ship now, we'll be stuck up here when the psychons start their next advance."

Rhett stood and glanced back over the railing. There was no sign of the sea monster, not even a shadow.

"How do we get back in?" he asked, gesturing to the crumpled heap of metal that had been the bridge tower.

"What, you think this thing only has one door?" Basil said as Mak helped him up. Then he gripped her under her elbows and pulled her close. He kissed her for a long moment, with the rain pattering down around them and lightning flickering between the clouds. When the kiss finally broke, he said, "Are you all right, my love?"

Mak nodded, and for just a second Rhett thought she might be crying.

"Good," Basil said gently. "Then let's get out of here."

FOURTEEN

Running along the top deck of the *Harbinger* was like running across several city blocks in New York. Platforms rose and fell, sometimes in a fluid way, sometimes in a jarring, haphazard way. There were wide-open stretches, with the one remaining smokestack looming above them and the flat black canvas of the deck spread out around them. There were cramped, narrow alleys where they had to shuffle sideways between tall compartments with windows that were all blacked out. The amalgamation of all the different ships that had come together to create the *Harbinger* was less clean up here. It was like the pieces from a bunch of different jigsaw puzzles had all been jammed together.

Rhett followed Mak and Basil, the rain driving against them, soaking them, blinding them. From far behind, at the front of the ship, they could hear the banging of psychon claws against the hull and the distinct sound of their skeletal feet scraping against the metal as they ran. They were flooding the ship, trying to find a way through the thick steel to the lower decks. And they weren't far behind.

"Keep moving," Mak said.

After running for what felt like hours, Mak and Basil finally slowed their pace and ducked into a little alcove formed by rising stacks of metal shipping containers. Their colors were faded to varying shades of dark gray, but Rhett could see the subtle variations and the places where their ribbed sides didn't quite line up. Cables were strung over the tops of the stacks, pulled taut to keep them from toppling over. The three of them moved single-file between the containers.

Once they were inside the alcove, Rhett thought for a moment that he was looking at the set of some bad pirate movie. While the outer edge of the alcove was surrounded by stacks of shipping containers, hiding their view of the rest of the ship, the space *inside* the alcove was all wooden, made of badly swollen and warped boards that were frayed with splinters. There was a raised quarterdeck that was surrounded by a mostly destroyed railing, with stairs leading up to it that didn't look very reliable, either. Beneath the quarterdeck were the cracked and shattered windows looking into what would have been the captain's quarters themselves. There was a door in the center, though, that was made from the same riveted steel as the rest of the *Harbinger.*

"Secret passageway?" Rhett asked Basil.

"Secret passageway," Basil replied, looking proud.

"Yeah, except everyone on board knows about it," Mak said, slipping her fingers in the space between the door and its frame. It had been left ajar. "Someone's already been here."

"Henry?" Rhett offered.

Mak pushed the door the rest of the way open with an iron squeal. "Or Treeny."

From beyond the alcove, they heard the sound of booming thuds, three or four of them, one right after the other.

"They've started with the cannons again," Basil said with a sigh. "Luckily they won't be able to do much damage with those. It'd take about a million hits from one to break through the hull."

"I hope you're right," Rhett murmured, listening to the distant metal *ping* of the cannonballs bouncing off steel.

Mak disappeared into the shadows within the door. Basil and Rhett followed.

Inside there were no captain's quarters to be found. Only a sharply descending stairwell that went on burying itself deep into the ship for as far down as Rhett could see. He thought of the apartment building and decided he would be done with stairs for a while after this.

Once they were all inside, Mak pulled the door shut behind them, completing the darkness. Rhett heard something slide and then click into place. Mak had locked it.

"Everyone hold your breath," Basil murmured.

Rhett felt his way down, clinging to the wall and the railing. They all fumbled for a solid grip, sometimes bumping into or grabbing each other's shoulders. The darkness was total, unbreakable.

Rhett shuffled his feet across the occasional landing, looking for where the next set of steps began. He was blind, trying to imagine each step in his head before he took it. Each time they came to a new landing, he hoped that Mak or Basil would say that they had gone far enough. But they just kept going, seemingly unbothered by the complete absence of light.

After they had gone down at least ten or eleven sets of stairs, there was a violent clanging from above them, followed by a horrible screech that made Rhett think of a rake scratching along the hood of a car. Then another clang.

They stopped. Rhett looked up in the direction of the sound, knowing that the other two were doing the same.

"Damn," Mak whispered. "They found the door. We have to move."

They moved quicker, no longer reaching out delicately with their feet for the next step but letting themselves to half-fall down the stairs. Above them, the clanging got louder. So did the scratching.

"Will this take us to the steam room?" Rhett asked, allowing himself a little too much hope.

"Sort of," Mak said without pause.

Rhett lost track of how many steps they had gone down. Each new landing was at once a potential oasis, the end of their long descent, and then immediately became a fading, bitter memory. They were so far into the black now that Rhett wasn't sure they were even surrounded by walls anymore. For all he knew, the unending shadows could have stretched out in all directions forever.

From high up, there was a horrendous crumpling sound. A few seconds later, something large and heavy rushed past Rhett's head, tossing his hair, falling down the middle of the stairwell. He wasn't sure if he ever heard it hit the bottom.

He squinted up through the abyss, to where there was now a speck of gray light cutting into the black. He could hear the rain again and the thunder. And he could see the faint silhouettes of the psychons as they poured into the stairwell. They were like floating skulls racing down through the darkness to meet him. Really, all he could see were their frozen grins.

"*Run!*" Mak yelled, her voice deafening in the small space.

And now, by the scant light of the storm outside, the three of them ran down the steps, skipping over two and three at a time. Rhett could sense the psychons behind them, not bothering with the steps anymore but leaping from one landing to the next, darting across the opening in the middle of the stairwell. He could hear the ruffling of their cloaks and the scratching of their boney claws.

"*Faster!*" he cried at the other two. "*Go!*"

They went lower and lower. The darkness that they plunged deeper and deeper into was absolute. The psychons gained on them. Rhett thought he could hear one breathing just behind him.

Finally, as they came around to the next landing, Rhett saw the outline of another door. It was red and glowing, and thin wisps of smoke floated out of the cracks.

"*There! There!*" Mak yelled.

They all jumped down the last set of stairs, crashing into one another on the landing. Rhett turned back, clambering to his feet, and saw a psychon standing at the top of the steps, where he had just been a moment before.

Mak struggled with the door. Basil tried to help her. The psychon came down the steps toward them, its skull face looking eager and hungry. Behind it: more psychons, their limbs and claws flailing in a mass of bone and muscle.

Basil wrenched the door open, flooding the stairwell with hot, red light. Rhett followed him and Mak through it, just as the psychon stepped onto the landing. They fell in a heap together on the other side. Mak jumped up, Rhett with her, and the two of them slammed the heavy iron door shut. They spun the turnstile in the center of the door until it wouldn't turn any more. From the other side, the psychons banged and scratched and wailed.

Rhett and Mak stepped back, eyeing the door, making sure it was going to hold.

After a moment, Mak adjusted herself, checking her hip to make sure the lantern was still there. It was, dangling without so much as a spark within its case.

"I think they're stuck. For now," she said.

Basil was still lying on his back on the floor.

"They could have at least had the common courtesy to call ahead first," he said. "Don't you think?"

Mak helped him up.

They were in a long, high-ceilinged room lined with huge furnaces that cast the red glow out of their vents and windows. Behind the furnaces, giant pistons slammed up and down, puffing out steam. The whole room was loud and chaotic with the sounds of working machinery.

Rhett leaned into Mak.

"This wasn't what I meant when I asked you if that led to the steam room," he mumbled.

She shrugged. "I said 'sort of,' didn't I?" She pointed down at the end of the room. "There," she said. "That'll take us back up to the main part of the ship and back to the Column from below. From there we just have to get to the steam room."

"What are we supposed to do when we get there?" Rhett asked. "Make our last stand? We almost got torn apart back there."

"There's a fail-safe," she replied.

"A fail-safe?"

"There's a mechanism that gets the containment tank off the *Harbinger* in the event that she's under attack," Basil explained. "It's impenetrable if you're not a syllektor. So the safest place for it to be is as far away from the ship as possible."

"Especially now," Mak said, shooting a glance at Rhett.

They were almost at the other end of the room, leaving the hiss and thump of the pistons behind as well as the horde of psychons still trying to get through the door from the stairwell.

Rhett nodded. He understood what Mak was saying.

"If Urcena gets her hands on Rhett and the souls at the same time," Mak continued, "we have no idea what she could do."

"*Soul Keeper.*"

The voice. From behind him. From all around him. From *inside* him. It exploded out from within his mind. Her voice and hundreds of others, like a grenade going off right in the center of his brain. Rhett fell to his knees. On either side of him, Mak and Basil did the same, covering their ears, trying to block her out.

He looked over his shoulder.

She was there, standing in the middle of the corridor, with the red glow of the furnaces around her, dripping water onto the hot floor and receiving wafts of steam in return. Her matted hair, her hospital gown, her dead, black eyes with those pinpoints of white in the middle.

And then he saw Treeny, cowering in the space between two of the hulking furnaces, her arms wrapped around her knees, her glasses askew on her nose. Tears ran down her face.

"*It is time,*" Urcena said, her voice blasting into Rhett's head. "*You will come with me.*"

For the first time, Rhett fought through the agony of having the she-thing twisting around inside his mind and spoke to her.

"Why?" he said. His voice sounded feeble even to him. "What do you want with me?"

"*You have no idea what you're capable of,*" she replied, and Rhett doubled over under the force of her speech. She took a step toward them, cocking her head to the side. "*You have no idea what kind of power you hold.*" She came closer.

Rhett struggled to speak, and when he did, the words were little more than ragged whispers. "You're right. I don't. But why would I allow you to control a part of me that I don't even understand yet?"

Urcena stopped short. Her eyes widened, and the tiny white specks of her pupils seemed to almost completely disappear.

"*Do you defy me, Soul Keeper?*" she said, and even though the thing that looked like a girl was whispering, the other voices still boomed between Rhett's ears. *"Do you defy me as you defied your parents?"*

Those words broke through the pain in Rhett's head like an ice pick. He looked up, staring into the black abyss of Urcena's eyes. He understood why they had seemed so familiar back on the Golden Gate Bridge.

"You were there," he said. The images of that night—the night that Rhett perished along with his parents—came into focus behind his eyes. He could see the road and how empty it was. But the road hadn't been empty, not entirely. "You were standing in the road."

Urcena's face curled into an awful grin.

"Your power was wasted in life," she said. *"I could not wait around for you to die on your own."*

"You did this to me," Rhett said, the realization crashing down within his heart. "You did this to my parents."

Basil was moving beside him, reaching up to his shoulder, where his scythes jutted from their sheaths.

"You used me against my parents just like you used Treeny against us," Rhett went on. He glanced at Treeny, shaking and crying in the unsettled light of the furnaces' flames. She was just as scared and angry and vulnerable as Rhett had been. He hadn't killed his parents at all. And Treeny hadn't ghosted the captain. It was the she-thing. All of it. He saw Treeny's mouth moving and at the same time heard Urcena's raging voice.

"Do not look at her!" she snapped. *"Look here. To me. To your destiny."*

At the same moment that Basil was getting his grip on the scythe, Rhett was understanding Treeny's part in all this. She wasn't Urcena's assassin or her errand girl or her messenger. She was the conduit through which Urcena was able to manifest herself. She needed Treeny, to enter this world from wherever it was that she came from. That was why Rhett had heard the dripping water inside the *Harbinger*—in his room, in the halls of the crew quarters. Urcena had been there all along—with Treeny. She'd been with him from the very beginning.

"We're going to destroy you," Rhett said. Even to his own ears, his voice sounded viciously calm.

Rhett saw the blur of Basil's arm straightening out and the blur of the scythe leaving his hand, spinning in the air toward Urcena. She didn't look afraid. In fact, the touch of another sinister grin winked at the corner of her lips. And Rhett knew why. Even if the scythe hit her, it wouldn't do any damage. If they wanted to do that, they'd have to destroy . . .

From her spot between the furnaces, Treeny stood and ran. She dove in the air, screaming. She put herself between Basil's scythe and Urcena.

The scythe buried itself in Treeny's chest. She hit the floor and lay there for a moment, a look of pure relief spreading across her face. And then she crumbled into black ash, the shape of her falling apart into a pile of dust with the handle of the scythe protruding from it.

But Urcena remained, her face wild with rage. She stared at Basil, then fixed her eyes on Rhett again. She opened her mouth and screamed. The sound should have broken them all, but it was barely as potent as her whispers. With her connection to them gone, Urcena was stuttering in and out of reality.

Her scream tore through the compartment. Several furnaces crumpled in on themselves like balls of tinfoil. A piston broke free of its arm, vomiting steam and punching a hole in the wall, where it got stuck and began to whine, the pressure building. Flames erupted from the collapsed furnaces, filling the room with wavering heat.

Rhett stepped back, pulling at Basil, who pulled at Mak. Together, they backed away.

Urcena screamed. She let her fury ignite the compartment as it fell apart around her. Behind her, the psychons had folded the door in. Their arms and faces thrashed in the narrow hole they'd made, trying to get through. Urcena was their queen. They would continue trying to serve her, even if it meant being incinerated.

As Urcena continued to fade, the image of her body flashing and sputtering, the three syllektors stepped slowly through the door that they'd been trying to reach. The she-thing's halting effect on them had dwindled along with her presence in their world. Fire filled the compartment, and at the far end, Rhett could see the cloaks of the psychons catching some of the flames. They screamed right along with their queen.

"*YOU HAVE NOT ESCAPED ME, SOUL KEEPER!*" Urcena roared, her voice more *thing* now than *she*. "*YOU HAVE NOT ESCAPED ME!*"

And then Mak sealed the door to the compartment, locking the inferno on the other side.

More running. More stairs.

"Didn't anybody think to put a damn elevator in this thing?" Rhett asked, running up a flight of steps behind the other two. He was trying to put the image of Urcena out of his mind—Urcena back in the furnace room, Urcena on the road the night of his death. He'd be lucky if he never saw that horrible face ever again. He didn't think that would be the case, though. They may have weakened her connection to them by ghosting Treeny, but they hadn't gotten rid of her completely. He could feel it.

They came to a long hallway, brightly lit with fluorescents, nothing but dull gray metal.

"This will take us back to the Column," Mak said, an undeniable touch of relief in her voice.

They jogged down the hall. Rhett was unnerved by the quiet. He saw Basil give Mak a concerned glance. Rhett wanted to know why the hallway was deserted. Where was everybody?

"Guys—" was all Rhett got out before the wall and the floor behind him exploded inward. He heard ripping metal and gushing water. Something caught him, pulling him off his feet and slamming him hard into the wall. He was able to half turn. There were white sprays of water pouring in through a hole that was probably big enough to fit a minivan. The hallway was already filling up with dark water. Hiding out within the white froth of the incoming sea, Rhett saw the kymaker's tentacle—a smaller one but with the same basic anatomy, gross crab legs included.

The tentacle knocked into him again, shoving him into the wall. He heard a dull *smack* as his head collided with the solidity of it. The creeping crab legs on the underside of the tentacle reached for him, grabbed his leg, and pulled him in. There was already at least two feet of water flooding the hallway. Rhett went down and under.

He was caught in a swarm of bubbles. The noise of the rushing water was muffled into a quiet, steady roar. He tried to focus on the fluorescent bars on the ceiling, but they began to flicker and go out. He reached for his knuckle blade and found only an empty holster. He didn't know when he'd lost it—probably back up on the upper deck, when the bridge tower had collapsed. One of the tentacle's circles of slender legs had Rhett now. He could feel the rounded points of the legs as they crept across him, pulling him closer. They would get a good hold on him and then the tentacle would pull him back out of the ship and deposit him right into the toothy hole of the angry beast. Who knew if it would destroy his heart right away? He might have to wait around while the monster's teeth slashed into every other part of him, breaking him down, digesting him. It could take hours.

At least there would be no pain if he didn't want there to be. There was no pain now, even in his body's mangled state—broken ribs, damaged lungs, waterlogged and covered in scrapes and bruises. He felt none of it. And that, at least, was a blessing.

Rhett struggled against the kymaker's tentacle legs. His feet found something that was mostly solid but had a little give to it, something almost like rubber. He realized it was the tentacle itself.

Using it for leverage, he tried to pull free of the reaching legs and only succeeded in getting himself wrapped tighter in their rigid grasp. While his body was content to just float there, Rhett's brain was screaming, *Breathe, damn it! Breathe!*

He shut his eyes and prepared to inhale. He didn't know what was going to happen when the water flooded his lungs. Would it be the same as the smoke? Would he just keep going without the oxygen? Or would he sink, lost in a comatose state, left to lay at the bottom of the sea forever? That didn't sound so bad, actually.

But then something swiped through the water nearby, and he felt the squeeze of the legs loosen a bit. Another swipe. The tentacle squirmed and jerked. It knocked into Rhett again, only this time it flung him away. The crab legs released him, and he broke the surface, heaving in a deep breath.

He got to his feet just in time to see the tentacle squirm back out of the hole it had made, leaving behind a dozen or so of its spindly legs. They floated at the surface of the rising water, writhing on their own. Mak stood with Basil's remaining scythe in her hand, watching them. Basil was holding on to her belt and now let go. He'd been holding on to her in case they needed to make a quick escape, Rhett presumed. But still, they'd stayed. They'd saved him.

"Thanks," he said lamely.

"Don't mention it," Basil replied. "No, really. Don't mention it. That thing gives me the willies." He shivered dramatically.

The water was up to their elbows now and still pouring in. They sloshed the rest of the way down the hall. There was a flight of six or seven steps at the end. They crawled up them, pulling themselves out of the water.

"Because we weren't wet enough already, right?" Rhett said, shaking his arms out.

The water gurgled up the steps behind them.

"We have to seal this compartment," Mak said. She was wringing out a mass of her dark hair. "The engine room that we came from is compromised. It might have already blown more pistons, which means it's probably taking on water, too."

She pulled open another bulkhead door at the top of the steps, with the water lapping at their heels again already. When they were through, she pushed the door closed and spun the turnstile. Rhett helped her twist it until it wouldn't budge another inch.

When he turned around to get his bearings, he was glad to see that they had finally reached the bottom of the atrium and the winding staircase that made up the Column.

Down here, the banister was all flaking, rusted wrought iron, and the steps were some kind of marble. Rhett looked up and saw the familiar spiral of blue light and metal. At the top, though, the ceiling had come falling in. Some of the lights sparked, and it looked like there might be a fire burning. Everything else was twisted metal. When Rhett stepped forward to get a better look, he kicked something that clanged across the floor. He looked down and saw scattered pieces of debris that had fallen all the way from the top.

"Where is everybody?" Rhett asked, the question he'd wanted to ask way back before the kymaker struck again.

"Might have abandoned ship," Basil suggested.

"I don't think anybody would have done that without the captain's order," Mak said, nudging a sharp dagger of metal with the toe of her boot.

"Maybe Henry gave the order," Rhett said. He hadn't known Henry for very long, but even as he said the words, he knew they weren't true.

Mak shook her head. "Henry's skittish, but he's a fighter. He wouldn't have run away." She took her eyes off the debris and looked up through the atrium at the destruction. "Let's get up there," she said after a pause.

Before they could take to the stairs, something back in the direction they had come from exploded. The ship lurched and immediately began to list slightly. They now stood on an angle. Rhett gripped the banister to hold his balance, and he exchanged nervous glances with the other two.

More steps. Rhett decided that the *Harbinger* had to be at least 50 percent stairs. These ones, at least, were familiar.

They came to the steam-room deck and stared down the long tunnel that eventually devolved from sleek steel to rotted wood, with the steam room tucked under the trapdoor at the end. Now all the lights in the tunnel were out. Not even the torches at the very end were lit. The walls and floor and ceiling faded away into blackness after only a couple of feet. From far back in the cavernous hole, Rhett heard movement.

"Someone's in there," he whispered out of the corner of his mouth to the other two.

They both nodded. Basil slipped his scythe into his hand while Mak reached down, maneuvering around the lantern that was still miraculously attached to her empty sheath strap, and rolled up her pant leg. She pulled a dagger out of a smaller sheath on her ankle. Rhett gave her a look. She shrugged. All Rhett could do was stand there with his fists clenched, feeling stupid and defenseless.

In the tunnel, shadows began to take shape. There were several of them, spanning the width of the darkened corridor. They moved closer, trudging forward with purpose. It wasn't until their faces started to become visible that Rhett realized the shadows were too short and humanlike to be psychons. They were crew members, syllektors.

All three of them relaxed.

"Mak!" the one in front called. She was a tough-looking woman who appeared to be in her thirties. There was no way of telling how long she had actually been on the *Harbinger*, of course. She had short, reddish hair and a mammoth battle-ax that came up to her shoulders when she propped it on the floor. It reminded Rhett of Theo, and he couldn't quite bring himself to believe that he might never see the big lug again. "Damn, it's good to see you," the red-headed woman said. "And Basil, too!" She sauntered up, followed by a group of five or six other syllektors. They were all armed, and they all looked shaken.

"Edith," Mak said. She gripped the redheaded woman's hand for a moment. "Where's the rest of the crew?"

The woman—Edith—cocked her head back toward the tunnel. "What's left is back there. The tunnel's the best place to try to bottleneck the bastards and keep an eye on the steam room at the same time." She sounded casual, but there was something stiff in her voice that Rhett didn't like.

"What do you mean 'what's left'?" Rhett asked.

Edith gave him a temperamental look, but Mak nodded for her to go ahead.

"Everything's been chaos," Edith said. And as if to emphasize her point, there was another series of booms followed by the hollow pinging of cannonballs knocking against the ship's hull. "We didn't know what our orders were. Some of the crew tried to evacuate. Most stayed and fought."

It was only then that Rhett saw the piles of black ash that littered the floor around the entrance to the tunnel. Weapons gleamed out of the mounds, the remnants of syllektors that were no more.

"What about Henry?" Basil asked. "Did he ever make it back down?"

There was a long, uncomfortable silence among the syllektors who had emerged from the tunnel.

"Not in one piece," Edith said, her voice finally softening. "When we saw him, he was . . . a mess. Psychons followed him down. We held them off until we couldn't anymore. Henry didn't make it." She lowered her gaze.

"We lost Captain Trier, as well," Mak said. "Did Henry tell you?"

Edith nodded. "Yeah. That traitor is gonna get it if she crosses my path."

"She won't be crossing anybody's path anymore," Basil murmured, looking down at his scythe.

There was another pause.

"So . . . wait," Rhett said. Something concerning had crossed his mind. "If Trier and Henry have both been ghosted . . . who's in charge now?"

Mak and Edith exchanged a look and then Edith tilted her head at Basil.

"He is," she said.

Rhett looked at her, looked at Basil. He chuckled. "No, seriously. Who's the captain?"

Mak let a subtle grin steal across her lips.

"I'm afraid Edith's right," she said. "Basil was the second mate. His primary duties were to bring new syllektors on board. Like he did with you, with me. A lot of us." She regarded Basil with a look of loving admiration. Edith was nodding in agreement. "But he was also in line to become captain."

"I just never thought it would come down to that," Basil said in a hushed voice. He looked up at Rhett, at Mak, at the rest of the syllektors. "Damn," he said. "Now I've got to be responsible and stuff, don't I?"

Edith and the other crew members behind her looked antsy, but Rhett and Mak grinned. It felt good to do it, despite the ever-growing tilt of the ship and the attack from the *Cyclops* and the psychons that were probably still lurking on board somewhere, preparing for their next assault.

"If you're done being impressed with yourself," Edith said with an edge to her tone, "we have souls to protect." Her eyes darted to the left. Rhett saw the quick flick of her irises. He also saw her hand squeezing in and out of a fist. She flicked her eyes again.

It wasn't long before Mak saw it, too. Rhett elbowed Basil softly, and he nodded in the direction of Edith's eyes. It was a warning. She was trying to move their attention behind her, to the tunnel.

Rhett took a quick inventory of the weapons that were lying among the piles of ash and spotted a decent-looking sword. He would have had more control with his own knuckle blade, but that was long gone. The sword would have to do.

Edith stepped forward, flicking her eyes one last time. She leaned between Basil and Rhett and barely whispered.

"They're in the tunnel," she said. "The rest of the crew are hostages. We were—"

But she was cut off by the all-too-recognizable screech of a psychon, a noise that erupted from the deep black throat of the tunnel. There was a rush of movement from back there, and a wall of shadows moved quickly toward them.

Rhett darted over to where the sword lay amid the other fallen syllektors. He grabbed the hilt and lifted it, testing the weight. Definitely more than he was capable of dealing with, but he had no time to shop for other options. He put himself flat up against the wall beside the tunnel entrance, holding the sword up in front of him. His breath fogged against the polished blade.

A swarm of psychons burst out of the tunnel in a singular mass of bones and torn fabric. Rhett noticed something else with them, something big and muscular and clad in dark suspenders. Theo.

But it wasn't Theo. Not really. Because this version of Theo used a fist to crush the face of one of the syllektors who had left the tunnel with Edith. The syllektor stumbled backward, lost his footing on the stairs, and rolled down them. Then Theo knocked the hatchet out of the hand of another syllektor, bent, and wrapped his arms around her torso. Theo turned with the girl still struggling in his arms and looked right at Rhett. Theo's eyes were gone, replaced by flat black emptiness and pinpricks of white.

Theo hadn't just been Treeny's leverage to get off the bridge. He'd also been Urcena's backup plan, another connection to try and destroy them with.

As Rhett watched, the thing that looked like Theo squeezed the girl in his arms. The cords in Theo's neck strained under his skin, the muscles in his arms warbled. There was a snapping sound, like a tree branch breaking, and then the syllektor girl sank to the floor, limp, her spine no longer in exactly the right place.

After the psychons, more syllektors came running out of the tunnel in a panic—the hostages that Edith had mentioned. These ones were weaponless and scared. Most of them ran for the stairs, climbing over one another to move up the atrium and get away from the madness.

"*Get your asses back down here!*" Edith hollered. She got the words out just before a psychon's claw slid into her chest, almost calmly, without any hurry. She evaporated into a cloud of black dust.

Basil and Mak had their hands full with two psychons of their own. Mak was fending one off with just her little hidden dagger. Basil was doing his best with a single scythe. The other syllektors who had weapons sparred with the psychons to the extent that they could. But the psychons towered over them and began to overtake them. There was a reason the syllektors chose to outrun the psychons instead of fight them, Rhett realized. This was it.

"*This is what happens when you defy me, Soul Keeper,*" the Theo-thing said. The words came out in the same maddening tangle of voices, this time overlaid by Theo's own New York accent.

There was a psychon between Theo and Rhett. Rhett stepped up to it and swung at it with the sword. The psychon caught the first two swings with its claw, but Rhett faked to the left and came back in an arching swing to remove the psychon's arm. It stepped back, squealing in pain. Rhett swung again, severing the top half of the psychon from the bottom half. Its ugly, muscle-strewn torso and skull fell to the floor, where it stared up at Rhett, motionless. When Rhett looked up again, Theo was barreling toward him.

Rhett dove sideways and rolled. Theo, controlled now by an entity that typically presented itself as a frail, petite young girl, was clumsy. He toppled over the dispatched psychon and hit the floor with a hard thud.

Rhett didn't waste a second. He lunged, bringing the sword down in a tall arc, aiming for Theo's chest. He had no intention of ghosting Theo. He just wanted to use the sword to pin Theo to the floor. He aimed as far away from the heart as he could.

But Theo's hands rose up to meet the sword. They clapped together on either side of the blade and held it where it was, halfway between Rhett and Theo.

"*You would destroy your friend?*" the Theo-thing said.

"Only if it meant destroying you," Rhett grunted, pushing with all his strength—and there wasn't much left—against the hilt of the sword. He was bluffing. Or trying to, anyway. Trying to get the advantage, to surprise the demon that now existed in Theo and set him free.

"Then you are more foolish than I thought."

Theo's hands moved a few inches, repositioning the sword, still with all of Rhett's weight on it. Rhett didn't have time to let up. Theo let go of the sword, and the blade fell straight down. It stabbed into Theo's chest, right at his heart. The Theo-thing looked up at Rhett, laughing, and then disintegrated. The sword jutted out of a huge mound of ash like a flag stuck into a hill of dirt. Rhett could only stare at it, consumed by shock.

A moment later, Basil and Mak came up behind him and gripped his elbows.

"C'mon, mate," Basil said. "We have to go. We have to get to the steam room."

"There's nothing you could have done," Mak said. "That wasn't Theo." But she gave the pile of ash a weak, sick look anyway.

FIFTEEN

They went headlong into the shadows for the last time, leaving the battle behind them. They all knew the way.

The *Harbinger* continued to sink. It tilted into the water, and everything inside the ship listed drastically. As Rhett and Mak and Basil ran down the tunnel, it became almost like running *up* a hill.

Rhett had left the sword behind. He didn't have the will to pick it back up again. It hadn't been his weapon of choice to begin with. The image of Theo's face breaking up into all those miniscule specks of dust wouldn't leave him. Having the sword in his hand just would have made it worse.

The end of the tunnel almost seemed to come to meet them. As did the two psychons that stood guard above the trapdoor.

Mak didn't stop. Even in the darkness, Rhett heard her drop and slide across the uneven wooden floor between the psychons' legs. She threw the trapdoor open, and the faint blue light from the steam room illuminated the back of the tunnel just enough for Rhett and Basil to see what they were doing.

Basil dug the end of his scythe into the first psychon's hollow eye socket. Shards of bone and gristly tendrils of muscle flew. The blade cracked into the cavity of the skull, and black ooze came dripping out. The psychon dropped to its knees, then fell flat on its chest. In the next instant, Basil tossed the slime-covered scythe to Rhett. Rhett caught it, bent down below the swipe of the second psychon's claws, and took off its legs below the knee. It fell, squirming, to the floor. Rhett inserted the blade into that one's skull, too.

Rhett held on to the scythe as he stepped down through the trap-door and said, "This has an awesome swing to it."

"You have no idea," Basil replied.

Mak was already halfway down the ladder into the steam room when Rhett and Basil caught up to her. But by now the ladder had been angled to the point that it was almost like traversing a set of monkey bars. The ship was going down. Fast.

From far-off, they could hear iron wrenching and twisting, the haunted moan of things bending out of place and being swallowed by the waves. There were more explosions, and the sound of the battle back in the atrium was growing. The psychons were pushing the syllektors back into the tunnel, making their last run to capture the souls.

Inside the steam room, the walls groaned and cracked under the pressure of being forced out of true. The wood was old and weak. It wouldn't stand up to the discord for very long.

"How does this work?" Rhett asked. For the moment, he was able to put Theo out of his thoughts.

Mak didn't reply. Instead, she sidestepped over to the cube, its size making her look like a tiny action figure standing next to a huge toy chest. The tank gave off its ephemeral glow; the cloud of life lost pulsed behind its glass walls. Mak put her hand on the cube's door, and for one horrible second, Rhett thought she was going to open it and let all the souls out. But this time, the door didn't open.

There was a sucking sound, like something being slurped up by a vacuum, and the extension tube that jutted out from the side of the cube and disappeared into the wall was suddenly emptied. All the souls that had been moving throughout the *Harbinger*, helping to give it power, were pulled back into the main tank. With a hiss, the extension tube detached itself from the tank. Now the cube was on its own. And so was the *Harbinger*.

Along with the continued sounds of the ship struggling to keep itself afloat, there was a sound of engines and machines powering down, of propellers ceasing to spin and whole sections of lights going dark. The glass cube filled with souls was the *Harbinger*'s life support. And Mak had just pulled the plug.

"Okay," she said, stepping back. "The containment tank is secure. Even if there's a breach in the circulation system somewhere else on the ship, the souls are safe. Nothing but a syllektor is getting in there now."

"You forget, love," Basil said. "That she-devil back there can *control* syllektors. Look what she did to Theo." He paused, looking away. "And Treeny."

Rhett was grateful to Basil for laying the blame on Urcena. Truly, that's where it belonged. But that didn't help with the guilt. From the look of it, Basil was dealing with some guilt of his own.

"And what about the ship?" Rhett said. "We just cut the power when she needs it the most."

Mak only shook her head. "She's going down anyway, Rhett."

As if to solidify her point, the floor beneath them shuddered and buckled. Splintered boards sprang free, flipping up like snapped bones and spinning into the air, showering the room with dust. The containment tank dropped about a foot into the floor with a teeth-rattling crunch.

When everything settled, all three of them let out a breath.

"Shit," Rhett whispered.

Above their heads, the battle raged on as if nothing had happened. Rhett could hear metal stabbing into bone and bone stabbing into flesh. Someone slammed the trapdoor shut. A second later, the door exploded inward. The dimly lit shape of a syllektor formed out of the shower of splinters. The syllektor, a guy with shoulder-length white hair, fell into the steam room. His body clanged against the nearly sideways ladder and fell some more, until he hit the damaged floor and broke through it, disappearing below.

"If we're getting the tank off the ship," Rhett said, "we better do it now."

"Mak," Basil said. "Go. *Go.*"

Rhett and Basil took up positions on either side of her, almost as if they were out gathering a soul. In a way, they were. They were gathering all the souls.

Mak placed her hand on the glass of the tank again, and the faint, foggy image of her handprint appeared on the smooth surface.

Rhett had deposited enough souls into the cube now to know how cool that glass was, even without his senses. It wasn't even really a sensation or a feeling. It was more like an assurance. An assurance that within that block of glass and steel, there were no hard edges or boiling rooms. That there was comfort in death.

From this angle, there was a narrow gap where the trapdoor had been that Rhett could see through. He could see the fluttering cloaks of psychons and the winking blades of syllektors.

"Whatever you're doing, you need to do it n—" a voice up top started to yell before it was cut off.

They waited.

A few seconds later, Mak stepped back from the tank, looking at it, then looking at her hand. Confusion and panic were etched all over her face.

"What's wrong?" Basil said frantically.

"It's not working," Mak replied. It sounded almost like a question.

"What's not working?" Rhett asked.

"The fail-safe. It's supposed to . . . to disappear. Go somewhere else." She was still staring at her hand. "The way we do, when we go out to collect a soul. There's supposed to be a door, and it's supposed to disappear."

"So what's wrong with it?" Rhett heard the edge in his own voice.

"I don't know!" She stepped up to the cube and planted her hand on it again. She waited. Then she stepped back, frustrated. Fury took over her face and she started banging on the glass with her fists, creating an odd bonging sound that echoed around the room. *"Fucking piece of shit!"* she screamed.

Basil came up behind her and caught her by the wrists.

"Whoa, whoa, whoa," he said, pulling her back gently. "It's okay. We'll figure something out."

Mak whirled around. "Figure what out? Huh? What are we going to figure out?" With a finger that was shaking just slightly, Mak pointed up at the trapdoor. "They're *coming*. For *this*." She moved the same finger so that it was directed at the cube. "And we are not enough to stop that from happening."

She sank to the floor, surrounded by bent and twisted boards. The glow of the cube behind her stretched her shadow into a long, thin line.

Another syllektor fell through the trapdoor but caught herself on the ladder. She continued to swing with a sword up through the hole, clashing with a psychon that fought to get through. The sword might have been the same one that had ghosted Theo, but Rhett couldn't tell for sure.

The *Harbinger* screamed and whined and tilted. Everything was turned now, leaning dangerously. In other parts of the ship, Rhett imagined furniture sliding across floors, knickknacks tumbling off shelves. He imagined the old wooden parts of the ship snapping apart just like the steam room was. He imagined the dark shape of the ship as it began to point upward out of the water, lights flickering, the surviving smokestack coughing up its last dark clouds, the kymaker and the *Cyclops* nearby, the storm hammering on around them all.

It was a car wreck all over again, this one on a monstrous scale. This one concerning the lives—or afterlives—of thousands instead of just three.

Because they *were* lives, even if they were lives that had ended. Their souls had continued to be, either as the glowing white cloud inside the cube or as syllektors. Life echoed on in those faint remains, doing good, *being* good. And they deserved better than this.

Rhett looked down at the scythe that was still in his hand. His washed-out, scraped-up face looked back at him. He thought about the night of the crash, about the moment he swerved the car in front of the truck. He could clearly see Urcena in his memory now, standing in the middle of the road, her desperately evil glare connecting with his for just an instant. Of course he wouldn't have remembered that, not after everything else—he had barely been able to remember his own name in those first moments after his death. He was angry now. So angry. But it was also a relief to know that his anger hadn't killed him, or his parents, in the first place.

Maybe it had been a sudden, too-early death for him. But to think about all the good that he'd done with it, all the good he could *still* do with it, was comfort enough to make it okay.

Rhett held the scythe out to Basil, who just looked back, confused.

"Use it," Rhett said. "On me."

"I'm sorry," Basil said. "I'm not sure I got that. Because all I heard was *fucking bollocks*!"

Rhett pulled the scythe toward him, laying it against his chest.

"Think about it," Rhett said. "Urcena came after *me* first. She can't do anything with the souls in the tank without me. You heard Mak—only a syllektor can get into it, and the *Harbinger* is sinking anyway. Let it. Even if the psychons could somehow get the tank off the ship in time, there's no way that Urcena would let them have any of the souls until she's done with them. We make it as hard as we possibly can for her to get her hands on the tank, and in the meantime, we get me and . . . and whatever it is I can do as far out of her reach as we can. *This* is the fail-safe."

Mak was still on the floor, staring at a dark knot in the wood.

"So you want us to ghost you," she said, "and let the ship take the containment tank down with it."

"Exactly," Rhett replied. "It was stupid for me to come here in the first place. If I'm gone, Urcena can't use this power that I have. Defend the tank for as long as you can. Once the psychons realize they can't get to it without drowning themselves, they'll give up and regroup. Then you two and whoever else is still on board can abandon ship."

Basil took a step back, taking the scythe with him but letting it fall to his side.

"And go where?" he asked. "Do what? What are we supposed to do with the rest of the souls?"

Rhett could only blink at him. "The rest . . . ?"

Basil chuckled. "Just because the *Harbinger* sinks, mate, doesn't mean that people are going to stop dying."

From the trapdoor, they heard more clashing. The girl who had fallen onto the ladder had managed to get herself back up into the tunnel, but the fight was still close, and there was no way of knowing how many psychons were still trying to get through.

Rhett wasn't paying any attention to the fight, though. He ran a hand through his hair. Now that he was standing still, he could focus on it. It wasn't nearly as strong or insistent as it had been earlier in that impossibly long day, but it was here, nagging at the edges of his mind: the invisible lasso. The push.

Basil was right. Nothing that was happening here had any effect on the real world. There were people out there who were still dying, who still needed their souls protected.

He looked from Basil to Mak, then back again.

"I don't know what else to do," he whispered.

"It doesn't matter what happens to us, mate," Basil said. "If there aren't any syllektors to gather the souls of the dead, then the psychons win anyway. They get a feast one way or the other."

"What about Urcena?" Mak said, finally standing again. "We can't just pretend she doesn't exist. Rhett's right. She needs him *and* the tank if she wants control over anything. And whatever she has planned is going to be way worse than anything a bunch of psychons are capable of."

"So that's it?" Basil asked. His voice rose, cracked a little. "We're just supposed to give up? I already had to ghost one of my teammates today. I . . . I can't take another one. I just can't."

"Once you guys are safe," Rhett went on, a strange certainty overwhelming him, "you can find me. Captain Trier said that the part of my soul that's still attached to the living world will go back there. Find me. We can fix this."

"*Fix* it?" Basil cried. "Mate, this ship is dead!" He pointed at the containment tank, which was turned almost completely on its side now. "*They* are dead! *You'll* be dead! Like, *dead* dead! And nobody can—"

"I can," Rhett said, cutting him off. "I can. I don't know how or why, but I know it the way that I know my parents loved each other, that they loved me even as we all died together. I know it the way that I know you love Mak. I have the power to fix all of this. All I need is a chance."

Basil looked at Mak. She reached out and squeezed his hand, then she reached out with her other hand and squeezed Rhett's. Rhett was surprised but comforted. He was also afraid.

"That power is what Urcena wants," Mak said. "We won't let her have it."

The ship was canted at a sharp angle. The three of them struggled to even stand up straight. The walls continued to groan and flex. Water began to seep through the cracks in them and drip from the ceiling. The battle in the tunnel seemed to fade for a moment and then came back full force. Rhett could see the movement in the shadows through the trapdoor.

He leaned down and grabbed Basil's hand, the one that was holding the scythe, completing the circle of their grips. He lifted the hand. He leveled the point of the blade at his chest.

Mak and Basil stood in front of him, their eyes red and wet and angry and sad.

"We'll find you," Mak said. She opened her mouth, as if there was something more she wanted to say, then closed it again.

"I'll be the one that looks like a ghost," Rhett replied. And, somehow, they all choked out a little bit of laughter.

There was a strange pressure pushing against him—not like the push, but something nearly as strong. He pushed back, and when he looked down, the curved blade of the scythe was buried in his chest, slipped between his ribs to the left.

"See you soon, mate," Basil whispered.

All around them, the floor began to get soft, began to crumble into liquid tendrils that floated into the air. Rhett watched them burst into tiny fragments and continue floating up. Beneath the floor and behind the walls, there was only solid black.

As the world disintegrated around him, Rhett saw a psychon leap down through the trapdoor. Mak let go, pulling her dagger out. When he lost his hold on her, Rhett fell to his knees. Basil sank down with him and then Mak was there again, and they were both staring at him. Mak ran a hand through his hair, and he was sure that she was crying now, unable to keep the force of her emotions at bay, the way he'd been unable to keep his emotions back that night on the bridge, when he told the captain about his parents.

The blue light from the tank darkened, plunged into a deep hue, somehow bright and dark at the same time, an antishadow. And under that light, the ship continued to break apart into those atom-like pieces and float away into the nothing.

For a while he could still see Mak's and Basil's faces. And then they were Theo's and Treeny's faces, and then they were his parents' faces. They were talking to him, saying his name, the way they'd been trying to communicate with him from the tank where their souls now lived. They were still in there. He knew that he would save them somehow. If he had nothing else to fight for, he had them.

The last specks of reality funneled themselves away, vanishing into the wide-open black. He wondered if this was what being in space felt like. Probably not. At least in space there would have been the stars to keep him company. When the two faces in front of him broke apart and disappeared, Rhett Snyder was alone.

In the great distance, a circle of intense, almost blinding light appeared. It grew and grew. It consumed the black and turned it white. As it drew closer, preparing to swallow him, all he could think was *Finally*. Then it washed over him—the light, the warmth.

And all the world was brilliance.

EPILOGUE

From where he stood, the house was clearly visible.

It might have been painted blue at one time, but the sun had beaten all the color out of it. It leaned under the firm and constant hands of weather and gravity. Some of the windows were boarded up; others were just missing. Roof tiles had peeled away like ancient scabs, leaving sagging spots in the wood underneath. The chimney stood tall, even if the top of it had eroded slightly, but it had been years since any smoke had come curling out of it.

The field stretched away from the house in all directions, making it look small and lonely. There was a wall of brown, leafless trees not far behind the house. Above it, the faint specter of a daytime moon hung like a cradle in the pallid sky.

He stood in the grass, surrounded by dwindling patches of snow, while the others fussed with the crate. They were just a few that he'd brought with him, quiet and cooperative. They shimmied the crate across the bed of the truck.

He waited patiently, his hands stuffed into the pockets of his overcoat, the collar turned up to cover his ears. The effects of the ship had gradually been wearing off, something that they hadn't seen coming. He could feel the cold, he could feel the pain in his numb fingertips. The longer they stayed in the physical plane, the worse it was going to get. Time was catching up with them, and eventually, when it came nose-to-nose, they would all know what real death felt like. They would be nothing.

He worried for them and for himself. Their last hope was inside that house.

A few more minutes passed. The gray day seemed to linger in a constant, pale light. There were no clouds, but he was sure it was going to snow some more.

The crew got the crate down off the truck and started carrying it across the field to the house. The brittle grass crunched under their feet. One of them—Jon—slammed the tailgate shut and then came up beside him.

"Captain Winthrop," Jon said. "That was the last of it."

"Good," Basil replied. "Everything else is already in place?"

"Yes, sir." Jon had a red baseball hat in his hands that he wrung like the neck of some small animal. The color was jarring against the paleness around them.

They watched the other guys lug the crate up the front steps. After a moment Jon cleared his throat.

"Captain, sir?" he said.

"Yes, Jon."

"If you don't mind me asking . . . I mean, if it's something you're able to share . . ."

"You want to know what all this is about." It wasn't a question. Basil kicked at the hard earth with the toe of his boot.

Jon hesitated, then said, "Yes, sir."

Basil waited, scratching at his chin, pondering his words. Somewhere over beyond the tree line, a crow called out.

"What do you remember about the day the *Harbinger* sank, Jon?" Basil finally asked.

Jon thought about it. "Not a hell of a lot, sir. It happened so fast."

Basil nodded. "We lost a lot of good people. Good syllektors."

"It was awful," Jon murmured, his focus suddenly distancing, the memories of that day playing back behind his eyes.

"How long has it been?" Basil knew the answer, but he was trying to make a point.

"A long time," Jon replied. "Years."

"Yes." Basil licked his lips. "We lost something else when the ship went down. Something very important."

"The cube," Jon said. At the house, the other guys were sliding the crate, a big, tall, rectangular box, through the front door. "We lost the containment tank. It went down with the ship."

"Correct," Basil said, nodding again. "And the world's a different place now because of it." The images of everything that had happened after, of fighting their way up out of the steam room, of fleeing the ship through the last active door they could find, the dead psychons, the ghosted syllektors. By the time it finally went under, the *Harbinger* had been so full of ash that it was more like a giant urn than a ship. Maybe that was fitting. But the thought of that cube, still packed with souls, lost out in the water somewhere, had unnerved him from the second they left it behind.

"With all due respect, Captain," Jon continued. "What does all that have to do with what we're doing now?"

He'd asked himself that question, too. Maybe they didn't need to go through any of this to accomplish what they wanted to. It had taken long enough to get here, enough searching and fighting and hiding to bring them to this doorstep, nowhere near New York City, not even in the same state. For what? This whole plan had been built on nothing but what-ifs. And Basil had another one for Jon.

"What if we could get it all back?" he said.

Jon looked at him with his eyes narrowed. When he decided that Basil was serious, he said slowly, "Is that possible?"

"Maybe," Basil replied. "That's what we're here to find out." He nodded at the house, at the empty doorway that led to more shadows and more dust. "There's a ghost in there. He's my friend," he said. "And he's coming out alive."

ACKNOWLEDGMENTS

When you write a book, you do most of that part by yourself. When you *publish* a book, you're suddenly part of a team. And I'm lucky enough to have the most amazing, genuine, hardworking group of people on my side at Swoon Reads and Macmillan. Swoon Reads as an imprint wouldn't even exist without its legendary creator, Jean Feiwel, and its fearless director, Lauren Scobell—a huge thanks to them for overseeing not just the imprint but also this amazing community of writers and readers. And this *book* wouldn't exist without the work of my brilliant, hilarious, and immensely patient editor, Emily Settle. She's had my back since Day One. She's also the queen of including appropriate GIFs in her emails.

To everyone else at Swoon Reads who read and loved and supported my book, I thank you from the bottom of my heart.

When my book was selected for publication, I was welcomed into a group of amazingly supportive and courageous authors, some of whom went out of their way to offer their help and friendship, including (but not limited to) Tarun Shanker, Melinda Grace, Maggie

Ann Martin, Danika Stone, and my fellow Season 10 authors, Tiana Smith, Caitlin Lochner, and Dee Garretson.

I swung for the fences when I posted the original manuscript for this book on the Swoon Reads website—I didn't let anybody else read it. So to all the readers on Swoon who aren't related to me in any way and haven't known me for several years, who read the book and rated it and offered their invaluable feedback, a huge thank-you.

There's also a massive support system of family and friends behind me, and I owe many of them a debt of gratitude that I can never hope to repay:

My friend of many years, Cait, who officiated my wedding and is one of the most inspirational people I know.

My sister-in-law, Morgan, who's a friend (and babysitter) whenever she's needed, and my brother-in-law, Michael, who can slap a set of brakes and a new radio into a car without breaking a sweat.

My siblings, Kaydance, Chloe, Marcus, Shane, and Brandon, who are never too far away to inject some fun and love into my life.

My in-laws, Dynel and Eric, who never say no and always put everyone else before themselves.

My stepmom, Michele, who wouldn't let me quit on this dream and was one of the only people to patiently read the 108-page poem I wrote in high school.

My mom, Mylinda, who's seen some of the darkest corners life has to offer and still has the wherewithal to be a pillar of support and positivity in her kids' lives.

My dad, Brian, who taught me more about the art of storytelling than he probably realizes.

My astounding and beautiful wife, Kelsey. This book is dedicated to her because she exists as much within these pages as I do.

And to my daughters, Rylan and Norrie, thank you for giving me a reason to laugh every day and for smiling the best smiles I've ever seen in my life. I love you.

If I left you out, I promise it's not because you don't matter. There's more to come from here, and there's a place for you in those books if you're willing to make the journey with me.

With love,
Devon

Check out more books chosen for publication by readers like you.

DID YOU KNOW...

readers like you helped to get this book published?

Join our book-obsessed community and help us discover awesome new writing talent.

1 **Write it.**
Share your original YA manuscript.

2 **Read it.**
Discover bright new bookish talent.

3 **Share it.**
Discuss, rate, and share your faves.

4 **Love it.**
Help us publish the books you love.

Share your own manuscript or dive between the pages at **swoonreads.com** or by downloading the **Swoon Reads app.**